Lovers' Vows

'How did it go?' Dewar asked merrily.

'Wretched!' She continued without stopping, till Dewar's arm caught her wrist and drew her back.

'Don't tell me he turned violent on you! Swithin is a tame man in a carriage.'

'That's what you think!'

'Surely he didn't. . . . Just what happened?' he asked, startled out of his merriment.

'We have taken a vow of mutual celibacy, *eternal* celibacy at that.'

A slow smile formed on his lips as he glanced to Swithin's carriage, where his cousin's helmeted head projected from the window waving a kiss to Holly. 'That won't last long,' he prophesied.

'It had better last till you get him out of here!'

Lovers' Vows

Joan Smith

ROBERT HALE · LONDON

ISBN 978-0-7090-7930-9

Robert Hale Limited
Clerkenwell House
Clerkenwell Green
London EC1R 0HT

www.halebooks.com

2 4 6 8 10 9 7 5 3 1

To Marg and Bill Hawken

Typeset in 11/14½pt Souvenir
by Derek Doyle & Associates, Shaw Heath
Printed and bound in Great Britain
by Biddles Limited, King's Lynn

at lovers' vows
They say, Jove laughs.

Romeo and Juliet
act 2, scene 2

CHAPTER 1

$\mathcal{T}$he highest tribute ever paid Miss McCormack's appearance was that she was not a bad-looking girl. Even the most well wishing of her friends never so stretched credulity as to imply she was a beauty. Oh, not ugly! No indeed. No squint, no butter tooth or platter face marred her plainness. Her hair was brown, hair-coloured hair that did not hold a curl nor even a hairpin very well, with the result that there was often a wisp of a tail hanging down her back. Her eyes were hazel, neither beautifully large and lustrous nor heavily fringed with lashes nor even, truth to tell, so very effective as organs of vision. In the privacy of her room, she occasionally resorted to a pair of spectacles to read her Bible, whose print was extremely fine. Her teeth, while regular and in good repair, had never been likened to pearls. Her figure, too, was average, neither gracefully willowy nor pleasingly plump. It was compact, on the thin side. All in all, she was not a bad-looking girl.

In the opinion of her Aunt Elsa, under whose roof Holly McCormack had found a home upon the death of her widowed father a few years before, this lack of physical distinction was a desirable attribute. Holly had slid into their lives like a minnow into a pond, without causing a ripple of trouble. In a short space of time, she had become indispensable, rather like a comfortable grey gown in which one always appears respectable and can wear anywhere. She was not noisily distracting; neither was she so shy as to cause pity. She was just there, speaking when spoken to and occasionally making a sensible comment on her own. She could be put forward without shame for her appearance and manners, but certainly she was no threat to her cousin Jane. Her age, too, was a convenient thing, somewhere in the mid-twenties. Old enough to preclude having to have a husband found for her, and old enough to act as a chaperon for Jane, but not so ancient as to require any special care for her health. She was fully young enough to run an errand upstairs or into the village, but old enough not to require a footman on the latter.

It was really very strange, had anyone thought to consider it, how Miss McCormack was exactly the right age for everything but marriage. When the nursemaid contracted the measles, Miss McCormack's youth made her the one to enjoy a romp in the nursery with the youngsters, yet in a week she had so far matured as to be a respectable chaperon for Jane at the Assembly Room. By the time she returned from there, she had become forty or so, and enjoyed an hour-long coze with her aunt on the trials and tribulations of raising a family. She arose the next morning rejuvenated to her twenties, and just the proper age to hem up Jane's suit for church on Sunday.

Holly was engaged in this task when her Aunt Elsa (Papa's sister) entered the morning room, wearing her habitual air of distraction. Elsa Proctor was a faded beauty of another decade. She felt in some vague and undefined way that life had been hard on her to have given her a doting husband, a ravishing daughter and two rowdy sons, a fine country mansion, and good health. Life had recently rectified its error, however, and bestowed on her spouse an increase in fortune upon the death of a relative, and a knighthood upon the judicious spending of a small portion of the increase. Lady Proctor felt the full weight of her new dignity, and meant for the village to feel it as well. To this end, her natural bent for elegance of toilette had recently increased, as had her aspirations in the sphere of a husband for Jane.

'Holly, my dear,' she said, pausing at the doorway with a lace wisp of handkerchief held aloft to add refinement to her new status, 'perhaps you should just put Jane's skirt away for the moment. Lady Dewar is coming by for a visit. You will stay to meet her, of course. It would not do for her to catch us at work.'

Lady Dewar was not likely to catch the speaker at work unless she arrived at the door of her bedchamber, to find her occupied with her rouge pot and powder box. 'She will be coming to congratulate us on Bertie's being knighted. Dear me, what does one say to a countess? I wish Bertie were here, but there, he never is when one needs him.'

'Uncle has gone into the village. He won't be home to luncheon,' Holly informed her aunt. She was the main medium of communication between them from eight in the morning till six in the evening, when Sir Egbert arrived at the table for his dinner, which he insisted on calling his mutton, as though he were still a mere country squire. His lady thought it would not hurt him to call it dinner now that he was a knight. Sir Egbert was an early riser and a hard worker about his estate, where he raised excellent hogs. His wife never came downstairs before ten. Lately, eleven was deemed a more dignified hour.

'Pity. I would have liked him to bring me some souchong tea for Lady Dewar's visit, but men never think of anything useful.'

'Why don't you sit down and be calm, Aunt? There is no reason to be upset only because the countess is coming to call. I'm sure Lady Dewar has been here half a dozen times the past year. You will have no trouble speaking to her.'

'Yes, I will, Holly.' The niece thought that Lady Proctor felt some superior method of speech was expected of her due to her elevation, but she was soon corrected. 'It is plain as a pikestaff why she is coming.'

'You have only to say "Thank you, it is kind of you to have come", or something of the sort, when she offers her congratulations.'

'Congratulations? My dear, that is only her excuse! Now that Bertie is knighted, and with all the money from his Uncle Thomas, she means to push for a match between Jane and her son.'

A trill of spontaneous laughter caused Lady Proctor to frown in displeasure. It could not have been the quality of the sound that accounted for it. Miss McCormack's voice was the best part of her. It had a throaty, sensuous quality entirely lacking in her appearance. Heads (masculine heads) had been known to turn with interest at the sound of it, and to turn away again when they saw from whence the voice issued. In a fit of lyricism, Mr Johnson, the local minister, once said she sounded as though she were laughing when she spoke, and as though she were singing when she laughed. Neither flight of poetry was quite accurate, but he had caught the essence of her voice.

'You worry for nothing, Aunt,' she said. 'Dewar is old enough to be her father.' She was too polite to state any of the other impediments to the match. Certainly Jane was very pretty, and the best-natured child in the world, but to think she would appeal to a clever, mature, blue gentleman like Lord Dewar stretched imagination too far. Any romantic mention made of him by his mother featured ladies of exalted birth and fortune. The very diamonds of society were his female companions, and even these gems had failed to raise him to an offer of marriage.

'Dewar is not so much above thirty,' Lady Proctor countered. 'And Jane, while she is only seventeen, is so pretty you know, and now with her dowry increased. . . . I expect my decision to present her in London next spring had something to do with it. It will be a vast bother. Bertie is already complaining of the expense of hiring a house too; but it will pay off in the long run, I'm sure the countess's visit is to foster a match between them.'

Holly listened, and sought to deflate her aunt's hopes painlessly. 'Dewar would hardly have had time to learn of Uncle Bertie's new great fortune, would he?' she asked. 'I cannot think Lady Dewar would be suggesting a match to you without her son's concurrence.'

'Bertie has only been a knight for two weeks to be sure, but I expect Dewar may have heard of it before we did ourselves. He would be frequently at St James's, you must know, where such matters are spoken of.'

'I had not thought of that,' Holly replied mildly, yet she could not feel a wealthy nobleman had been so impressed with her uncle's knighthood that he had sat down on the spot and posted off a note to his mama. 'Dewar so seldom visits his mother that I don't suppose he realizes Jane is a young lady now. She was still in the schoolroom the last time he was home, was she not? It was two or more years ago. I know she did not go to the assembly. It was spoken of, you recall, but you felt fifteen too young.'

'I expect he knows how to count,' was the reply. 'In any case, we shall see, for she will be here in five minutes, and I wish you will put that skirt away, Holly. It will look so underbred for us to be working when she is shown in. Do you think this gown good enough? I put on my new lace jabot, and this dab of a cameo pin. The fashion papers are saying gem stones are not eligible for morning calls.'

This speech was really only a bid for a compliment. Lady Proctor knew better than to take advice on sartorial matters from a girl who was herself wearing a faded bombazine gown and jean slippers. As she folded up the skirt and set it aside, Holly said, 'You will look five times as fine as Lady Dewar.' To herself she added silently, 'and so will I.'

When the noble dame was shown in, Holly mentally noted that ten times as fine would have been no exaggeration. The countess, being a countess, felt it suitable to pay a morning call on her inferiors in a well-worn greatcoat which had belonged, some several years previously, to her son. About her head she had wrapped a shawl. Beneath the greatcoat she wore a gown that had known what it was to be a curtain in one of its previous incarnations. If one did not recognize in this shabby ensemble the unmistakable gaunt anatomy of Lady Dewar, one might well take the apparition for a beggar. Strands of grey hair had blown forward over the plain, lined face. A pair of brightly intelligent eyes were the lady's only claim to physical distinction.

'Well now, Elsa, ain't you fine!' was the jocular shout from the doorway when Her Ladyship was shown in by the butler. 'Sitting idle like a lady, now that that husband of yours has set up as a knight. Good day, Holly. You've nothing better to do than to sit moping on a nice day like this either, eh? Sit down, gel. Don't bother hopping up like a puppet for me. I'll find myself a seat. I may be getting long in the tooth, but I don't need to be helped into a chair yet.' She dropped her body into the most comfortable chair in the room as she spoke and reached down to pull off her boots, which she then kicked aside. They looked remarkably like a pair of gentlemen's Hessians that had been cut off with a pair of large scissors till they reached no higher than the ankle. 'Corns,' she explained briefly; then, looking down at her toes, she wiggled them, with a luxurious sigh of relief.

'So kind of you to call,' Lady Proctor said, in her most elegant voice, pretending all this gross exhibition was not going forth.

'Kind? I was bored to tears and had nowhere to go, so I decided to see if Holly has that receipt for Folkstone pudding she mentioned to me. I am fagged with plain rice. Old Dr John has got me on rice pudding, trying to cure this bellyache that keeps recurring on me. He threatens me with custard as well, the wretched man. I think myself it is no more than constipation that ails me, but he don't believe in purges. What do you think, Elsa?'

Elsa thought it a great shame people had to have interiors at all, and certainly had no notion of discussing their functions in her best morning gown. 'Dr John is a little old-fashioned,' she decreed, and racked her brain for a more elevated topic of conversation. Knighthoods, presentations of daughters to court, eligible sons, and dowries occurred to her, but she saw no polite way of raising them.

'Try prunes, Lady Dewar,' Holly suggested. 'Stewed prunes in the morning might help, or a mild aperient – Scots perhaps. Certainly you don't want custard, if your problem is what you think.'

'Just what I said! Nothing is so binding as boiled milk, and what is custard but boiled milk and eggs and sugar?' She turned her full attention to Miss McCormack then, for she never could find two words to say to Elsa Proctor. 'You're looking a little peaky, gel,' she announced. 'Too much sitting in. I suppose Mr Johnson has burdened you with those demmed woolen undershirts for the orphans. He gave me two dozen of 'em to do. I passed them along to my woman. I refuse to burn my eyes out on stitching when I could be burning them out on a good spicy novel.'

'Yes, he gave us two dozen as well. We have finished one dozen.' The word 'we' was used in a nominal sense, for of course it was her own fingers that had wielded the needle.

'Don't hurry or he'll land another dozen in on you. Mrs Wheeler won't be able to do her share. She has sprained her wrist, did you hear?'

'Yes, I heard it in the village,' Holly answered, then looked to her aunt, for she did not wish to monopolize the guest's attention.

Lady Dewar followed her glance, and said to Elsa, 'Well, is there any other news?'

What was called 'news' in the village of Harknell was really no more than gossip. They discussed the latest floral miracle of the Misses Hall, keen horticulturalists who were forever cross-pollinating and grafting. There was Mrs Raymond's newest pelisse to be analysed. Elsa thought, though she could not be positive till she saw it closer up, that it was last year's with a new fur collar added. Before long, Elsa was saying, 'We have decided to give Jane a Season next spring.'

'Have you indeed? What on earth for?' was the reply. 'Waste of time and money. She's pretty enough to get a husband without the bother. Why, I thought she was meant for her cousin in Sussex. You used to speak of it, did you not?'

'Oh, but that was before . . . before. . . .' She could not bring herself to utter the bald truth.

'Before Bertie got his uncle's money you mean. Aye, that will make some difference I daresay. You will be looking a little higher for a match. My son is coming home next week.'

A cunning smile alit on Lady Proctor's face at the significance of this statement, coming so close on the heels of talk about Jane. After one glance at that expression, Lady Dewar rapidly spoke on. 'Chubbie is bringing some young folks with him. There might be a *parti* in the lot for Jane.'

'Chubbie?' Lady Proctor asked.

'Dewar. I still call him Chubbie once in a while. I'm getting old and dotty, you see. Funny how you revert to the old days when you're approaching senility. Dewar was a chubby baby. A regular little roly-poly fellow. I don't see how he grew into such a string bean. I really don't know why he's coming to the Abbey. I thought he'd stay in town for the fall little season, and maybe come home for a few days at Christmas, but he comes this week-end with a party of young folks. It will be lively to have them around. He might be bringing home a lady for my approval,' she added in a seemingly careless way, dashing the hopes in her hostess's bosom.

'Is he thinking of marriage?' Elsa asked.

'I'll be the last to know. His aunt tells me he's been running around town with some beauty. Lady Alicia Grover I believe it is. She's mentioned it twice over the past few months, so there may be something in it. We shall see.'

This disheartening talk was interrupted by the arrival of the tea tray. 'My word, you *do* do things up nicely, Elsa. Say that for you,' the countess exclaimed, eying the tray with greedy interest. 'Hot scones and cream for the tea. That's a good-looking preserve too. Strawberry, is it?' She spooned a gob on to her place as she spoke, and stuck the serving spoon into her mouth to confirm her guess. At least she did not return it to the communal jam pot.

She single-handedly consumed two-thirds of the scones and drank three cups of tea before bending over, with a mild oath, to ease her aching feet into her boots for departure. 'Write up that Folkstone pudding receipt for me, Holly, and have a servant bring it to me. Nice visit, Elsa. I'll come back soon,' she said as she went toward the door. As an afterthought she added, 'And I'll have Dewar bring his company to call if there's a likely-looking match in the young men for Janie. Where is she?'

'She is having her piano lesson in the village with Miss Carroll,' the mother answered. 'I'll tell her you were asking for her.'

'Hah, much she'll care, the minx. Tell her to curl her hair and I'll find her a beau to save you dragging her off to. London. Good day to you. Good day, Holly,' she shouted as she went out the door, lumbering at an awkward gait, as the damp autumn weather invaded her corns.

'There, you see, it is just as I said,' Lady Proctor told her niece, as soon as they were alone. 'She means to foster a match between Dewar and Jane.' Holly looked at her blankly, wondering how desire could so warp one's reading of reality. 'She mentioned we would be looking higher than formerly. And telling us Dewar's baby name – that is the sort of family familiarity she has never mentioned before.'

'She said one of Dewar's *guests* might be suitable.'

'Guests? It is Dewar himself she has in mind. Not a doubt of it. Why else would she ask to be remembered to Jane, and caution her to get her hair done? Dewar fancies elegant women, you must know. I begin to understand her scheme now. She has not spoken of it to Dewar. She means to send him down to call, and let him see for himself how pretty Jane is become. That is clever of her, to be sure. Very clever. I shall do the same with Jane, and not say a word about it, except to tell her to get her hair done, of course. And she had better have a new gown. Is that skirt hemmed yet, my dear?'

'I was just about to finish it,' Holly said, reaching down for the garment.

'It is all those orphan shirts that holds us up so. How we shall ever find time to get a new gown made up as well I don't know. You had better take Jane into the village this afternoon, and speak to the modiste. Oh, and you will have to stop at the draper's and select some material. Much too cold for muslin. Get her a good quality of silk – some of that new georgette they have got in. The rose or blue, whichever Jane wants. In fact, get both. With Dewar in residence, there are bound to be plenty of balls and parties. We shall have one ourselves. A rout do you think, Holly, or a real ball? Make up a list of guests, will you? You know where the old list is. My, so busy as I shall be. I think I'll have a lie-down to prepare myself for it all.' She dragged herself from her chair, trailing the lace wisp after her. She was fatigued with the weight of all these pending exertions. So fortunate she had dear Holly to help her a little.

CHAPTER 2

*L*ord Dewar sat at an ornate japanned desk in his bedchamber on Grosvenor Square with a cup of black coffee at his elbow, and the *Morning Chronicle* open before him. It was his custom to begin at page one of this journal and quickly read it through each morning before he dressed. Today, he stopped at page seven, his eyes scanning the social columns. One would be forgiven for thinking him ill-pleased with the world. There was an expression of weary disdain on his chiselled countenance. His black brows, as finely etched and groomed as any lady's, rose a fraction as his grey orbs settled on an item in the column. Without looking up, he reached out his hand for a pencil, and drew a circle around the item, then lounged back in his padded chair and sighed luxuriously. A smile of satisfaction settled on his lean cheeks. Then he shoved the paper aside and took up his coffee.

Really a dead bore, the daily papers. When you'd read one you'd read them all. Always a tirade against the government, and usually another against the Prince Regent in this Whig paper. Prices were high and rising daily, the roads were a national disgrace, and one or another of the Royal Family was ill. On the editorial pages there would be an article against the low academic standards pertaining at the universities, the low moral values of the aristrocracy, and the high unemployment. Really, the world was a demmed bore. He would be happy to get away to the Abbey for a few months and recuperate his spirits. Even if that notice had not appeared in the paper he would have gone. In fact, especially if it had not appeared, he would have gone.

He picked the *Chronicle* up once more and reread the item. Lady Congrave was pleased to announce the betrothal of her niece, Lady Alicia Grover, to the Hon. Hanley Healey Smith-Daiches. . . . Folks would take the shatter-brained idea he was running to hide his grief, when the visit (to say nothing of the betrothal) had been arranged a week before, to escape the lady's clutches. That was the trouble with women. Flirt with them for a few weeks, and they took the cork-brained idea you wanted to spend the rest of your life with them. Marriage was for fools and clergymen. What man would willingly shackle himself to one woman for the rest of his days, when every Season brought forth a new batch of beauties? One month had proved the invariable length of time it took him to become tired of a young lady. One week to learn her tricks, two to admire them, one to become disenchanted. Strange when one came to consider it for, with male friends, the longer you knew them the better you liked them. But with women it was the reverse. There was nothing so fascinating as a new flirt. It was not likely he would find any to his liking at Harknell, in the very heart of Kent, where his Abbey was situated. Should he invite a few along? No, this would be an all-male party, he decided. To be inviting females to one's ancestral home had a serious air he sought to avoid in his affairs.

He had invited Luke Altmore for rational conversation; George Foxworth for riding and hunting; old Sir Laurence Digby to amuse his mama; and Rex Homberly, a cousin, had invited himself. He would amuse no one, but never mind. He was a harmless fool. Kings of old were accustomed to have midgets and clowns about them, and Rex filled the dual capacity, being only slightly above five feet in height and an acknowledged idiot. It did not occur to Dewar that he had mentally assigned himself a monarch's crown in this analogy, nor would it have seemed out of place to him if he had thought of it. He was considered a sort of monarch of society.

He was disturbed by a scratching sound at the door, as of a cat sharpening its claws. Curious, Dewar arose and went to open his door. There was no cat there, but a stumpy, slightly overweight gentleman with a pink face and bright blue eyes. 'Morning, Dewar. Mind if I come in?' he asked, and pushed his way past, into the elegant chamber.

'Why were you scratching at my door? Why did you not knock or, better, await below and have word sent up you were here?' his cousin demanded, never in a terribly good mood before he had finished the ritual of paper and coffee.

'Did,' Homberly answered with a sniffling sound. 'Been waiting half an hour. In a bit of a hurry, Dewar, if you want the truth.'

'By all means, let us have no evasions,' Dewar answered, in a bored voice.

Rex sat down at the chair just vacated by his host and began to glance at the paper. As he turned a page, he heedlessly reached out for the cup of coffee and raised it to his lips, while Dewar looked on, first in vexation, finally giving way to resignation, as one always did in the end with Homberly.

After another moment, Dewar went to the door and called his valet. While he made a careful toilette, taking quite ten minutes to tie his cravat to his liking, and another two or three to select from amongst his blue jackets, Homberly read on silently, his lips forming each syllable, stopping only to sip from time to time. The dressing and drinking were concluded simultaneously.

'Next time you mean to honour me by coming for breakfast you must let me know, Rex, and I shall provide you gammon and eggs, or a nice beefsteak if you prefer,' his cousin said.

'That'd be dandy, Dewar. Just dandy. The coffee was good, but I prefer more sugar, and a lot of cream – at least half a cup. Foxey is such a jokesmith, he says I take a little coffee in my cream.'

'A dangerous man with his tongue, Foxey.'

'So he is. Think I could handle a second cup all the same,' Rex said magnanimously, and reached for the pot.

'Help yourself. And, when you are finished, we shall discuss what brought you here. There was talk of a great hurry.'

'So there was, by Jove. Slipped my mind. Got to reading about that woman that cleaved her man's head open with an axe. They say there was brains spilt on the floor. Ain't that an awful thing for a woman to do. You ever seen brains, Dew?'

'As a matter of fact I have, but I cannot ever recall seeing any evidence of them when I am with you, Rex,' he answered in a kindly tone. 'About that hurry. . . .'

'Have to let Roper to know what to pack for the visit. Thing is, only wanted to ask you if there's anything in particular I'll be needing. Outside of horses and clothes, I mean. Got any rigs running is what I'm asking you.'

'You want to know the nature of the diversions planned to amuse you?' Dewar asked.

'That's it. Know you often make your guests take part in a play or a pageant or whatnot. Got a dandy horse's outfit at home. Me and Foxey wore it to a masquerade party at Wilmot's last night. Had a jolly time. Mind if we go as a horse again, I mean to be the front end, for it's not only hot as Jehoshaphat at the rear – it puts a crick in your back, bending over so long.'

'I try to avoid the obvious, so shan't say a word about the suitability of your outfit. I see no need for the costume at the Abbey, Rex. Thoughtful of you to ask.'

'Not at all. Very happy to help you out any way I can. Thought your mama might enjoy it. Just what is on then? Mean to say, when Dewar takes a party off to St Alton's Abbey for a month at the beginning of the little season, folks wonder what you're up to. Can't be just Alicia's getting buckled to old Smith-Daiches, for you had the visit planned before that. Was yourself pushed Daiches at her head, as far as that goes. You ain't taking any ladies, so it don't look like one of your famous dramatical presentations. Wish you'd asked me to take a part in the last one, with all the devils and stuff in it.'

'I have no drama planned this trip. Some hunting, riding, a few routs, a ball perhaps. . . .'

'Sure you ain't going to make us write?' Homberly asked, with a suspicious eye. 'I remember the time you locked all your guests up and made us each write a one-act play. Ain't going to write no silly play, Dewar.'

'You have already done that, One silly play from you is more than enough. And if you will recall, Cousin, I did not invite you on that literary sojourn held at the Abbey. A bunch of us – Leigh Hunt it was, Byron, Tom Moore, and a couple of blue ladies – wanted to compare how different writers would tackle the idea of a modern morality play. It was Byron's idea. It was not a success, however. Byron claimed none of us knew enough about the subject to do it justice.'

'Don't intend to sit around painting pictures either. Didn't invite myself the week-end you had us to your hunting box and made us all paint each other as some famous painting. You invited me. Didn't know you didn't plan to hunt. Mean to say, a man invites you to his hunting box. . . . And you turned that pretty little Frances Webster into an ugly old Mona Lisa. Made a very poor Julius Caesar yourself too, I can tell you.'

'I have given up taking an active part in the arts, Rex. Mother Nature has played a cruel prank on me. It is ironic that I, who perhaps appreciate music, painting, and poetry more than any other man in England, should be endowed with no talent to execute any of them. I am a mere critic. I don't mean to subject my guests or myself to any of that form of torture you speak of. If you have misgivings, however, I shall be very happy to make your excuses to Mama . . .' he said politely.

'Well, I'll go then, if you're sure we won't have to *do* anything. Mean to say, not a bad time of the year to be in the country. Hunting good. Excellent cellar at St Alton's. Your chef – Bernier – will be going with you?' he asked eagerly.

'Certainly he will, I never move without him.'

'Settles it. Be there for dinner this evening. What does he mean to serve us, do you happen to know?'

'He mentioned *soupe à la bonne femme, dindon à la*

Perigueuse, poule a la Condé. . . .'

'Pity. Was hoping for bubble and squeak,' Rex said, and pulled himself from the chair with a sigh, his back hunched forward at an awkward angle. 'Devilish crick in my back from that costume. Sure you won't be needing it at the Abbey?'

'Quite sure.'

Homberly wandered out the door, and Dewar rang for a fresh pot of coffee and a clean cup. He sat long over it, thinking in a sad, nostalgic way of times gone by. The good old days when he had associated with the people who did things. His mind wandered to the Hunt brothers, Leigh and John, who had been incarcerated for libeling their Prince Regent in the Examiner, their influential though small paper. 'A libertine over head and ears in debt and disgrace' they had called him, among other things. It had been fun to decorate Leigh's prison cell, which was in fact a very fine room, complete with piano and his books. They had contrived to make him quite comfortable, painting the ceiling like a sky with clouds, covering the walls with a rose-trellis design, and always keeping him supplied with good wine and fresh flowers. Some snug little dinners they had held there.

Then there had been the season he had been involved in art, and the exhibitions of the Royal Academy. What a fuss they had raised about showing Turner's superb *Snowstorm: Hannibal and His Army Crossing the Alps.* The latter part of the title was added to get it through the hanging committee, who could not see their way clear to exhibit 'a huge and violent sky' as art. The best, and certainly the most influential, painting of that year – or decade. Some folks called Dewar a dilettante; he did not consider it an appropriate term, indicating as it did a lack of seriousness, a trifling sort of interest. He was keenly interested in all manifestations of beauty. His greatest regret was that he did not excel in any of the arts. He was relegated to the post of patron, seeking out the new and talented people, and encouraging them. If he occasionally stepped on a few toes by deriding the old and fusty in the process, it was regrettable but necessary. His valet entered and began picking up his discarded dressing-gown and ruined cravats. This bustling about displeased His Lordship, which aggravation was conveyed to his valet by one scathing glance from his eye. He would retire to his study, to peruse the long rows of books for something light and simple to amuse the local folks at Harknell.

'If I may remind you, my lord, there was the letter from Her Ladyship, your mother, you meant to do something about before leaving,' the servant said in a timorous tone.

'Letter? Ah yes, it slipped my mind. Some neighbour has bought himself a knighthood. Have my secretary send him a congratulatory note, Wickens, and sign my name. I do not wish to be disturbed.' He strode from the room, muttering under his breath, 'Moliere, perhaps, would be amusing. . . .'

CHAPTER 3

*D*ewar and his party had been at the Abbey for three days, without venturing farther afield than into the woods and parklands for some shooting. Homberly had been well entertained plundering his lordship's well-stocked coverts, in company with George Foxworth, and accidentally shooting a foxhound as well when he discharged a gun into the bush by mistake. The surreptitious burial of this animal took up a full hour, and another thirty minutes were used in concocting a story to account for its vanishing if Dewar happened to count his hounds and find one missing. Dewar had met for very brief and casual reports from his steward, nodding his head in a lazy sort of half-listening way to hear that all was in order, generally speaking, with a few details awaiting his own settlement.

'The local townspeople are after one of your tenants, old Arthur Evans, to give them a footpath through his land, to save them a few steps,' the steward mentioned.

'Is there any reason, outside of sheer ill nature, why he doesn't do it? I never met such a bad-humoured man as Evans.'

'He says the path would go through his rose garden.'

'I would not encourage him to destroy a lovely rose garden, only to save the lazy pedestrians a few yards. Anything else?'

'There's the schoolmaster in the village who is getting on in years. He is about due to retire, and a replacement will be needed. You will want a hand in that, I fancy.'

'What leads you to fancy anything of the sort?' Dewar asked, with a startled look on his face. There was no answer. 'Has he asked to be retired?'

'No, but a few of the parents have suggested it. He is more learned than most of the gentlemen in these parts, but he is a bit hard of hearing.'

'That will be a marked advantage in a room full of rowdy young-sters. We'll let him suggest it when he feels ready to hang up his rod. I do not approve of turning the old boys out to pasture prematurely. They so often cock up their toes and die within a twelvemonth. Is there anything else, Roots?'

'I'll leave the books with you, to look over at your leisure.'

'What an abuse of leisure,' Dewar sighed.

'Your clergyman, Johnson, will want to speak to you. He is always after me for more money for the orphanage, but it seems to me the young lads have what they need. The local ladies are all active in helping tend to their needs. They have a committee to make up the clothing and hold little parties at Christmas, and so on.'

'We do not want to deprive the ladies of their good deeds. Don't stint the boys on food and clothing and lessons, however. The last is the most important of the lot. It might be a nice gesture to have the charity ladies to tea at the Abbey one afternoon. I shall suggest it to Mama.'

'That's it then,' Roots said, shuffling up his papers. 'I'll do as we agreed. Try the west acres in clean, fallow tares next season to see if we can improve the soil. Seems to me it ought to be yielding more than it is. And I'll get you a price on Dutch-glazed tiles for the dairy.'

'I want to see the pattern and price before you proceed with the ordering, Roots. There is no reason my dairy cannot be pretty while we are about renovating it. The dairy girls spend a good deal of time there. I saw an interesting set-up at Beaton Hall – a foun-tain of fresh-running water set in the middle of the big stone table used for creaming and ripening the milk for churning. It seemed to keep the whole place clean and fresh-smelling. Most dairies have an odour that does not encourage one to linger. My own is no exception, I fear. I shall have a barn built out back too, for cheese.'

'How was this fresh water kept running?' Roots asked skeptically.

'By means of a pump, I expect. Unless there was one of those wells of the sort they have at Artois, where the water swells without pumping.'

'There's no such quantity of water hereabouts.'

'I would like you to look into it all the same. I shall be in touch with my friends at Beaton Hall, and discover from them how it was done. A dairy should be quaintly pastoral in character – pretty milk maids all in a row, in clean aprons. Yes, the babble of freshly running water will add to the rustic character I strive for. And it will keep the place fresh-smelling. I know your theory that every penny spent must bring in two, Roots, but I wish you will humour me in this matter,' Dewar said in a mild enough way, but the imperative glance he levelled on his steward did not encourage the man to argue further. 'Thank you so much,' Dewar said, showing him to the door. 'We shall take a day off very soon for a tour of the estate, and to say good day to all my tenants.'

'I'll introduce you to them,' Roots could not desist from saying.

'Oh I am not quite a stranger to most of them.'

'No, sir, only the five families that have come the past two years. It is two years since you have made a tour.'

'Is it really so long? *Tempus fugit*, does it not? It seems only yesterday we ploughed through those muddy fields, you and I, ruining our topboots. I must remember not to wear my white-trimmed ones.'

'I'd been telling you for six months that field wanted tilling.'

'I had been telling you for longer than six years to tend to such matters for me. What horrors have you in store for me this time, I wonder, that you are so eager to lure me off into the wilderness?'

'No horrors, I hope, but it is a good idea to be acquainted with your own estate and tenants. They like to feel you take an interest.'

'My dear Roots, would I have hired such an excellent and expensive steward if I did not care for their welfare? And, of course, my own. Pray consider yourself *in loco Dewaris* in my absence. Do as you see fit for anything under a thousand pounds, and don't hesitate to write me in London for anything above that sum. I always answer your *billets-doux*, do I not?'

'Eventually. It would be handy if you could get an answer back to me inside of a week or two. When cattle is up for sale, or a planting of trees is to be chopped, six months is a long time to wait.'

'Those are the very sort of details I pay you so handsomely to tend to, Roots. Don't be shy in the matter of earning your money. Should an important matter arise, I shall bear in mind your love of promptness. Good day, Roots.'

Rex Homberly was straggling past the doorway as Roots strode out. 'Oh, there you are, Dew,' he said, drawing up to chat. Then he happened to notice the earth on his hands from burying the hound, and pulled them hastily behind his back.

'Come in, Rex, and we shall have a glass of wine. A new case I have got hold of from France. Burgundy – my wine steward tells me it is unexceptionable. He likes it so well it is half gone already, and I have not tried it yet.'

'Burgundy, eh? Don't mind if I do,' Rex answered, giving his hands a surreptitious wipe on the seat of his trousers, while Dewar busied himself pouring the wine and admired its deep red glow by holding his glass in front of the window.

Homberly took a mouthful and proceeded to chew it. 'Did I get a piece of cork in it?' Dewar asked.

'Nope. Testing the taste,' Rex gurgled, then swallowed the mouthful and took another, somewhat larger one, emptying the glass. 'Good stuff,' he congratulated. 'Not a forward, encroaching type. Musigny, I think?' He proferred his glass for a refill, while Dewar regarded him with amusement. 'Alvanley taught me the trick. You chew it, to get the taste.'

'I see. What is it you look for?'

'Well – for the taste,' Homberly repeated. 'Tastes very good, but you've got to say more than that, you see. It's got to taste *like* something.'

'Something other than grapes?'

'Yes – like cloth or people. It can be smooth as velvet or satin, if you like, or it can be impertinent or shy – or even argumentative if you don't like it. Well, there's no fight in this bottle, is there? Have another, Dew. Have several. Something I want to tell you.'

'Preparing me for good news, are you?'

'Good news? Hardly call it good news. Not that a man needs thirty-six hounds. In a kind of a way, it is good news to have one less mouth to feed. . . .'

'You've shot a hound!' Dewar said. 'Now how the devil did you come to do that, Rex? Those are a specially trained pack!'

'Accident. And it ain't the leader of the pack or anything like it. In fact, it's a dashed troublemaker. Sneaked out of the enclosure and came pelting after me and Foxey, scaring the hares so we didn't catch a thing. Didn't shoot it on purpose, whatever Foxey may tell you. Well – white and brown – took it for a hare.'

'And the hunting season about to begin!' Dewar rolled up his eyes in vexation, then was struck with inspiration. 'Rex,' he went on in a pleasant voice, 'I have an excellent idea. Why don't you and Foxey run into the village for me and . . . and go to the lending library.'

'Foxey don't care for reading.'

'I want you to see if you can find a play for us to put on. Take your time! No hurry.'

'A play? You promised you wouldn't. Besides, I've left the horse suit in London.'

'You can send for it. Or, for that matter, you need not feel compelled to participate.'

'I ain't lending that suit to nobody. Well, I'll see if I can find a play about a horse then, but it won't be easy, Dew. I know there is one. *My Horse, My Horse, My Kingdom for a Horse.* Think that's the name of it.'

The knocker of the front door sounded, and within a minute a servant was at the study, informing his lordship that Mr Johnson, the incumbent parson of St Alton's, was come to call.

'That prosy old bore! Tell him I just stepped out. I'll go with you, Rex.' Dewar snatched up his hat and cane and slipped out the French doors, to disappear around the corner to the stables.

The two were soon strolling along the main street of Harknell. Dewar's eyes focused on the old Gothic church that was visible on a slight promontory at the street's end. He admired its clean, soaring lines, its lancet windows, and found the stark black branches of nude trees added just the right touch of gloom to the view. It might do as an illustration for a gothic novel. Even the heavy grey sky was in keeping with the atmosphere. At such moments of contemplating the harmony of Man's and Nature's work, Dewar preferred silence. Wrapped up in the joys of artistic appreciation as he was, he failed to notice the cause of Homberly's unusual reticence, and was only grateful for it. After he had gazed his fill, however, he looked to his companion, and observed that his blue eyes were popping, and his lower lip hanging loose. He followed the line of vision, smiling to himself at the fellow's lack of facial control. His own lips did not open, nor did his eyes pop, but they narrowed slightly, as they settled on the vision of loveliness that was passing them by across the street.

He suddenly felt Rex's elbow poke him on the hip. 'Who's that?' Rex asked in a smitten voice. There was no other word for it. Rex was in love again.

'No idea, but it won't be hard to find out.' With no more words spoken, they both headed across the road, just as the vision and her companion turned in at the drapery shop.

'Can't go in there. Pity,' Rex said, and leaned against the window to await the girl's exit.

'I can go anywhere. It is my village,' was the bland answer as Dewar pushed the door open and strolled in, with Rex nipping eagerly at his heels.

Once inside, he had some reservations about accosting the beauty, however. He contented himself to stand back and observe her as she discussed with her companion the purchase of ribbons and thread. After the two ladies had left, he mentioned to the proprietor that he did not believe he recognized the young ladies.

'That is Sir Egbert Proctor's daughter and her cousin,' Mr Rogers told him. 'Miss Proctor is to be presented in London next spring, milord.'

'She is not out yet then?' Dewar asked, a little disappointed to hear the girl was so young.

'Out?' Rogers asked uncertainly. 'Well, she goes to the assemblies and dancing parties. She is out in Harknell, if you see what I mean.'

'I understand. When is the next assembly in the village, Mr Rogers?'

'There is one this Friday evening, sir. At the Assembly Rooms. Will you be taking a look in, as you are here for a visit?'

That His Lordship should 'visit' his own home was an odd way to put it, but it did not strike either speaker or listener as odd, as Dewar was so seldom in the neighbourhood. 'Certainly I shall,' he replied, then left, without bothering to pretend he had entered to make a purchase. When Mr Johnson was spotted across the street, Dewar and Homberly turned and went back to the Abbey, without so much as a thought for the lending library.

The young ladies did not go directly home. They stopped to chat to friends, and visited a few more stores. Before they climbed into the carriage, they were accosted by Mr Johnson. It was his custom to accost Miss McCormack at every possible opportunity. He was not precisely a suitor – he never called on her without the excuse of church or orphanage work to discuss. He never drove out with her, or even offered his arm if they happened to walk along a street together, but he did not take it amiss to be teased in a discreet way about her. It was quite settled by custom that he would be her first partner and her last at the local assemblies. He was a tall, lanky gentleman with sandy hair and sloping shoulders. He had rather more nose than his face could well accommodate, and less chin, but he was not downright ugly. His excesses and deficiencies were noticeable without being disfiguring. His smile was rather pleasant, and his conversation rational, if repetitive. The latter was due more to circumstances than anything else. In the dull routine of Harknell, it was hard to find new topics of conversation, but he certainly had one today.

'Well, ladies, you have heard Lord Dewar is in residence?' he asked, lifting his hat.

'Good afternoon, Mr Johnson. We saw him in the drapery shop half an hour ago,' Miss McCormack replied.

'Then you have heard that he plans to attend the assembly.'

'No, we did not hear it. We were not speaking to him. I have not met Lord Dewar.'

'But you have been here an age now. How does it come you have not made his acquaintance?'

'He is here so seldom, and I have not chanced to be anywhere to be presented to him. I have seen him in the village before, and recognize him by sight. I was surprised he did not recognize Jane, but he did not appear to do so.'

'I've only met him two times myself,' Jane pointed out. 'I was young then. Did you happen to hear who the gentleman with him is, Mr Johnson?'

'Not by name, but I heard he has four gentlemen with him – all bachelors – or one is a widower, I believe, an older gentleman. You girls will have a fine time at the assembly. I will be lucky to have a partner at all. I hope you will do me the honour of reserving the first dance for me, as usual, Miss McCormack?'

Holly felt a jab of annoyance. It was not so much the certainty of missing out on the interesting newcomers that vexed her as the possessive sound of 'as usual.' The daughter of a clergyman herself, she placed great importance on the position, and could not screw herself up to any rude or sharp answer. 'I look forward to it,' she replied, with no great enthusiasm.

'Excellent. Excellent. I am just back from the Abbey. I went to speak to Lord Dewar about getting some increase in the orphanage funds, but he had just left. I seem to have missed him in the village as well. He is very generous. He will raise the funding when he comes to realize we have not had an increase in ten years. Costs have risen sharply in that time. It is not a raise in my own salary as the director I speak of, of course. I have sufficient from my position as rector of the church. It is the boys I am concerned about. The building wants some repairs.'

'This would be an excellent opportunity to speak to Lord Dewar about taking Billie McAuley to see a specialist in London as well,' Holly suggested. 'That leg of his – I am sure a good specialist could alleviate his pain, and perhaps even make it easier for him to walk. He is so bright, and so brave – never complaining. An orphan – his only chance for help is through the orphanage.'

'I shall certainly speak to him about it, if I can manage an interview.'

'He will surely return your call,' Holly said.

Johnson looked surprised at this idea. 'I don't count on it, but I shall certainly go after him again. He is reasonable, not clutch-fisted, really; it is only that it is difficult to get hold of him. I have written to him twice in London, but his man of business wrote back that Dewar would speak to me when he came to the Abbey. I wonder how long he means to stay.'

'I didn't hear,' Holly answered. 'He will not leave without attending to business. I expect that is why he is home – to get matters in hand here in the village.'

Again Johnson looked at her with some surprise on his face, though he did not actually refute her statement. 'There are several items wanting his attention, certainly.'

'Yes, there is the school with old Mr Parsons, well into his seventies, trying to teach, while Mr Prendergast is graduated from Oxford with nothing better to do than clerk for Mr Raymond.'

'Your friend will be happy when Mr Prendergast is appointed schoolmaster, eh Miss Proctor?' Johnson asked in a bantering way. Jane's friend, Miss Peabody, was engaged to Mr Prendergast, impatiently awaiting the day he could find a good position and marry her. Jane nodded and smiled her agreement.

It then occurred to Johnson he had not made any congratulatory reference to Proctor's recent knighthood. He had formally sent his delight in writing and speech, called Proctor Sir Egbert every time he met him, and satisfied even Lady Proctor by using her proper prefix several times when they met. For the next month or so, the matter must also be raised with all members of the family upon each meeting. 'How are Sir Egbert and Lady Proctor?' he asked, to get it all rolled up in one shot.

'They're fine.'

'While you, I know, are busy as a bee preparing yourself for the jaunt to the big city. You will set all the men's heads awhirl. You'll be the prettiest girl there. The belle of all the balls.'

'I wish Holly could come with me,' Jane said.

'She will be required to manage those brothers of yours at home, while your parents take you to make your bows at Court. They are fortunate to have her. Indeed we all appreciate Miss McCormack's many excellent qualities,' he finished, pushing his gallantry about as far as it ever went.

'You remind me of my duty, Mr Johnson,' Holly said, to get away as neatly as she could. 'I am to cut the boys' hair before dinner.'

'Remember to save me the first dance Friday evening!' he said, and lifted his hat again, before turning his steps toward the rectory.

CHAPTER 4

$\mathcal{R}$ex Homberly lived for riding, hunting, drinking, and falling in love. In the normal way, his preference followed the order given, but occasionally he fell in love with a female the pursuit of whom took precedence over all other pastimes. His annual drop into the abyss of love occurred the day he set his eyes on Miss Proctor in the village. It could not have happened at a worse time either, for the autumn hunting season was opening, and he had brought three hunters with him to St Alton's Abbey. Foxworth and Dewar would not let him off, he was forced to participate, and enjoyed it very much too once he got into the field. It was a long run, with what Rex called 'the slyest old Reynard ever let out of its kennel.' He incurred no wrath from his fellow hunters for, while Rex could usually make a mess of most things, he was a dusting good rider. Brooks, banks, fence, woods, open meadows, or a neighbour's garden – it was all one and the same to him. It was 'forrard,' so long as the hounds had the scent. He cared for neither his new Bedford cords nor his hunting jacket. On the field, he thought of three things: his horse, the hounds, and Mr Fox. With single-minded tenacity, he followed his own nose to Ellsworth Craig when over half the field went west to the woods. He was in on the kill, and had the great fortune to get a few drops of blood on his coat. These he treasured as though they were diamonds. No denying, as he pointed out to Foxey, it took the look of the amateur off his jacket to have it splattered up a bit. He smiled happily on the unsightly stains, and offered to run the tails of his jacket on Foxey's, to share the glory, 'seeing as how you didn't know enough to stay with me. You might have known Altmore would lead you astray.'

'I felt like landing him a facer,' Foxey said. 'Here I thought he was following the hounds, but he was only shearing off to a farm to change mounts, for he managed to cripple his, the flat.'

'Should have done it.'

'I would have, but he's such a gudgeon he fell right off his nag, and I never hit a man when he's down.'

'Good idea. Neither do I. Don't know how big he might be when he gets up.'

After distinguishing himself on the first day; it was expected he would be as miserable as the rest of the party when the next morning showed them lead grey skies, with a virtual curtain of rain cascading down, accompanied by rumbles of thunder that augured a continuance of the weather for some hours. He had been known to urge going on with the hunt in such cases, but on this morning he settled quite happily into his beefsteak and ale, congratulating his hostess on a good country breakfast. Lady Dewar nodded jealously as she helped herself to a dish of Folkstone pudding. She would have preferred the steak and ale, but Dr John was adamant.

'As the hunt is cancelled, this will be a good opportunity for us to select a work for our little dramatic presentation,' Dewar said, speaking across the table to Mr Altmore, the friend he had invited along to ensure one agreeable companion.

'That must depend on what people in the neighbourhood will be available to perform for you,' he said. 'Lady Dewar can tell us how many of the youngsters would be interested in taking part.'

'You don't know Chubbie very well, do you?' she asked, bluntly. 'It don't matter whether they want to take part or no. He will make them. There are a dozen young chits will be happy to throw their caps at you bucks, and as to men – why there are all of yourselves, and the parson and Mr Prendergast. You can use footmen to fill in the little bits of parts. Just see you don't cast me as anything,' she warned her son. 'I don't act.'

'And here I thought you were all set to take the male lead, Mama, as you are wearing my old jacket,' Dewar said, lifting a brow to admire her ensemble. 'What do you think about Moliére, Luke?' he went on, turning to Altmore.

'Do you really think French is a good idea?'

Rex was chewing with a look of fierce concentration on his pudgy face. He suddenly laid down his fork. 'Thought it was all set we was to do *My Horse, My Horse, My Kingdom for a Horse,* Dew. Sent off to London for the outfit yesterday.'

'Surely not *Richard the Third* – so heavy,' Altmore objected.

'Miss Proctor would not like it,' Dewar agreed.

Rex frowned to consider this difficulty, and began chewing his ale.

'You will want to have Jane Proctor and her cousin,' Lady Dewar said. 'But don't go dangling after the chit,' she added to her son. 'Since Bertie has been knighted, his fool of a wife is casting her eyes about for a title for the gel. She's a taking little thing, but not suitable for you, Dewar.'

'A title, you say?' Rex asked, his eyes narrowing. 'Daresay an abbey would suit her as well.'

'Our title goes with the Abbey,' the hostess pointed out to him.

'So it does,' he said, blushing.

'Rex refers to his own abbey, Mama. What a bore. He is in love again.'

'No such a thing!' Rex insisted, then immediately suggested they all take a dash into Harknell, asking just which house had the honour of holding Miss Proctor, and whether she had a fellow on the string at all.

'I am not about to swim into the village,' Dewar told him. 'Proctor's place is the rather ugly stone one on the right side of the road, just east of Harknell.'

'Can't go alone. Don't know her. Look a fool, barging in and saying I was your cousin. She'd wonder you hadn't come with me. Ought to come, Dew,' Rex told him.

'Mama will provide you with an excuse,' was the best answer he could get.

After a good deal of prodding, Lady Dewar had the inspired notion of sending half a dozen of the orphans' shirts down to Miss Proctor to sew, but Rex did not feel this was a romantic enough errand, and delayed his visit till he could go without arriving soaked to the skin. He felt instinctively too that it would add to his consequence if he could arrive at the door with Dewar in tow, but throughout the day his cousin obstinately refused to budge from his study, where he and Altmore thumbed through books, discarding each after reading it for five minutes. Everything had been done, or was too long, or too dull, or had too many characters. By nightfall there was still no decision taken. Friday the sky had cleared and, though the ground was sodden, the hunt continued, making a visit to Miss Proctor impossible. When the hour for the assembly rolled around, Rex had still not made her acquaintance, and was champing at the bit to get to the party.

A similar state of eagerness prevailed at Stonecroft, where Lady Proctor was very peeved indeed that neither Dewar nor his mama had come to ask for Jane's hand, and His Lordship in residence for five days now. 'At least he will be at the assembly,' she consoled herself. 'Mr Johnson said he would attend, did he not, Holly?'

'Yes, he did.' Holly, too, felt a greater than usual eagerness to get to the party. Lord Dewar's being at the Abbey with a party of bachelors lent a brighter lustre to the evening. There was a feeling in the air that anything might happen. It was highly improbable that Dewar would fall in love with Jane, less likely that he would even so much as stand up with herself, but Mr Johnson had spoken of four other gentlemen. The short, funny-looking little man with him was of course one of them, but that still left three unknown quantities. Three London gentlemen, one of whom might be partial to herself – that was something to look forward to.

She glanced into the mirror, where Jane was seen to stand

behind her, wearing a white gown, befitting her status as a young lady making her bows. Her blond curls shone in an aura around her face – such a pretty little face, with large, dark blue eyes, and a small, child-like pair of lips. Holly's heart sank to compare herself to Jane. She was tall, her arms too long, her hair undistinguished, and her gown an unfashionable dark green. She looked like a chaperon. She often was one, but this evening Lady Proctor came with them, so she was free to be a young lady. On the threshold of twenty-seven, she no longer felt like one. She looked a suitable dancing partner for Mr Johnson, and that, very likely, was what she would be.

'You look nice, Holly,' Jane said, and smiled sweetly. On top of her other advantages, Jane also had a charming disposition.

Lady Proctor looked them both over approvingly, then went to the mirror for a final appraisal of her own gown. It was a new one, made up since Bertie's elevation in the world. It was of cinnamon crepe, with great swaths of silk fringe attached to the gown, after a pattern seen in *La Belle Assemblée*. One had not thought, to look at it in a frozen sketch, that it would jiggle about so when one walked. Really, it was extraordinarily uncomfortable, and she had paid a very good price for it. 'We had better go. We don't want to miss the opening minuet,' she declared, and called for her fur wrap.

As they jogged along into Harknell in the carriage, Lady Proctor gave her daughter such bits of motherly advice as she found suitable. 'If Dewar should happen to ask you for the first dance, Jane dear, you want to show your appreciation in a proper manner. Don't giggle or smirk or lord it over the other girls and, for goodness sake, don't be shy. You may have two dances with him. If he encourages you to stand up for a third, you must refuse. Do it gently, but firmly. And of course you must not waltz. He will not ask you, when he learns from his mama you are to make your bows in London. The only young lady from Harknell who is doing so, and it is a pity, in a way, that you cannot waltz, but there will be the opening minuet, and perhaps a cotillion or quadrille, or a country dance. Not that he will bother with the country dances, I expect. They are sad romps, lacking in dignity. Dewar stands very high on his dignity.'

The evening began auspiciously enough. Dewar and his party, even including his mama, had arrived at the Assembly Hall before the dance began. Lady Proctor had no way of knowing this was due to the unabashed hounding of Mr Homberly, who had begun his gentle insistings an hour before they were due to leave the Abbey. She took it, strangely enough, as a personal compliment. There was surely great significance in the fact that both Lady Dewar and herself, neither of whom normally came to these dos, chose to attend on this occasion: the former with her eligible son, the latter with her nubile daughter. It was pretty clear as well that Dewar was standing close by the doorway on purpose to greet the Proctor party, and she regretted deeply that Sir Egbert had elected to stay home and play cards with his bailiff. One would think a knight would have a more proper notion of his duties. But there, she had suspected all along it would be up to herself to make the evening run smoothly.

The countess sat across the room, ensconced in the warmest corner of the hall, the one that backed against the kitchen and got the heat from the stove. Her son had not permitted her to leave the house in a gentleman's jacket, but had promised to secure this warm corner for her. Dewar's attention, though he stood near the doorway, had been temporarily distracted across the room to Miss Lacey, who looked as vulgar as usual in a gown cut much too low for a young lady, and with an overly elaborate coiffure that sent Lady Proctor's eyes darting to Jane's plain curls for a comparison. For one horrible moment, it seemed Dewar did not realize Jane had entered but, fortunately, one of his companions, likely warned to the job, tugged at his elbow and said in quite an audible voice, 'She's here.'

This finally got Dewar's eyes off Miss Lacey and on to his future bride. No mama could like to have a gentleman ogle her daughter in such an open way, with his quizzing glass raised, running noticeably from head to toe. As soon as he smiled and advanced towards them, however, this solecism was forgiven. The 'Good evening, Mrs Proctor,' that followed immediately was harder to forgive, despite the graceful bow that accompanied it. Dewar stared as the woman's expression changed from delight to offence. For a full thirty seconds he was stopped dead, racking his brain to discover where he had gone amiss.

From the dame's left shoulder, a pleasant voice spoke up. 'Oh, Lady Proctor, your shawl is slipping,' it said. Without glancing to follow the voice to its source, Dewar recovered his *faux pas*. 'What a forgetful fellow I am!' he explained. 'For years I was used to call you Lady Proctor when speaking of you to Mama, and have heard myself corrected so often that the old name slipped out. Do forgive me, Lady Proctor. Now at last I can address you in the way that always seemed most natural to me.'

There was so much blarney wrapped up in this speech, and such swift, clever thinking, that Miss McCormack was momentarily overcome. She looked to her aunt, seeing with amusement that the blarney had gone down very well. A broad smile beamed. It was of all things the most acceptable he could have said – to intimate frequent references to her at the Abbey and to include a neat compliment on Egbert's knighthood all in one. She was forced to admit it was skillfully done. There was a flurry of introductions, while Dewar expressed the proper amount of surprise and pleasure at Jane's having achieved maturity and an acknowledgement of Miss McCormack's being amongst them. Then Homberly was put forward. It was such a rosy beginning for the evening that really there seemed nothing more to be desired, till the musicians began scraping their bows, indicating the dance was about to begin. Then things began to get out of hand. Somehow, it was the insignificant little fellow with the popping eyes that was leading Jane to the floor, while Dewar hastened across the room to offer his arm to Miss Lacey. Holly hardly had time to assure her aunt it was all a mistake before Mr Johnson was at her elbow, reminding her of her promise. 'Dewar intended to ask Jane first, but the

Homberly man beat him to it. She will surely have the second dance with Dewar. Why don't you go and speak to his mother?' Holly said before leaving her aunt's side.

There was little consolation to be gained from the countess. 'I see Homberly achieved his wish. It is all we hear at the Abbey, Elsa, how he is smitten with your gel. You will have an offer from the fellow if you play your cards right. A very eligible parti he is too. Has an Abbey in Surrey. A good old family. There – I told you I'd save you the bother of hauling her off to the city.'

'Is Dewar looking to make a match with Sally Lacey?' Elsa retaliated. 'Quite a feather in her cap, for a miller's daughter to nab a peer.'

'That he ain't! But it will do her no harm to claim him for her flirt for the month or so he is home. She's a looker. Dewar likes that. Tell me, Elsa, what the deuce are all those strings doing hanging off your gown? They will have a pair of scissors in the ladies' room to trim them for you,' the countess suggested, with a malicious little smile on her gaunt face.

'This is a fringe, Lady Dewar. The latest style from London but, then, you are not interested in style.' This was not the way the talk was supposed to go at all. They should be discussing visits by now.

'I have better things to do. When we get to be our age it is time to give over to the youngsters.' Another blow, for a lady of sixty-five to be claiming herself coeval with a dame scarcely forty. 'You've got Jane rigged up to the nines tonight. A part of her London wardrobe, I fancy?'

This unpromising beginning soon went even further downhill, to become immersed in bellyaches and cures. At the end of the first set, Lady Proctor excused herself with thin-lipped civility, and went after her daughter. She scarcely nodded to Homberly when he returned Jane to her. Had it not been for his kinship to the Dewars, and of course his Abbey, she would have forgone the nod as well.

Mr Johnson soon added himself to the list of persons out to defeat Lady Proctor. What must the gudgeon do but claim Jane for the second set, when that rather good-looking gentleman who had come with Dewar – Altmore they were calling him – was advancing towards the Proctor party. As he was deprived of Jane's company, he asked Miss McCormack to stand up with him, bringing some little joy to Holly at least. She had noticed him amid the throng – tall, dark, not precisely handsome, but with the unmistakable aura of the city about his hair and jacket. She was soon in possession of all the important facts regarding Dewar's company at the Abbey – their names, backgrounds, and the intended length of their visit. The next set was whiled away for Holly by putting Lady Proctor in possession of these same facts, and by trying to calm her wrath at Dewar's standing up with Mrs Raymond when Jane was at loose ends. Jane was not long free, however. Mr Altmore at last claimed her for a dance, and Foxey was hot on his heels.

The evening was well advanced before Elsa had the pleasure of seeing her first-born in the arms of Dewar. What vestige of relief this might have brought was largely destroyed by its being a simple country dance. It would take an active imagination to find any intimacy or chance for romantic dalliance during a country dance. Jane appeared a perfect fright at its end, with her face bright pink, little beads of perspiration on her forehead, and her curls all shaken about on her head, till she looked nearly as common as Miss Lacey.

'Well, what had Dewar to say?' she was asked, as soon as she resumed her seat.

'He said he would like to call on us tomorrow, if it is all right. I gave him permission. I hope you don't mind?'

Miss Lacey, Mrs Raymond, Mr Homberly, and Mr Johnson – all were forgiven in the burst of hope that followed these words. 'Mind? *Mind*? No indeed, I have nothing to say against it. Morning or afternoon?'

'He didn't say, Mama. I hope he comes in the morning, for Holly and I wanted to go into the village in the afternoon.'

'Go and brush your hair, Jane, and wipe off your face. See if

Holly has any rice powder. You are overheated with all that hard jigging.' This speech was accompanied by a most doting smile and a gentle, motherly pat on the wrist. When Jane returned to the hall, she saw her mama sitting beside Lady Dewar, her head back, laughing gaily. It really was an excellent party. 'We should come more often to these little local assemblies, Lady Dewar,' Elsa said. 'It keeps up the ton for the slightly older ladies to attend, do you not agree?'

What 'ton' Lady Dewar lent was all in her title and her reputation, for her physical presence in a grey gown oddly resembling a gunnysack lent no distinction.

Jane was not singled out at Dewar's dinner party, but the two families were all at the same table, with the Laceys and their like excluded. That odious little Mr Homberly had an encroaching way of putting himself forward, and of cutting Jane off from the other gentlemen by seating her at the end of the table. But, all in all, the meal was not unpleasant and, afterwards, there was the visit to the ladies' room to mention in a loud voice to Holly that Dewar would be calling tomorrow, while Mrs Lacey looked on angrily. Then in a lower voice she added, 'See if you can keep that pesky Homberly fellow away from Jane, dear, for there is no saying Dewar won't stand up with her again if he gets the chance.'

This request proved impossible of fulfilling. It was Mr Homberly who stood up again with Jane. Later, Dewar was returned to the family circle. When he passed Lady Proctor's chair between sets, she called out to him in a loud voice, 'Ah, Dewar, I forgot to tell your mama – perhaps you will be kind enough to mention it to her when you get home. . . .' There was sufficient noise that he had to walk up to her chair to hear her, and once he was within an arm's length she was soon urging him on to the empty chair beside her. Jane was in the card room, as a waltzing session was next to come.

'Yes, ma'am?' he asked, just a trifle impatiently. The prettier girls were already being led to the floor. She refused to recognize any hints. Quick darts of the eye to the far wall, a jiggling knee –

all were ignored, while she launched into a recital of Sir Egbert's dislike of assemblies. Suddenly she was struck with inspiration. There was Holly unpartnered; if he stood up with her, he would be back in this spot when Jane returned after the waltzes.

'I see you are eager to dance, Dewar. My niece will be happy to oblige you. She has hardly had a dance all evening.' This speech sent Holly into a fit of the dismals, which she did her best to conceal as she accepted the black-sleeved arm that was held to her, rather stiffly, as though under protest. She felt an utter fool. Her hopes had risen insensibly when first Dewar strolled towards them. She took the idea he was coming to ask her to dance, but as his steps veered off to the left, she had recovered her disappointment without much trouble. It would have been nice to stand up with a lord, particularly a tall, elegant, eligible lord, but she had not really expected it. Especially it would have been flattering as he chose the prettier ladies for his partners, but to be foisted on to him as a duty – she would a thousand times rather not have stood up with anyone at all. Suddenly he looked down at her and smiled, and all her disappointment faded. That lean, aristocratic, supercilious mask came to life when he smiled. It was the eyes that did it.

'I have not had an opportunity to thank you for saving my face earlier this evening, ma'am,' he said, pitching his voice low so that it sounded intimate. 'Thank you.'

Their arrival at the dance was several hours ago; she could not recall what he referred to. The waltz began, and he gathered her up in his arms. Waltzing had but recently arrived in Harknell from the city. It was still considered a trifle dashing, new enough to cause a flush on a young lady's cheeks, to feel a man's arms around her, and in front of the whole village too. The only man Holly had waltzed with before was Mr Prendergast and, really, when one's partner is engaged to another lady the recklessness of it is greatly diminished. It seemed much more exciting to be waltzing with Lord Dewar.

'I am referring to my regrettable accident in forgetting your aunt is now entitled to be called Lady Proctor. I thought for a minute there she was going to brain me with her fan, till you so adroitly brought my error to my attention. Neat, Miss McCormack.'

'You deserve congratulations on your recovery as well, sir.'

'That was rather well done, was it not? I have gained a certain expertise in disentangling folks, not least myself, from tight corners. If you have met my cousin, Rex Homberly, you will understand my meaning.'

'Is he the little short, fat . . . the not very tall . . . that is. . . .'

'He is the tall, handsome midget who has been dogging Miss Proctor's steps all evening. As I have just been boasting a little of my skill, it is the least I can do to rescue you from that verbal morass you are sinking in. If you have not had much chance to become acquainted with Rex, you soon will. I have a presentiment he will become a fixture in your aunt's saloon. He has coerced me into delivering him there tomorrow morning, in any case. He has taken the unaccountable notion the mama don't care for him, and he would be more welcome if he went under my auspices. I do hope it is not true – that Lady Proctor has taken him in dislike, I mean.'

'Oh no!' Holly said, her mind foreseeing all manner of unpleasantness when the truth of the much-looked-forward-to visit was revealed.

'You are wearing a very woe-is-meish face all of a sudden, ma'am,' he said, whirling around in time to the music, making the waltz seem a whole new experience from the two times she had marched it with Mr Prendergast. 'Never mind. You will soon love Rex. He has an insinuating way about him, like a puppy. Odd how we come to love those who cause us the most trouble.'

'I have never noticed that.'

'Think about it,' he suggested. Then they were silent for a few moments. After a while, he said, 'I did not mean necessarily to devote your mind to a study of it at this moment. Please feel free to think of anything you like, and even to mention it.'

She took this, as indeed it was intended, as a hint to talk to him.

'A pity the weather has been so bad for the hunting,' she said.

This platitude may as well have remained unspoken. He did not acknowledge it at all, but said, 'I hope you too will be home when we call tomorrow morning. There is a matter we would like to discuss with you. I think you are the more likely one than your cousin to discuss it with.'

'What matter is that?' she asked, curious.

'It's a long story. We shan't go into it tonight, but that voice of yours is superb.'

This cryptic statement left her wondering what on earth he could have in mind. He went right on to another subject before she could gain any idea what he meant and, too soon, the waltz was over.

Lady Proctor's spirits were so high on the way home that Holly did not wish to depress them with a recital of the truth. It would be learned soon enough and, meanwhile, she could hug the memory of the evening to herself, and cosset her little mystery and her few rags of compliments.

It really does not do to worry a trivial conversation too much, she discovered. Dewar spoke of not having had an opportunity to thank her, but he had taken no step to make the opportunity. He had not intended dancing with her till Aunt Elsa forced the issue. She soon came to think it was ill-done of him to leave her wondering for hours what he wished to discuss on the morrow. He might have given a hint. It was inconsiderate to leave a person wondering all night. What on earth could it be?

CHAPTER 5

$\mathcal{J}$t was unthinkable that anyone leave the house when Lord Dewar had promised to call. Even when morning grew into afternoon, and still he did not come, there was no mention by Lady Proctor of doing anything but sitting in the saloon in her second-best gown, waiting for him. Jane, deeply into a novel, had little objection to this. Holly, with her mind half on the orphans' shirts awaiting her needle, resented the waste of time for, of course, it was impossible to be caught sewing by such prestigious callers. Long before luncheon, she had deserted the saloon and gone to her own room, to sew and wonder and, finally, to resent such thoughtless treatment. It was not long after luncheon when she was called down, but the visitor was not Dewar. It was only Mr Johnson, ostensibly come to check on the progress of the shirts but, in fact, to gossip over the assembly, like any old maid.

'Quite an addition to our little society, Lord Dewar's party. The girls are all twittering this morning. I expected to see you in Harknell on a Saturday morning, ladies,' he said, lifting his coat-tails to take a seat.

'We were waiting for Lord Dewar to call. Holly thought he said he would come in the morning, but it seems she was mistaken, for he did not come,' Lady Proctor told him.

'Very likely,' Johnson answered, but Holly knew she was not mistaken. 'He was so very busy this morning in the village that I had not a chance to talk to him about the money for the orphanage. I hoped when I saw him in the village that he would call on me, return, my call, that is, but he didn't get round to it.'

'What was he doing?' Lady Proctor asked, with shameless curiosity.

'He was at the post office and in the shops.'

'He would be tending to business for his mama,' she decided. 'He called on Mr Raymond, her solicitor, I warrant.'

'No, he did not. I happened to be speaking to Mr Raymond, and he had some hopes Dewar would drop in, for there are some papers requiring his signature, but he didn't get round to it. He was too busy. He was in the drapery shop chatting to the Cockburne girls, and he took his visitors to have a look at the church. Unfortunately, I was not around at the time. He didn't call at the rectory, but my housekeeper tells me he was outside the church, pointing out the gargoyles and features of interest to his visitors. He will likely call on me this afternoon. Or, if not, I'll try if I can pin him after service on Sunday. I expect I may be asked to the Abbey for luncheon, to meet his guests. I often dine with the countess on a Sunday.'

Mr Johnson was not invited to remain and discuss his business with Dewar when he called, nor was he obtuse enough to suggest it when he saw Jane sitting in her good blue gown, with every curl in place. Turning to Holly, he continued speaking. 'I am happy to see Dewar plans to remain a while at the Abbey. There are several matters requiring his attention.'

'A pity he wouldn't attend to them, instead of gossiping in the village,' she answered tartly, becoming a little tired of everyone's making excuses for him.

'You may be sure he will. That is why he is come, certainly: to see to the running of the family orphanage, and to replacing the schoolmaster – all the details that need his personal decision. I shall speak to him about having a specialist look at young McAuley's leg while he is here. I am very happy he has come at last. The roof of the church could do with a few new slates as well.'

They continued talking for half an hour, at which time Johnson took his leave, peering down the road hopefully as he turned his mount homeward, to see if there was any chance of buttonholing Dewar. But the only person in sight was Mr Raymond, returning from the Abbey, where he had been to get Dewar's signature on the required document.

'He was sorry he hadn't known when he was in the village this morning,' Mr Raymond said. 'If he had known, he would have stopped at my office and spared me the trip. Odd he didn't know, as I left a message yesterday, but he didn't get it. He was very obliging.'

'Oh yes, he is always very obliging,' Johnson agreed. It was the opinion generally stated of Dewar, that he was very obliging.

He finally obliged Lady Proctor at five o'clock, coming just as she had abandoned hope of seeing him, and had removed her uncomfortable lace collar (that scratched the neck due to an excess of sugar used to stiffen it). Jane's careful toilette had suffered as well. With her muscles cramped from sitting up straight for hours, she finally pulled her feet up beneath her on the sofa and lounged against the pillows, creasing her gown beyond elegance. When Holly joined them at four-thirty, Lady Proctor ordered tea to help pass the vigil. The empty cups sat on the tray when Dewar and Homberly were finally shown in.

Lady Proctor was determined to be a ladylike and affable, but it took all her self-control to do it. When she looked at the untidy tray, and at her lace collar hanging over the arm of the chair, a frown pleated her brow. And when she observed that Mr Homberly was of the party her eyes snapped angrily. 'Lord Dewar, we were beginning to think you had forgotten all about us,' she said, her tone tinged with annoyance.

'Not for one moment, I promise you,' he replied, with an appreciative smile at Jane that calmed the mother's ruffled feathers in a wonderful hurry. 'I have been trying to get here all day, but something always interrupts me. It is the fact of so many details awaiting my attention that delays me.'

'I am sure you are very busy,' Lady Proctor said, sliding the lace collar in behind a cushion, and ringing the bell for a fresh tea tray. 'Mr Johnson was mentioning only this morning that he was expecting a call from you.'

'Mr Johnson?' he asked, frowning, and quite obviously not familiar with the name of his own rector.

'Feller we ducked out the side door to miss t'other day,' Rex reminded him helpfully. 'Rector, I think your butler said he is. Ain't that right, ma'am?'

'Yes, the rector of St Alton's,' the astonished dame replied.

'That was the day I had to spend with my steward,' Dewar explained, in an effort to gloss it over. 'Roots becomes very vexed with me if I interrupt our business chats.'

'Day we saw Miss Jane in the village,' Rex added, with a fond smile at the girl.

There was an uncomfortable moment's silence while the two elder ladies regarded him in a measuring fashion. Into the silence, Rex spoke up. 'See you're reading, Miss Proctor.' He used the comment as an excuse to join her on the sofa, reaching out to see the title of her book. *Necromancer of the Black Forest*, he read. 'Sounds pretty heavy stuff for a young lady. Daresay you're blue. Wearing blue anyway.'

'Oh no, it is only a novel,' she assured him, dismayed at the charge of being an intellectual.

'That so? A new one on me. Like reading myself. Read *The Castle of Otranto* once. You read *The Castle of Otranto*, Miss Proctor?'

'I'm not sure. I don't recall the title.'

'Like me,' he told her, nodding his head sagely. 'Have no mind for what I've read, except for Otranto. Dewar – he could tell you what I've read. I always borrow my books from him.'

'It would take me all of a minute if you are interested in the list,' Dewar said, with a satirical smile.

Neither Miss Proctor nor anyone else displayed the least interest in either the list or the ill-natured remark. Lady Proctor enquired for Lady Dewar's health, after which Dewar conveyed his mother's imaginary compliments to his hostess. These civilities taken care of, he turned to Miss McCormack, who was regarding him with scanty approval. She had not been mistaken to think him unkind in his remarks the preceding evening. He was nasty to Homberly, heedless of his duties and, she suspected, not quite truthful in trying to hide his faults.

'You have not forgotten, I hope, that you and I have something to discuss today, Miss McCormack,' he said.

'I have not forgotten. I am curious as to what it can be,' she answered.

'What is this? You did not tell me of this, Holly,' her aunt said, leaning forward, her eyes bright with interest.

'I did not know what matter Lord Dewar had in mind,' she explained, looking to him for enlightenment.

'Putting on a play,' Rex told them. 'Something to do to get in the days till we go back to London, you know.'

This was not the manner in which Dewar had planned to broach the subject but, as he considered it very much a treat for the ladies, he was not much dismayed. He looked to the three for the expected approval. He saw Jane blinking her eyes in astonishment, Lady Proctor glancing to the doorway for signs of the tea tray, and Miss McCormack regarding him in stony disapproval. The thought struck him that the household might be Methodist, though he had not heard anyone say so. 'A classical drama – something to bring a little culture to Harknell,' he explained hastily.

Holly's expression softened into interest at this. 'How nice,' she said. 'The school put on *The Search after Happiness* a few years ago, a pastoral play by Hannah More, you know,' she said, nodding her approval at this high aim. 'What play is it you plan to bring to the village, sir? The travelling troupes seldom stop here, as we are a small community, and cannot scrape together sufficient audience to make it worth their while.' It seemed a suitable charity venture to her that Dewar should finance this scheme.

'Actually it is our intention to mount the production ourselves,' he said.

'Oh! That is why you brought those gentlemen with you. What play is it you are going to put on for us?' she asked, still satisfied.

'That is what I hope to discuss with you ladies today,' he answered. 'What play would you enjoy to do?'

'We?' Jane asked. 'Lord Dewar, we are not actresses!' She laughed aloud at the very idea of herself or Holly standing on a stage in front of everyone, making cakes of themselves.

Holly remembered his remark regarding her fine voice. She looked at him, incredulous. 'Certainly not! It is not to be thought of.' she seconded.

'Thank God for that!' Homberly sighed, at peace with the world. 'Rubbishing idea. Tell me, Miss Proctor, you ride at all?'

Her answer was not heard by Holly, or her mother either. These two ladies were immediately subjected to a verbal barrage from Dewar that did not leave them an ear free to listen. 'Of course it is only an amateur performance we have in mind,' he began persuasively, 'for a small group of friends.'

'That won't bring much culture to the local people in general, will it?' Holly asked. 'Not to the ones who need it, I mean, and would enjoy it as a great novelty. The gentry you speak of may go to a play in London as often as they like.'

'As a local resident, you would have a better idea of who might enjoy it,' he agreed instantly. 'It is why I especially wanted to talk to you – all you ladies at Stonecroft. Mama suggested you as being very active in all the goings-on in the village. The charity work, the church projects, and so on.'

'That is true,' Lady Proctor nodded, taking some credit for her niece's active involvement. 'The sewing, for instance, we do a great deal of, and when Mr Johnson had his bazaar last spring we did three-quarters of the preparing. The notices for the shop windows, the setting up of the stalls, the prizes. . . .'

'We are much too busy to spend any considerable amount of time in preparing a play,' Holly said. 'I, personally, have not a moment free.'

'With that voice of yours, you must take part, Miss McCormack,'

Dewar objected. 'It struck me the moment you spoke last evening that it was made for the stage. A deep, carrying tone, but still very musical. I have not heard a finer voice anywhere, and I include Mrs Siddons in that. Your voice reminds me of her.'

If he thought to cut any ice with this comparison he was out. Lady Proctor could not quite place the name, though she was sure she had heard it before, and Holly knew when she was being cozzened. 'Thank you for the compliment, sir, but I have never acted on a stage, and never intend to. I know it takes up a great deal of time, and I am too busy.'

'What is it you do that doesn't leave you a free moment?' he asked.

'Charity work. I also help my aunt here at home.' She reached down and picked up an orphan's shirt as she spoke, to prove her point.

'As to that, Holly, there are plenty of servants, if you want to help Lord Dewar put on his little play,' Lady Proctor said. From the corner of her eye, she saw that nig-nog of a Jane discussing riding with Mr Homberly, whom she sincerely hoped would not take part in the dramatic presentation. Jane must be in the play to keep her under Dewar's eyes and, as chaperoning would be required, Holly too would participate. It was just the sort of occupation she did so well – dignified, genteel work. 'You could always stitch on the shirts while you chaperon, Holly.'

Dewar looked startled at this speech. 'I hope you will take a more active part than only chaperoning,' he said.

'No, really, I am not at all sure I can even do that. I help Mr Johnson with the church arrangements. I usually spend an afternoon a week with the church committee, and one or more with the charity work.'

'That leaves five afternoons and seven mornings,' he pointed out.

'And when Mr Parsons fell ill last winter, you remember, Aunt, I took the school for a full month. Mr Prendergast wanted to do it, but he had just undertaken to help Mr Raymond and could not get away.'

'Is Mr Parsons ill at the moment? I had not heard it,' Dewar said, becoming more determined with every obstacle thrown in his way. This was the one he wanted for his leading lady. Her voice enchanted the ear, the more so as she became angry and spoke more forcefully. There was a timbre to it – almost a vibrato – that would show to advantage in a great dramatic tragedy. Her form, too, while not of a feminine fullness, was tall and straight. The last success of Mrs Siddons was in his mind – Lady Macbeth. A more difficult piece than he had originally intended, but by no means beyond doing.

'No, but he is very old, and might fall ill at any moment,' she answered.

'If that occurs, I shall appoint a permanent replacement for him,' Dewar answered simply. 'Now, what we must settle on is what play we are to do. What do you think, Lady Proctor?' He turned to this dame, not because he felt for a moment she would have interesting views on the subject, but because she was in charge of the young ladies, and must be buttered into compliance.

'I once saw *The Rivals* played in Bath,' she told him, thus emptying half of her dramatic budget. 'It was ever so amusing.'

'So it is. I like it enormously,' he agreed readily.

'Then, of course, there is always Shakespeare,' she added. 'Jane's seminary that she went to two years ago put on something by Shakespeare. What was it, Jane dear, that play you were in at Miss Kinnear's?'

'*Romeo and Juliet*, Mama.'

'Yes, that has been done very often,' Dewar said in a dismissing way. 'I thought perhaps *Macbeth* would be interesting.'

'I cannot think Jane would like playing Lady Macbeth,' the girl's mother answered. 'She is not old enough, and she has all the speeches of Juliet by heart from Miss Kinnear's play, you know.'

With a dazed look on his face, Dewar said, 'Indeed,' then he sat rapidly revising his cast and even his play. Between Miss McCormack's reluctance and Lady Proctor's pushing of Jane, he saw he was not going to get his own way, but he would not abandon the whole project. He would still put on a play. He turned to examine Jane with a new interest. 'Now that is odd. You disclaimed being an actress when I first mentioned it, Miss Proctor.'

'It was only for the school. I have never acted in public,' she pointed out. She did not think to add that it was only the balcony scene she had been called upon to perform, with Miss Ewart, dressed in her brother's trousers, playing Romeo.

'Make a dashed pretty Juliet,' Rex said, his fond eyes melting, his voice mellowed with love.

Dewar continued to scrutinize the young girl. She was remarkably pretty and young enough, too, to play Juliet without the audience bursting into guffaws when the girl's age of fourteen years was mentioned in the play. Her voice was not strong, but it had a clear, bell-like quality that was pleasing. In a smallish room – the refectory hall at the Abbey, for instance – it would be loud enough. Yes, it would be interesting to mount a truly stunning production of *Romeo and Juliet* to raise it from the depths of its latest producer, Romeo Coates, who had brought a farcical version of it to London not long ago. And if this girl already knew the role it would save time. Altmore, of course, would play Romeo. With one last, reluctant glance back at Miss McCormack, he decided to try once more for her services in a tragedy.

Before he uttered a word, she spoke up. 'I don't see how you can possibly hope to have people learn a whole play in a month, and rehearse them. If Jane knows the role, common sense would dictate putting on *Romeo and Juliet*, providing one of your friends could undertake to learn Romeo's part.'

'Altmore,' Rex said, crossing his legs and jiggling his Hessians up and down, while he admired the gloss of his toes. 'Altmore played Romeo at Chatsworth two years ago. Daresay he remembers the lines. Devilish long-headed, Altmore. Knows everything. Memory like an elephant.'

'Will you be in the play, Mr Homberly?' Jane asked.

'Nope.'

Lady Proctor smiled in blissful contentment.

'Why not?' Jane asked him.

'Too clumsy. Trip over things. Don't like getting rigged out in silly costumes either. Ain't saying I wouldn't stand at the back of the stage to make up a crowd scene. Can't talk in front of people though. Haven't got the knack of it. Can't learn lines either. Offered Dew my horse's outfit. Glad to let him make use of it if he likes. Help any way I can. Won't act.' This speech dwindled into a mumble that was nearly inaudible toward its end.

When his lips stopped moving, Lady Proctor turned to Dewar to enquire what role he would take in the play.

'I will direct and produce,' he answered, which satisfied her as putting him in close contact with Jane for the duration.

The fresh tea tray arrived. Lady Proctor served with great daintiness, pushing biscuits and cakes on everyone but Mr Homberly, who could not wait to be offered. He slid over to the end of the sofa that put him within arm's reach of the tray and ate his way steadily through a Chinese cake, one piece at a time. While he ate, Dewar explained that his refectory hall would be the scene for the play, with rehearsals to begin a few days hence, after casting was completed.

'Will this leave you time to attend to all your estate business?' Holly enquired.

'I am pretty well finished it already,' he answered.

She could not believe he had seen Mr Johnson and Mr Raymond and attended to the half-dozen other matters requiring his decision in the half day since Mr Johnson had been with them.

CHAPTER 6

The village of Harknell looked forward to the novelty of hearing Lord Dewar perform the reading in church on Sun-day, but they were disappointed. It was raining, and he did not attend the service. Neither did Mr Johnson receive an invitation to the Abbey for luncheon. He accepted an invitation to Stonecroft instead to take his mutton with Sir Egbert and his family. Disappointment lent a peevish touch to his conversation that day. He had looked forward to introducing Lord Dewar in church, more to dining at the Abbey.

'It sets a bad tone, for his lordship to stay away from service only for a few drops of rain,' he said, feeling rather daring to utter this mild reproach.

'I don't think you should look to Dewar for any raising of the moral standards, Mr Johnson,' Holly said curtly. 'Did he return your call yesterday?'

'No, he did not. He didn't call on Raymond either. Raymond had to drive out to the Abbey to get him to look at some papers.'

'He had time to go into the shops though, and to plan a play to amuse himself during the visit,' Holly said.

'A play? I heard nothing of that!' he replied, a little vexed that he was not the first to know. He soon had all the details, and showed not a jot of approval at the scheme, though he could not like to condemn it outright. 'At least it is Shakespeare – something decent. It is no secret he put on a Restoration comedy five years ago at the Abbey. One of those bawdy things that is considered too risqué even for London.'

'Demmed fine play it was too,' Sir Egbert laughed. 'The ladies didn't care for it, I recollect. It is a pity he has switched to Shakespeare. I like a good comedy myself. So you are to be Juliet, eh, Minx?' he asked, turning to Jane to tease her on her glory.

After dessert, Mrs Abercrombie, a neighbour, dropped in on her way to visit a friend and, while Lady Proctor regaled her with an account of the play, Johnson turned to Holly for a little more mild complaining. 'I hope this play won't interfere with Dewar's attending to business. It is really quite lamentable the way he lets things run to ruin here. It seems a shame he should divert everyone's time from the work that needs doing at the orphanage. With Christmas coming on, we usually have our Christmas pageant, and there are the Christmas baskets to be made up. The local ladies could be more gainfully occupied than spending their time in an entertainment for the gentry.'

'I don't intend to waste *my* time, Mr Johnson,' Holly assured him. 'He asked me to take part, and I told him I would not. My aunt expects me to chaperon, but I believe once the rehearsals begin there will be others who can do it as well. Someone will have to play the Ladies Montague and Capulet – some mature ladies, and there is no reason they cannot chaperon Jane.'

'Who is to play the roles, have you heard?' he asked, with more interest than Holly felt the matter warranted though, upon consideration, she felt it was only a concern that some of his other good workers might be stolen away from him.

'I'm sure Mrs Raymond will not, nor Miss Boggs. Don't fear we will desert you at such a busy season, Mr Johnson.'

'That is kind of you. I knew I might depend on your good sense in this business. I only hope it does not go to Jane's head, all the attention. But she is a good little girl. She will keep her feet on the ground.'

'Dewar has not been in touch with you at all about business – the orphanage, the church roof?' Holly confirmed.

'Not so much as a note putting off our meeting. I might as well never have written to him. I have been ignored entirely, after hounding him till I am ashamed of it. It is really too bad of him.'

'I shall undertake to remind him, next time he comes here prating of plays,' Holly said, with a martial light glowing in her eye.

'You might just mention it in a discreet way, if the opportunity should arise.'

'The opportunity will arise, Mr Johnson. I guarantee it.'

While this conversation was going forth at Stonecroft, Lord Dewar was scouring his library for copies of the play, and when he could find only two he dashed an express off to Hatchard's in London for the rest. He then held a conference with his guests to decide on roles. Miss McCormack, without knowing it, was cast in the role of Lady Capulet, while Rex flipped through the pages to see which of the minor personages shared a scene with Juliet. He noticed the name Friar Laurence often occurred on the same page with her, but mouthing such impossibly long speeches that he did not volunteer.

'It would be appropriate to have Mr Johnson play Friar Laurence,' his mother suggested. 'A churchman and all. Excellent casting.'

'Would he be willing to do anything so daring?' Dewar asked.

'He'll leap at the chance, and he could learn the lines easily too, for he has half the scriptures by heart. He rattles them off on Sunday without hardly a glance at his book. Has a good loud voice. You can't catch a wink of sleep in church when he is talking.'

'I'll go and see him this afternoon,' Dewar said. 'I could do with a little exercise.'

'What about Rex and me?' Foxworth asked him.

'Come along if you like.'

'I mean, what parts are we to have in the play? Been looking it over. A dandy duel scene here in the third act. Tybalt and Mercutio. Me and Rex could do that. Not too many words you know, but a good rousing sword fight.'

'Not a bad idea. Smallish parts. Practicing their duel will keep 'em out of mischief,' Altmore said aside to Dewar.

'I seem to recall Mercutio survives the duel, and has a fair speaking part,' Dewar countered.

'So he does. Rex is the more inarticulate. He must be Tybalt. He will enjoy dying. Grunts and groans are not beyond him.'

'We shall try them, and see how it works out,' Dewar decreed.

The next mention of *Romeo and Juliet* heard by Holly, other than a few reminders each day from Lady Proctor to her daughter that she ought to start looking over her lines, if only they could find the book, occurred on Monday afternoonwhen Mr Johnson once more came to call. The Proctors, mother and daughter, had gone into Harknell to try to find a copy of the play. It was Holly's lot to greet Mr Johnson alone.

His bright smile led her to believe he had achieved success with Dewar on the matter of augmented funds for the orphanage. 'Don't tell me Lord Dewar has called on you at last!' she exclaimed.

'Indeed he has. Most kind of him. He stayed the better part of an hour. Brought two of his guests with him, a Mr Homberly and Mr Altmore. Altmore seems a very gentlemanly sort of a man.'

'I was well impressed with him at the assembly.'

'An excellent fellow. He is to play the role of Romeo. A little old for Jane's Juliet but then, as Dewar says, at a distance from the stage it will not be noticed. Altmore has a youthful, lithesome figure and a wonderful voice.'

'I see he bored you with his wretched play! Of more importance, Mr Johnson, are the funds for the orphanage. What sum has he given?'

'The orphanage? We did not discuss it. We are to have a good coze very soon about that.'

'You cannot mean you sat for an hour and let him away without dunning him for more money!' she exclaimed, nonplussed.

'The time was not appropriate. Dewar could only speak of his play. He is very enthusiastic about it. And, as he says, it will be a very good cultural influence on the villagers. We do not get enough intellectual stimulation here in Harknell. I daresay I ought to do more along that line.'

'You scarcely have time to tend to the church and the orphanage. I'm sure no one expects you to raise the level of culture as well.'

'Still, it is a pity that we are all sunk into an intellectual apathy here. I did not realize the extent of it till I spoke with Dewar and Altmore. They are certainly very stimulating conversational companions. How seldom it occurs to us here in the village to read the latest book – philosophical work or poetry, I mean, for of course you ladies all read novels. We are very behindhand in such matters, and I must include ourselves there, Miss McCormack. Oh, we will occasionally order a new sheet of music, or a book of sermons, but the real intellectual life of the country passes us by. We live in a stagnant backwater, and do virtually nothing to keep abreast of the times.'

'I don't see that putting on Shakespeare brings us right up to the minute,' she answered sharply, not liking the slurs on her mental torpor.

'Shakespeare? He is for all times. Each age finds its own meaning in him. That is what makes him a classic. But our talk was not limited to Shakespeare by a long shot. Philosophy, music, art – those were our topics of conversation. Very stimulating. It quite took me back to my university days. I am very happy indeed they mean to stay a while, and I shall be seeing a good bit of them, with this play.'

'Surely the play will occupy Dewar a good deal, having quite the opposite effect from what you say. He will not have much time to discuss cultural matters with you.'

'Oh, I am to be in the play! Did I not tell you? He asked me to take the part of Friar Laurence. Quite a pivotal character, next in importance only to Romeo and Juliet. Indeed, according to certain views, he is even more important – the only well-developed mature character in the play, actually. Dewar feels my real-life role as a clergyman of the church adds a depth to the characterization as well. Sort of a role within a role for me, if you see the point. A clergyman playing a friar. A very profound part. Fortunately, I have a copy of the play in my library. I was used to be quite active in reading and studying, once upon a time.'

'But what of the Christmas pageant? And the baskets – to say nothing of the sewing!'

'The play will take the place of the pageant this year. We have the same old pageant every year, with the same old stock figures. This will be a pleasant change. We shall put on a special performance for the orphans in the afternoon, and it will serve double duty as a dress rehearsal. It is all arranged. You must not take the notion I have forgotten my orphans, Miss McCormack.'

'The children won't be amused by Shakespeare! They are too young for a love story.'

'They will adore the duel scenes. And the costumes and sets – very elaborate plans he has for them – will be a novelty. Just getting to the Abbey for a day will be a great treat, you know. I trust you good ladies will find a moment to help stitch up the costumes.'

'These elaborate outfits you speak of will take more than a moment, Mr Johnson! I thought you felt as I do about the play,' she charged angrily. She saw all his former chagrin had to do with his own exclusion, not with wasted or misspent time.

'I did think it a bit of a waste of time at first but, as I reconsider the matter, I come to think it is just what has been lacking in Harknell. We want shaking up, and Dewar is the very one to do it. As he pointed out, it will really waste very little time. Stitching can be done as well at rehearsals as at home, and listening to the immortal words of Shakespeare instead of gossiping will be good for you. Always with the exception of the Good Book, you will not find more good sense more eloquently spoken than in Shakespeare. Indeed, I often find it difficult to know for sure whether certain quotations come from the one source or the other. Shakespeare has quite a Biblical style. I daresay he was a regular reader of the book.' This fabrication seemed to set the seal of approval on the scheme. No words she could speak moved him an inch from his position. Before he left, the play had become not only a pleasure, but a positive duty.

Over the next day and a half, Holly came to realize that if she was not to spend the next two months in utter isolation she would involve herself in the dramatic presentation. It was the only item discussed in the village. Ladies who should have been tending to charity work were holding reading parties to familiarize themselves with the play. Dewar did not come. to Stonecroft in person, but he sent his eager ambassador, Mr Homberly, to inform Miss McCormack she was to play Lady Capulet, and to enquire whether Lady Proctor would have any objection to holding the first few rehearsals in her saloon, as his own hall was in the carpenter's hands, with a stage and proscenium arch under erection. Lady Proctor gave her much-gratified consent. Miss McCormack did not.

'I am much too busy,' she told Rex.

'Not that many lines,' he pointed out.

'I am not interested,' she insisted mulishly.

Lady Proctor, thumbing through Jane's copy, began to wonder whether it would not be interesting for her as well as Johnson to play a role within a role, and be Juliet's mama, as she was Jane's. It could not be a contemptible thing to do, for certainly Mr Johnson had mentioned a dozen titled ladies who had appeared in private theatricals. Mr Johnson seldom spoke of anything but theatricals nowadays. She mentioned this matter to Homberly who said, by Jove, it was just the ticket, and he'd tell Dew it was all set.

He took his two answers back to the Abbey, where Dewar heard with satisfaction that he was to have *carte blanche* with the saloon and, with surprise, that Miss McCormack declined the honour. 'We'll see about that,' Dewar stated blandly.

'Already taken care of it,' Rex assured him, smiling smugly at his coup. 'Did a spot of casting myself. Never guess what, Dew.

Jane's mother is going to play Juliet's mother. Dashed good idea.'

Dewar turned his head very slowly and levelled a dark eye on his cousin. 'I might have known better!' he said in a voice of suppressed anger.

CHAPTER 7

*T*he next morning, Lord Dewar called at Stonecroft, his stated purpose being to decide whether Lady Proctor's saloon would do for a few rehearsals. While there, however, he handed Miss McCormack her copy of the play, with her role ticked off in red.

Three days is rather a long time to hear all one's friends discuss a new project with the keenest enthusiasm, and not become a little infected oneself. To a conscientious daughter of a clergyman, it also seemed improper that the whole village be laid low with play-acting fever, particularly when there was more worthwhile work to be done. She knew that ladies who quibbled about a pound for charity baskets were spending several times that amount on extravagant materials to make themselves up outfits to be worn once. Mrs Raymond, for instance, alias Lady Montague, had actually sent off to London for a length of Italian crepe, and spoke of going to London herself to have it made up by a city modiste. Miss Lacey, who was to play Juliet's vulgar nurse, had come twice to confer with Juliet on their respective roles, and to discover as well how often Dewar came to call. She knew he was above her touch, and set her cap for Altmore instead. Holly's interest was also awake in that direction, and when she thought of the many hours the actors would be spending together she experienced a deep-seated and unworthy wish to join them. This wish rendered her very sensible to Lady Proctor's unsuitability to appear on stage in any capacity. She would never learn her lines, nor speak them with sufficient force to extend beyond the stage.

In short, she was prepared to be persuaded into participating, but she was not ready to have it taken for granted, When Dewar handed her the book and said nonchalantly, 'I have marked off your part in red,' she felt an angry flush warm her neck. Dewar spoke on rapidly. 'You will notice it is a smallish part. It will not occupy a great deal of your time to learn it.'

'It will not take a moment of my time. I do not mean to take part in the play, Lord Dewar,' she said in a firm voice.

'Why not?'

'I have already explained my reasons. I am too busy.'

'Mr Johnson says the sewing can be done at rehearsals.'

'Mr Johnson is not the one who does the sewing,' she said, still angry at his defection.

'He feels, as I do myself, that the play will be a very good thing for the village. Surely you will not be so selfish as to ruin the project for us all by refusing to act.'

'I am not ruining it for anyone!' she answered, astonished at this importance being put on her refusal. 'Get someone else to play Lady Capulet. My aunt. . . .'

'With a careful, quick look in that lady's direction, Dewar spoke on in a low, urgent voice, while Altmore held Lady Proctor captive on the sofa across the room, as he had been instructed to do. 'That is precisely why you *must* take the part. Your aunt is an admirable woman, perfectly well-meaning but, with all due respect, she is no actress.'

'Neither am I. Besides, I am too young to play Juliet's mother,' she added, this piece of casting having occurred to her more than once as inappropriate, if not downright insulting.

'No, no. Juliet is scarcely more than a child. I mean to emphasize her youth, in subtle ways. It is appropriate that Lady Capulet be portrayed by a woman who is not yet in her middle years. They married young in those days. Juliet will be fourteen years "come Lammas-eve at night," according to the script. Providing her mother married as young, as she says in the play she did, you are about the right age. Twenty-nine or thirty.'

A quick jerk of her head told him he had erred, to mention age to a spinster. Looking at her, he added, 'Give or take a few years, I mean.' This rider, being so ambiguous, naturally did not have the effect he hoped for. Scrutinizing her more closely, he began to think he had miscalculated her years. She was not quite so old as he had thought earlier. No child, but not quite pushing thirty either. It was her calm, confident manner that made her seem older than she was. Perhaps hobnobbing with old Johnson added to the illusion.

'In any case, it won't take much *maquillage* to make you look old enough. Oh dear, I do just stumble on from bad to worse, do I not? You are too young for the role, and your aunt is too old. I hope to do a version of the play emphasizing that Romeo and Juliet are scarcely more than children, which adds a pathetic touch to the tragedy, I think, and I want Lady Capulet to be youngish.'

'You will soon have me convinced I am too old for the part.'

'No, you are just right. I want you for the part. I have quite set my heart on it. If you refuse, I must, for civility's sake, accept Lady Proctor's offer, which I refuse to do. In short, if you refuse, I shall cancel the whole project.'

'Lord Dewar! You cannot be so – so. . . . Oh, everyone is looking forward to it!' she was betrayed into admitting.

'I would certainly regret to have to give it up. It is your decision.'

'You don't leave me much choice in the matter.'

'You have the choice of accepting or not. No one is compelling you to take the part.'

'This is little short of blackmail,' she said, yet she was aware of a feeling of relief at the outcome.

'You are a hard judge,' he answered wearily, his tone indicating he was bored with the affair already.

'It's a pity you aren't as determined to achieve other goals, more worthwhile goals, as you are to direct this play,' she charged.

He looked at her and blinked twice slowly. 'What worthy goals are these you speak of?'

'Why – taking care of your estate. We thought when you came here it was to attend to the orphanage and the roof of the church.'

'There is some disparity in our opinions of what constitutes my estate. I have got my affairs in order.'

'You haven't dealt with the orphanage. It has always been your family's charity, and you own the church.'

'The church belongs to the village. It doesn't do to treat people like children. They will appreciate their church more if they see to repairing its roof themselves. It is true it was built by my ancestors, but for the villagers. In fact, it is deeded to the Church of England, and the land for several acres round it is glebe land. As to the funding of St Alton's Orphanage, Johnson and I are looking after it.'

'When? As soon as you convinced Johnson he was Friar Laurence, he stopped worrying about the orphanage,' she replied, still vexed over this.

'Miss McCormack, there is really no need for you to concern yourself in my affairs,' he answered, with a stiffness of the spine indicating that great umbrage had been taken.

'Someone must concern herself in them, for it is pretty clear you do not and, since you've convinced Johnson he is an actor, he doesn't care much either.'

'Very well then, we shall strike a bargain. I shall speak to Johnson on my way back to the Abbey about what funds he needs if you will accept the role of Lady Capulet. Agreed?'

She looked to see if he were serious, for it seemed such an odd bargain to be making. There was no sign of facetiousness about him. 'All right, I agree,' she said, still startled.

'Excellent! I was afraid you'd haggle me into a new roof for the church as well. No doubt it will come before we get this play on the stage. Is your cousin finding much difficulty in recalling her lines? Fortunate her having played the role before.'

'She has the balcony scene down verbatim, Lord Dewar,' Holly replied, with a smile barely suppressed at the corners of her lips.

'The lines will come quickly back to her. At least she knows the story. I was toying with the idea of presenting it in the manner of the *commedia dell'arte*, but it would be rash to venture so far with amateurs. You perhaps could carry it off, and Altmore, but the others. . . .'

'It would be above my talents, sir. I don't even know what you are talking about.'

'*Ad lib*, as the Italian street players did in the fourteenth century. They settle on the story in advance, and present it in their own words. An intriguing idea. I might do something with it at Drury Lane when I return to London.'

'I would suggest you try this technique with some other play-wright than Shakespeare. With him, the wording – the poetry – is all. Take away that and what are you left with? It would no longer be Shakespeare, but a rather mawkish, sentimental tragedy by Bandello, from whom Shakespeare stole his plot.'

'A good point. It would work better with a fair storyteller like Vanbrugh, whose language is not his forte, thought it is not bad either,' he answered, then settled in quite comfortably for a chat, happy to find his companion a little knowledgeable about literary matters. Or had she been swotting up, and pretending she had no interest in the play? 'Tell me, Miss McCormack, did you happen to have the source of Shakespeare's play at your fingertips, or have you been doing some reading since my coming?'

'I read it, just recently, in Jane's copy of her play,' she answered, with no effort to pass herself off as a scholar. 'It is very interesting. They show a sketch of the old Globe Theatre, too.

'I see. You were not totally uninterested in the play then. I wonder if I was not too easily shoved into agreeing to your terms of blackmail.'

'I was not interested in performing. It is just that everyone's talking about it led me to read it – that's all.'

'That usually happens. You may well find yourself studying up a little Italian to see where Bandello got his idea, or reading some-thing of the history of the theatre. One thing leads to another. It is important to keep the cultural pot simmering, as it were. My own area of interest at the moment has to do with Shakespeare's theatre – the actual physical building I mean. I am very much interested in duplicating a theatre such as the Globe, but I daresay they won't agree to try it at Drury Lane.'

'Pity you had not thought of it a few years ago, when it was burned to the ground. That would have been the time to do it.'

'Very true, but then I was not with the theatre.'

'Do you – do you *work* at Drury Lane?' she asked, in some confusion as to these repeated references to it.

'I am a director, a member of the Directors' Committee. I will occasionally select a play for presentation, or commission one, and assist at its production. I enjoy to involve myself in the arts.'

'That's interesting.'

'I hope I do not flatter myself to feel I can offer something to the cultural life of the village.'

They were interrupted by a shout from Homberly, who was seated across the room. 'Did you talk her into it? I see you have got her to stop frowning, at least.' He was in poor spirits. Altmore had got Jane's ear, and he was forced to sit with the mother till Holly was talked round to accepting her role.

'Miss McCormack has been kind enough to take the part,' Dewar answered, with a repressive stare.

'Good. Can we go then?'

This question went unheeded, but as wine was soon being passed Homberly settled in happily enough to chew it up and pass judgement. Unhappy with the behaviour of the company, he assessed the wine to be 'a commoner.' Finally, Dewar outlined to Lady Proctor what arrangement of the seating he would like to prevail when he arrived on the morrow at eleven o'clock for the first reading, with all the cast assembled.

CHAPTER 8

a holiday mood settled over Harknell with the beginning of the play rehearsals. This showed itself in various ways, the most common way, of course, being in conversation. Nothing else was spoken of. With so few roles for ladies, the majority of the women had to devise some other ruse to get themselves invited to Stonecroft to watch the daily proceedings. Mrs Lacey had the excellent excuse of chaperoning her daughter, who was to be Nurse to Juliet. Mrs Abercrombie let on she was writing up an essay on Shakespeare's tragedies, and elected to do it in a neighbour's saloon, where half the village was assembled, making a great deal of noise. The less imaginative volunteered help with the costumes and prompting, till finally there was such a squeeze Sir Egbert threatened to bar the door and make them have their rehearsals in the barn. This scene got rid of all but the most persistent spectators.

But on the first day only the cast met to sit in a circle around the fire and read their lines aloud, while the director jotted down notes in a black leather copy book. Holly assumed, when Jane had twice to be urged to 'speak up', that there would be a re-casting of this major role at the reading's end. When Dewar went over to Jane for a private word later on, she was sure this was the reason, and felt sorry for her cousin, who took a strong delight in the whole business. Mr Altmore strolled toward Holly and took up a seat beside her. By this time, of course, they were all in a fair way to calling each other by their stage names. 'Lady Capulet, may I join you?' he asked, and sat down before she could do more than smile. 'How did you enjoy your first brush with play-acting?'

'Very much. I am concerned about Jane, though. Her voice is so weak – I hope Dewar is not telling her she must give up the part. I'm sure her voice can be strengthened somehow.'

'Don't worry your head on that score. He is very well pleased with Jane's reading. I believe he is, at the moment, explaining to her how to throw her voice a little more. He has no notion of changing Juliet. Your voice will need no work. As Dewar said a moment ago, you are ready for Drury Lane today.'

'I'm sure I don't know where I got such powerful lungs, for I don't sing much, or use my voice beyond the normal. My papa was a preacher. Perhaps I inherited it from him.'

'Was he indeed?' Altmore asked, feeling it time to become better acquainted with these new people he would be seeing much of. 'That would explain your championing of Johnson's cause then. Dewar wondered why it fell to your lot to lecture him into doing his duty, when Johnson himself neglected to mention it. He was a trifle put out – with himself, I mean, for not having attended to it sooner. He is a good fellow really, Dewar, but the artistic temperament – you know. He has his head full of poetry and painting, and now this play, along with the renovations at the Abbey. He will have the prettiest dairy in England. The tiles alone will cost five hundred pounds. Delft tiles from Holland.'

'That is extravagant for a dairy, is it not?'

'To us it seems extravagant, not to him. Though I think he is feeling a little foolish about the fountain to go with the tiles. We are all roasting him about it – a fancy carved statue in a dairy shed, the whole spouting water. I hate to think what he will have spent on it before he is finished. I know twenty-five hundred won't cover it.'

He chatted on for a few moments, at the end of which Holly was in possession of all the details of His Lordship's extravagant folly. When Altmore arose, Johnson took his place. 'You will be happy to hear Lord Dewar has increased our funding at St Alton's,' were his first words.

'I have heard it. How much did you get?'

'An extra thousand pounds a year.'

'He is more generous with his dairy cattle.'

'It is enough. Pray don't pester him for more. He told me you had spoken to him. I wish you had not. He found it very strange that you should do so.'

'Perhaps what he found strange was that you had *not* spoken to him, Mr Johnson.'

'The matter is settled. We agreed on a thousand pounds earlier, you will remember.'

'Yes, I remember you said one thousand was the *minimum*.'

'Well now, Lady Capulet,' he said, hastening on to happier topics, 'they are saying you are the best player amongst the lot of us. Congratulations! Dewar says I have the right quality for Friar Laurence. I'm not sure what he means, truth to tell, but I daresay he refers to my calling – the church. Poor Jane will soon be relegated to a lady-in-waiting, I fear. She has no voice. Pity. Miss Lacey, I fancy, will replace her.'

This opinion was generally held. When Rex Homberly took his turn by Lady Capulet, he said, 'There is no one can holler out the lines like you, Miss McCormack. You put us all to the blush. You would make a dandy Juliet. Pity Miss Proctor has no voice. Such a pretty little thing, she would make a much better . . . that is to say . . . younger, you know. Not to say you are ancient. Not a day over thirty, I warrant.'

'You are mistaken, Tybalt. I am thirty-nine,' she told him, with a very civil smile that hid all her anger.

'That so? Don't look it. In a high state of preservation. Daresay it is your rusticating here forever in the country, nothing to wear a body out.' He considered this a moment, then a worried frown creased his brow. 'Say – how old is Miss Proctor?' he asked.

'Only thirty-five,' she assured him gravely.

'Oh – *only* thirty-five, eh? Twenty-seven myself. Seven – eight

years' difference. Don't look her age. By the living jingo, what a
climate it is here. A body'd last forever. Must tell my mama. Very
worried about her wrinkles.' This was the end of his pleasantries.
He wandered into the hallway to lift up his sword and jab at the
fern that sat on a hall table. When he had dismembered several
fronds it occurred to him Lady Proctor might dislike it, and he
kicked them under the table.

The company finally left, after arranging the hour for meeting
on the morrow. Holly immediately asked Jane if Dewar had said
anything about her reading. 'He complimented me on it,' Jane
answered. 'He said you were very good too, Cousin.'

Holly thought Dewar might have offered her a word of praise
himself, as he had apparently thought well enough of her voice
that he had mentioned it to everyone else.

'He is going to give me lessons in projecting my voice, for it is
a little too light,' Jane added.

'Private lessons? Well, well, here is a new excuse for dalliance,'
Lady Proctor said, with an arch smile at her girl. 'Where are these
lessons to take place?'

'Here, if you will allow it, Mama.'

'Certainly. There can be no objection to it, but of course you
must be chaperoned.'

'He wants me to practice singing out loud too, to teach me to
throw my voice from the lungs, not the throat. That is the problem, that I don't use my lungs,' she added. 'Holly has the trick of
it.'

There was no mention of Holly giving the lessons instead of
Dewar coming to the house. 'You see what he is about,' Lady
Proctor said to her niece after Jane had taken her play to her
room to study. 'An excuse to be alone with her. He made up this
idea of a play to look her over, and now that he has decided he
likes what he sees he wishes to have some privacy without giving
rise to too much speculation. I do not fear he will soon tire of her.
Jane improves upon longer acquaintance. She is a bit shy at first,
but will soon overcome that. My, what a crowd of people we had

this morning. Quite like a party, and it will be the same every day.'

A happier affair even than the daily party, in the mother's view, was the nightly meeting when Dewar came alone to coach her daughter in private. She elected to play chaperon herself, as a special mark of condescension, a sort of recognition that his calls were appreciated as having to do with more than voice lessons. She could not but feel, after a second evening spent in tedious, quiet listening to him actually teaching Jane to breathe and throw her voice across the room, however, that her presence had the desired effect. He was shy in front of Jane's mother. Holly must take her place next time he came. Nobody paid any mind to Holly.

She would be told to keep herself in the background, and Dewar could get on with making love to Jane. Holly was curious enough by this time that she voiced no objection to the substitution. She had been sitting in her uncle's office helping him tote up his columns of figures for the men's quarterly wage, and was happy for an excuse to leave. She was dressed in an aging brown gown, and had thrown her uncle's old jacket round her shoulders as the room was chilly. She wore it still when she entered the room where the voice lessons were to take place. Dewar looked a little surprised when she replaced Lady Proctor but, as she settled quietly down with her sewing, he soon forgot her presence.

The lesson going forth seemed like the greatest nonsense to Miss McCormack. She could not understand how Jane could stand in a corner with her back to the room, whispering in a loud voice. The words she was told to speak too were utter nonsense, but Jane did it all with perfect, unquestioning obedience, just as she obeyed all her mother's injunctions. After forty-five minutes of this exercise, she was allowed to sit down and rest, while he outlined breathing exercises she must practice in her spare moments. What benefit was to be derived from placing her hands on her stomach to feel it rise and fall was not apparent to anyone but the teacher, but it held great importance in his view, the aim being to breathe in for a count of forty, which even Holly, doing the exercise by herself, found impossible. 'You might practice this one too, Miss

McCormack,' he said to her, 'Your voice is strong, but a little better control of your breathing would not go amiss. Oh, and as you are here I should like to discuss with you the costumes and staging. You recall we mentioned doing the play as it was staged in Shakespeare's time.'

'Yes, with seating on three sides, but have you not had the proscenium built already?'

'It is only begun. It is not too late to alter it. It seems to me an excellent time to try the circular stage – on a small scale, you know. Movable chairs will be used in the refectory hall, so it is only the stage that need be built. The requirement of a balcony for the famous balcony scene lends itself well to the Shakespearean stage. It will show to better advantage in the round than behind the proscenium. We'll have to have some spaces curtained off behind for changing. I read somewhere that singers entertained before a play, and of course there was some light juggling-type act as well to follow.'

'Tootles Seymour!' Jane exclaimed. 'He is a famous juggler in these parts, Lord Dewar. He can keep four balls aloft at once. He performs at the fairs. Why, when he was young, he once spent a season at Bartholomew Fair, in London.'

'Excellent! Where do I find him?'

'In your stable,' Holly told him. 'He is one of your stable boys. Strange you did not know it.'

Dewar said nothing, but a long glance directed on the speaker told her he was not happy with her comment. 'Is there any other talent lurking in the village?' he asked. 'Dancing dogs, clowns. . . .'

'I had not thought this the sort of cultural treat you had in store for us. Classical drama you mentioned in the beginning,' Holly pointed out.

'It was the custom in Shakespeare's day, and a custom we English have not strayed far from yet either. There is still a comedy to follow the tragedy at the licenced theatres. After the catharsis of a good tragedy, we want a laugh to put us back in spirits before

we go home. All seriousness and no fun makes Jack a dull boy.'
A passing glance at the sewing basket in her lap gave Holly the
idea she was being accused of dullness.

'I don't think you need worry about an excess of seriousness,
Lord Dewar,' she shot back hastily.

'I do not consider what I do as entertainment merely. If I were
not a nobleman, this would be my life's work. We cannot all be
seamstresses. To each his own talent.'

'Holly is an excellent seamstress,' Jane said, sensing some
tension in the atmosphere, and wanting to alleviate it.

'Thank you, Jane, but unlike Dewar, I would not spend my life
on my hobby, for choice.'

'What would you do, ma'am, if you had freedom to create a
profession for yourself?' he asked.

'I don't know, exactly,' she said, disconcerted to have become
suddenly the centre of attention. 'Something useful, worthwhile,
to help people.'

'Putting on entertainments helps people,' he said simply. 'Have
you not noticed all the bustling, happy activity in the village since
we began? Man does not live by bread alone. Bread and circuses
have long been recognized as man's twin needs. It is the latter that
caters to their higher instincts too. We have got Mrs Abercrombie
doing some heavy reading of Shakespeare, and that will do
anyone a world of good. Soon, we will have a musical committee
practicing up songs and instruments. Ladies are turning their
minds to Italy to discover what costumes will be appropriate, and
will incidentally expose themselves to something of Italian culture.
And our little Juliet is improving her lungs,' he finished up, with a
smile at Jane.

'Everyone *does* seem happier lately,' Jane pointed out to her
cousin.

'Everyone but Miss McCormack,' Dewar added, with a questioning look at Holly. 'That is very odd too, for since I have come,
Johnson has got his orphans' funding increased. I had thought my
failure to attend to that was the cause of your – disapproval?' he

said, selecting the last word with care. 'What else bothers you?'

'Nothing. Nothing at all.'

'When a lady says "nothing" in that tight-lipped way,' Dewar said, 'it usually means we have only scratched the surface of the problem. What is it? What else has not been done, Miss McCormack?'

'Well then, if you insist, I think one thousand pounds a paltry increase when you are spending more than twice that sum on your dairy. Some more of it might have gone to St Alton's.'

'It is not a question of either-or. One thousand was the sum Johnson mentioned.'

'Yes, and if you had made him Romeo instead of Friar Laurence, he would have said a hundred! What about the roof of the church, and Mr Prendergast. . . .'

'Holly!' Jane exclaimed, shocked at such plain speaking.

'I have not noticed anything amiss with the roof of the church, but I remember we discussed how it should be repaired on a former occasion.'

'I don't know how you expect us to raise the money when every spare minute is taken up with this play. And, if you had been at church on Sunday, you would have seen the rain pour in.'

'I rather wondered whether it was not my absence from church that had angered a clergyman's daughter,' he said, with a knowing nod.

'How did you know Holly's papa was a clergyman?' Jane asked.

'I believe Altmore mentioned it. Well, perhaps it is my duty to show some moral leadership. I shall be in church this Sunday, ma'am, rain or shine. Now, tit for tat! We were discussing Elizabethan theatrical. . . .'

'Excuse me, Lord Dewar, but we were discussing the leaking roof of the church, and not your attendance at it,' Holly corrected.

'You have led the horse to water – give him a chance to catch his breath before you make him drink. About the play, we shall have our thrust stage, with minstrels singing before, and possibly *entr'actes*, with a rustic entertainment afterwards if Tootles will oblige us. That will serve the triple purpose of cheering us up after the tragedy, of drawing the villagers into all our festivities, and – what will please you, Miss McCormack – it will amuse the orphans. More than those prickly shirts are likely to do, I dare to suggest. We'll give them sugarplums as well, to satisfy their physical hunger.'

'Oranges would be more appropriate,' Holly said, her temper abated at his plans. 'They used to sell oranges at the plays in those days, I believe.'

'So they did! A nice touch. We'll have some of the female servants carry them in baskets through the audience. Your maids, from Stonecroft. Mama has a knack for hiring the ugliest females in the country. The girl who brought your sewing down to you the other evening. . . .'

The two ladies exchanged a silent, knowing glance in mutual acknowledgement of Man's roving eye. 'I am not blind, after all!' he defended. 'Nor quite immune to female charms. I do not expend all my artistic appreciation on directing drama. I can see a barn by daylight.'

'By candlelight too,' Jane teased, her little white teeth sparkling, and a dimple showing in her left cheek.

'Even better by candlelight,' he agreed readily, with a close observation of her. For a long moment he looked at Jane, while a soft smile played on his lips. 'A pity the audience will not be able to see you at closer range,' was all he said, but it was said in a voice that set Jane to blushing, and that caused Holly to think it a wise precaution to provide a chaperon. Then he arose and took his leave of them both.

CHAPTER 9

*I*t was difficult to go on expressing wrath with Lord Dewar's pursuit of pleasure when it gave incidental pleasure to so many others along the way. Since he had driven into Harknell in his elegant travelling carriage and announced he meant to produce a play, the whole village had blossomed out in a way never seen before. The autumn used to be a time for hibernating in Harknell, for putting away the silken gowns of summer, for drawing into one's own house and waiting for spring. This autumn, the pattern was changed. Everyone, even including Mother Nature, conspired to defeat the autumn doldrums. St Martin's summer came and lingered for weeks. The ladies, a bit embarrassed to say outright they were buying new outfits to impress Dewar, made a mention of the warm autumn: so like spring, really, that one felt the urge to have a new chapeau. Bonnets were often chapeaux since his coming. Letters, too, had a way of turning into *billets-doux*, and mutton into a *ragoût*, at least in conversation that had assumed a Gallic air to match Dewar's.

But it was more than the accent that was French. A real *joie de vivre* had crept into their lives. It was impossible to say just how it had happened, but it was everywhere in evidence. Idle or latent talents came into full bloom under his encouraging aegis. Miss Lacey was discovered to have a bent for music. This came out one day when Dewar was seeking madrigals for the minstrels to sing before the play. Miss Lacey, whose name was Irene (and who was soon being called that as often as she was called Nurse), happened to know a few of these ancient tunes. Dewar immediately led her to the piano to play them for him, and to sing the words. She was reluctant at first but as his praise rose so did the volume and the quality of execution. Holly, observing silently, saw that his intention was to stick poor Irene with the job of teaching these airs to others, and practice them up for the concert, as he had indeed done before the day was over. Irene was also saddled with the task of seeking out other such tunes, as two were of course not sufficient for a half hour's performance. He was lavish with his praise. Miss Lacey's heart swelled to hear herself described, within her own hearing but behind her back, as 'marvelously talented – a very dab with the old Elizabethan music.'

It became evident that every member of the group had some formerly hidden accomplishment that could be of use to Dewar. Mrs Abercrombie, with her new interest in Shakespeare, was diversified into Elizabethan stage architecture, and put in charge of ferreting out the proper adornment to turn the refectory hall into a replica of Shakespeare's theatre. Mrs Raymond, who prided herself on the tricks she had taught her three poodles, was in the process of making them pink ruffles and urging them on to new heights of trickery. As she was possessed of this 'wonderful way with animals,' she was in charge of teaching them to dance, hop through hoops, and play leapfrog. Mr Homberly, who had made a very good horse's nether end, proved equally at home wrapped in a bearskin retrieved from Dewar's attic, and was learning to walk on his hands and balance a ball on his nose. 'Got the horse's rig beat all hollow, by the living jingo, but she's deuced hot.' Mrs Bartlett and her spouse (Citizens of Verona in the drama and retired innkeepers in the village) were set to discover the receipts for mead and Elizabethan victuals. Holly knew well enough her task was to be the most onerous of all, the overseeing of the costumes, and wondered that Dewar did not get on with praising her into work, as the job could not be done in a week. Lady Dewar's sole function was to deride everything and complain of the erratic comings and goings of her son and guests and, even more, of the infernal banging in the refectory hall where the stage, complete with balcony, was now in place and in the process of being painted, under the direction of Mrs Abercrombie.

On the first day the company met at the Abbey, they were taken into the hall to view the stage, and to hear the countess's litany of woes. 'Madge Abercrombie never did have two bits of wit to rub together,' she said, in no low voice. 'Why is the stage so high? That is what I would like to know. The seats are so far below it we'll see nothing but boots and buskins.'

This lament nudged Mrs Abercrombie into a defence of her set. 'The stage was always six feet above the ground,' she pointed out, ostensibly to Dewar, but aimed halfway between him and his mother.

'You have done a superb job, as we have come to expect from you,' Dewar answered, dismayed to think his mother was right about the stage being too high. He had no wish to make his audience stand, as they would have to do to get a proper view of the stage. 'A pity we cannot build galleries, to make optimum use of that wonderful stage you have designed. The little foot railing is exquisite, by the by. I wonder if it would not show to better advantage if we lowered the stage a bit.' It must, of course, be lowered at least three feet, but with the designer's sanction.

'Six feet was the height given in both books I used,' she assured him.

'Oh, quite! Exactly the right height, if we could only have the galleries. Mama, however, is very stubborn about it,' he said in a conspiratorial voice. 'To humour her, shall we just lower the stage a bit instead? I don't wish to deprive anyone of a good look at that foot railing. And the curtains and inner gallery as well are superb. Where did you come by that tapestry?'

'Just some curtains I had in a spare room upstairs,' she smiled happily. 'I must have them back when the performance is over.' Meanwhile, she and Harold made do with bed sheets on the windows of their own chamber. 'About the stage – perhaps I will lower it a trifle,' she conceded, as a pain shot through her neck from craning up to see the exquisite foot rail.

'I'll speak to the carpenters,' he told her. 'You will not want to go out to the barns where they are, at this moment, constructing the mausoleum you designed for us. The prie-dieu and crucifix you found in the attic here will be excellent for Friar Laurence's cell in the third act. We want to suggest a mood only, and let imagination do the rest.'

'Shakespeare was very sparing in his use of scenery and properties.'

'So he was. You are really to be congratulated for the grasp you have obtained on the subject, and for what you are accomplishing. Let me know your plans for the orchard scene. How we could use you at Drury Lane,' he finished up, setting her to blushes of delight.

He next turned his conning eye on a pair of sisters, the Misses Hall, who had thus far contributed nothing but their presence and vocal encouragement, though they were hopeful of being Citizens of Verona eventually. Their avocation, as all the village was coming to know, was horticulture. They had a conservatory that covered an acre, where several fruit trees resided. It was Dewar's intention to see a few of them on the stage for the second act, to suggest the orchard. He also had some hopes they would volunteer some of their oranges, as his own were sour as lemons.

'How are the plant ladies today?' he asked, with an admiring note in his voice. He had a real interest in plants, and knew enough that he had waxed lyrical when they took him to their conservatory the week before. Plants were fast becoming fashionable in Harknell as a result of his having begged some blooms and cuttings from them. 'Blooming as usual, I see,' he added to the fading pair.

'Oh, not in November, Lord Dewar. We do not bloom in the autumn,' the elder answered playfully. 'Not till April. We are the sort who remain dormant throughout the winter, like roses.'

'Does she always tell such whiskers?' he asked Miss Helen, in a playful aside. 'She must be a wicked trial to you. I know a rose in bloom when I see it.' Miss Helen twittered girlishly, and he continued his dalliance.

'I mean to adopt one of you two and put you in charge of my conservatory. Your skill might entice those oranges of mine to give me something other than lemon juice. Tell me now, Miss Hall, is it possible I have got lemons grafted on to my fruit trees by mistake?'

'It is not impossible, Lord Dewar. Folks will often graft lemon buds on seedlings of an orange tree – but you joke me,' Miss Hall replied. 'You would not have any good eating fruit from it for some time, however.'

'Pity. I blush to have our orange girls distribute such untantalizing fruits to the audience. The orphans in particular . . .' he finished, with a pitiful shake of his head.

Miss Helen twigged to it at once what she and Mary must do. By a quick jab of the elbow into her sister's ribs, and a narrowed eye, she conveyed her message. 'Lord Dewar, you must let us supply the oranges! We would be delighted to do it,' Miss Hall said. 'Ever so many we have ripening. We could not eat the half of them. We have more than enough marmalade made up to see us through the winter as well. We insist.'

'I feel a very beggar!' he exclaimed, in well-simulated chagrin.

'Nonsense. I wish I had thought of it myself,' Miss Hall said, and went on to say enough to convince him. An enquiry as to how his philodendron cuttings progressed brought their conversation to an end, and Dewar looked around to see who else he must sweet-talk into line. Miss McCormack, he noticed, was regarding him with her customary disdain.

He pinned his most cozzening smile in place and walked up to her. 'Good morrow, Lady Capulet,' he began, with a courtly bow. 'What do you think of our stage? A wonderful job Mrs Abercrombie has done, has she not?'

'A nine days' wonder. You are to be congratulated.'

'The congratulations are not owing to me,' he answered,

mistrusting her tone.

'I disagree. You deserve some credit for having bent the whole village to your will.'

'With one or two exceptions,' he answered mildly.

'I have been wondering when my turn for extravagant praise is to come. Don't forget to tell me what an exquisite stitch I set, or I shall be out of reason disappointed. It is past time we, meaning I, began the costumes, is it not?'

'You will have ample help. The ladies have been showing me materials and designs for approval, and can stitch their own costumes.'

'That leaves several gentlemen's outfits to be made. If the costumes are to be as elaborate as the sets, it is time we were working on them,' she persisted. 'I do hope it is yourself who has been studying the period style, for you did not ask me to do it, and I have really very little notion what sort of outfits would suit. We would not want to dress Juliet in a spencer if togas were the fashion of the day.'

'Togas were never the style for ladies,' he pointed out. 'Only men wore them. The *toga virilis* was adopted as a symbol of a fellow's having achieved manhood, at fourteen or so.'

'I stand corrected,' she answered, with no humility, but rather an angry sparkle from her eyes. It was irksome that Dewar seemed to consider himself an authority on everything.

'Shakespeare himself was not overly precise about such items,' he consoled her. 'He seldom bothered with period dress. Caesar, you recall, enters in his nightshirt, and Cleopatra has Charmian cut the laces of what must have been her corsets.'

'Still, I don't imagine Mr Altmore will be wearing his jacket of Bath cloth, nor Mr Homberly his large brass-buttoned jacket. I would like to know what has to be done as soon as possible.'

'I have a cousin who is considered an expert in these matters. He was to arrive last week, but was detained in London. He is to bring sketches and some materials with him. I shall bring him to confer with you as soon as he arrives.'

Miss McCormack brightened at this speech. She had had no luck in attracting Mr Altmore's attention. He had joined Jane's court of admirers, where he daily jostled with Dewar, Foxworth, and Homberly for her favours. Miss Lacey was having as bad luck as herself. Another cousin to Dewar, one who would come to confer with herself, sounded decidedly hopeful. 'What is his name?' she asked.

'Sir Swithin Idle, but he is not at all well named. Swith keeps himself very busy.'

'At designing stage costumes?' she asked, fearing he would turn out another dilettante.

'At everything,' was the comprehensive reply. 'He is remarkably adept in so many fields one hesitates to label him. Pleasing the ladies is not the least of his accomplishments either,' he added, with a little smile that sent her hopes soaring. 'You will like him, I think.'

She disliked to ask outright whether he were a bachelor, but the description sounded very much like it. 'Does Lady Idle come with him? I was just wondering, you know, whether I might have another pair of fingers to help with the sewing.'

'Swithin is a bachelor. A very eligible bachelor,' he added, with no particular emphasis, but a quick look to read her response.

'Pity,' she said, concealing her joy.

'You have some aversion to the breed, do you?'

'Oh no, they make the best husbands, one hears.'

'If you have designs on him, I hope you will not begin turning his head till we have the costumes in hand, on paper at least. Swithin is no good once he starts falling in love. I hope you will treat him with all the disdain you heap on me. Speaking of which. . . .' He paused a moment while he fixed her with a sapient eye, then said, 'How did you enjoy the service on Sunday? Friar Laurence did rather well, I thought.'

'I noticed you were at church, Lord Dewar. Am I to congratulate you on so ordinary an occurrence?'

'No, on my obedience. I was not only there, but Friar Laurence was here for luncheon as well. We have arranged for a man to come over from town to clamber up on the roof and see how big the holes are. If he tumbles off and breaks his head in the process, we shall lay it in your dish.'

'If he does not break his head, will the credit also be put in my dish? I am willing to accept full responsibility, if that is the case.'

'Welcome to it. You wouldn't care to take the responsibility for the bill while you are about it, I suppose? No, I didn't think so.'

'If you are feeling the pinch, you could postpone the fountain you are importing from Italy for your dairy,' she said reasonably.

'You have been misinformed. I sponsor English artists, though the design perhaps owes something to Italy.'

'It seems a shame to go to so much trouble only for cows. Why do you not put it in your garden?'

'There are fountains in the garden already,' was the answer. 'My dairy girls will appreciate it, as well as the cows. Beauty is important. It has a civilizing influence on mankind. Ladies, and gentlemen too, act better when they are in decent surroundings, and dressed up in their prettiest outfits. They try to live up to their costumes, I suppose.'

She was suddenly very aware of her own clothing, on which she never spent a thought but to see it was clean and decent. 'You must have Sir Swithin design your dairy girls an outfit while he is with you,' she said, as though bored with the whole subject.

'An excellent idea. Blue, to match the Delft tiles. Tell me, have you any more derelictions of duty to point out to me? If not, I shall speak to Lady Montague. I have just discovered a footman who is a perfect clown. She will be able to use him in our post-*drame* comedy routine. He falls well, and can somersault divinely.'

'He sounds a perfectly accomplished fellow. Before you go, one other item does occur to me. . . .'

'How much is it going to cost me?' he asked, taking a deep breath.

'It is not a matter of money.'

'There's a change. Well, spit it out,' he urged, with a peculiar little half smile on his face. She noticed that he had sunk from his usually elegant, mannered speech into an utterance that had very much the sound of Rex Homberly to it. 'What's the matter? What are you looking at?' he asked, noticing her frown.

'Nothing. What I meant to tell – ask you – is whether some-thing could not be done about Arthur Evans – one of your tenants.'

'The name is familiar to me. I do know some of my own people, particularly those who have been with me a long time. I even suspect what matter you have in mind. It is the business of a footpath through his rose garden?'

'Rose garden?' she asked, staring. 'I would not call one faded tea rose and a patch of weeds a rose garden. He is the most stubborn man in the county. The whole party who come here to rehearse each day must go a mile out of their way because Mr Evans refuses to let us use the footpath through his meadow. One corner of it does hold the tea rose, to be sure, and his cattle graze in the rest, but a roadway exists, and was always used, till three years ago. Then he suddenly went mad and took a gun to Sam Needles one day when he was scooting home from poaching in your woods. Since that time, hundreds of people have been inconvenienced from fear of being shot at. It is bad enough for those with a mount or carriage but, for pedestrians, a mile's extra walking is a considerable disadvantage. Especially in winter.'

'Do you know why he did this, shot the fellow?'

'Because he is not allowed to shoot game, I have heard.'

'Again, why?'

'You have consistently refused to lease him the measly acres he requires to qualify under the Game Laws. If a man leases, his lease must be worth one hundred and fifty pounds a year to qualify, and he is five acres short of it. You must have five idle acres you can let him lease.'

'Is the man actually insane?'

'To tell the truth, I think he has gone a little crazy, though he continues running his farm in a sane enough manner, and that's all Mr Roots cares for. Evans has made so many enemies that no one much talks to him.'

'I am expected to approach this lunatic and demand he open up the road, am I?' he asked.

'He will hardly dare to shoot *you*.'

'Lunatics don't much care where they point their guns.'

'If he is violent, then he must be put under restraint. It is *your* place. . . .'

'I thought it would be,' he said with a resigned sigh, and turned aside to accost Mrs Raymond as she walked past.

The troupe of players was soon on the stage, while the audience sat below, craning their necks up to see what they could of the goings-on. There was later a loud harangue by the director, who was not pleased with their reading their speeches, when they should have at least the first act by heart. Jane was particularly shy when she looked into the upturned faces, and could hardly bring herself to mumble, after all her lessons in projection.

Dewar's French chef did not deign to perform for such a motley crew of provincials, but Lady Dewar's own cook, Meg Appleby, made coffee and sandwiches and plum cake, which were as well received as gourmet fare by the undemanding actors.

Altmore strolled up to Dewar and said in a quiet voice, 'Do you really think Jane will do for this role, Dew?'

'Do?' he asked, astonished. 'My dear fellow, she is perfect for the part. She is the very essence, the soul of Juliet. So young, so beautiful and shy, with a soft, vulnerable quality, yet with some strength behind it to make her suicide credible. The voice needs more work, but I was never so enraptured with anyone as I am with Jane's Juliet. It is far and away the best thing in this play. Not to belittle you, my dear chap. You are an excellent Romeo too, but then you are half professional. You no longer require praise heaped on your head.'

'It is just that her voice is very small, and she doesn't always remember her lines either, or where she should be on stage.'

'That light voice is a part of what makes her performance so riveting. It will be tricky to increase it enough without losing the softness. The refectory hall is not large. She doesn't have to fill Drury Lane. She would never do in the real theatre but for this experiment in intimate theatre I am undertaking here her uncertainty is an advantage. Lady Capulet is a good foil for her too. Miss McCormack is more sure of herself, more forceful and everyday, down-to-earth. An excellent contrast to Jane's more timid quality. As to her forgetting her lines occasionally, I am ready to tolerate even that. It adds to her wistfulness, that helpless quality I am striving for. The scene where she is forced to have Count Paris, for instance! The audience will all be cheering her on without realizing they are doing it, or why they are doing it, at least. It will compound the tragedy when she finally kills herself. There will be plentiful tears in the hall, I promise you, including my own.'

'What can I do to bring out this effect you want?' Altmore asked.

'You do well now, Romeo. Just be madly in love with her. Who could be otherwise?'

'I might have known!' Altmore laughed. 'You can never put on a play without falling in love with your leading lady, can you?'

'My dear fellow, that is half the charm of it!' Dewar replied, with a fond glance across the room to Juliet.

CHAPTER 10

$\mathcal{M}$iss McCormack had had such good luck in bending Dewar to her bidding that she sat in hourly expectation of hearing the short cut through Evans's pasture was open to traffic. They arrived back at Stonecroft at four. Dewar, content that his Juliet was learning to project her voice, had absolved himself of further duty in her exercises, and assigned the task to Holly. It was a blow to Lady Proctor that the evening visits were ended, but she was fairly sure he would find some other excuse to present himself in her saloon. She held herself every bit as much ready as Miss McCormack to receive him. When the knocker sounded at eight-thirty there was a bustling of putting away the orphans' shirts by Holly, of straightening her lace collar and tidying her skirts by the mother, and of smiling with anticipation by Jane. The excited shouts in the hallway told them their caller was not Dewar, but Mr Homberly.

'That pest of a fellow. I hope he has left his sword at home,' Lady Proctor said. 'He has mangled my best fern; it will take eons to recover.'

'Tried to kill me, by Jove!' he was shouting. 'Call a sawbones, quick! Bleeding to death!'

This stark pronouncement soon had the three ladies in the hallway, where there was no evidence of blood, but a good deal of embarrassment. Rex stood, red-faced, with both hands clutching at the seat of his trousers, while his blue eyes popped in mute horror. 'Oh – evening, Lady Proctor, ladies,' he said, with a quick nod of his head. 'Fool of a fellow took a shot at me. Afraid he might have killed me. Ought to be in Bedlam. Crazy lunatic.'

'Mr Homberly, are you hurt?' Jane asked, running forward.

'No!' He leapt away, backing towards the door. 'That is – only a scratch.'

'But where were you hit? I don't see any blood,' she insisted, searching him from head to toe.

'Who shot at you?' Lady Proctor asked, seeing with relief that there was no sword in evidence this evening.

'Silly old fool who lives in that cottage a mile down the road. Took the short cut from the Abbey; out he comes with a gun, makes me dismount. No sooner turned my back on him than he discharged his shotgun on me.'

'Were you hit?' Jane asked, still seeing no evidence of his wounds.

'Certainly was! That is,' he added, again clutching the seat of his trousers, 'heh, heh – only a graze. Still, dashed uncomfortable. Wish you would call a sawbones.'

Holly had figured out the nature of his problem and took the matter in hand, shepherding the ladies back into the saloon while the butler shouted for footmen, for a message to be sent to the doctor, for water and basilicum powder, and for a bed to be prepared.

'Pair of Sir Egbert's trousers, if he can spare 'em,' Rex added.

'You had better go to bed and spend the night here, Mr Homberly,' Holly suggested.

'I wouldn't like to . . . that is . . . not a bad idea, actually,' he said, changing his tack as the possibilities this would present for throwing himself into Jane's path occurred to him.

'Shall I send a note up to the Abbey?' Holly asked him.

'Sorry to put you to so much trouble. Daresay they won't miss me. Roper, my valet, will worry.'

'I'll let them know where you are.'

Lady Proctor sighed in exasperation when she heard the plan, but was soon back in smiles. Dewar would naturally come down to see how his cousin progressed. Before Dewar arrived, however, Mr Homberly's valet was on the scene, bearing a valise that held enough garments for a week. The doctor was taken abovestairs to attend to the victim while Holly, satisfied that the wounds were not serious, foresaw the attack could be put to good use in bringing pressure to bear on Dewar to settle once for all the matter of Mr Evans.

It was just above an hour when Dewar finally arrived. 'I am most dreadfully sorry to have imposed on you in this way,' he told Lady Proctor.

'Not at all. What are friends for?' she asked merrily, after having complained for fifty of the sixty minutes while she was uncertain he would come. 'We are happy to be of service.'

'How is he?' was the next question.

'The doctor is not down yet, but the servants tell us it is not at all serious. Old Evans has run completely mad, and must be restrained before he kills someone,' Lady Proctor said, indicating a seat by the fireside for her guest.

'I'd like to run up and see Rex,' Dewar said, and was graciously given permission.

Dr John was soon down, explaining that Homberly's valet would see to his needs. 'A few days rest. He will recover quickly – just surface wounds. You will not long have him here,' he promised. 'Let him remain overnight, and by tomorrow he can be moved, but in a carriage. He will not be able to ride for a week or so.'

Dewar wasted very few moments upstairs. 'He'll live,' was his unsympathetic pronouncement when he came down. 'If the gudgeon hadn't popped back on his horse and ridden here, he would be in a lot less pain. The worst thing he could have done, but then Rex hardly realizes he has a pair of legs. He rides everywhere, and dislikes even to dismount to come to the table.'

'I'll run up and see if he needs anything. Is he able to see me?' Holly asked.

'Yes,' Dewar answered briefly, regarding her with a self-conscious expression. 'Then you will come down and see *me*. I hope the doctor has not left! I have an inkling I will have need of him.'

'Perhaps *now* you will do something about it,' she replied as she swept past him.

'You may be very sure I have! I would not have dared to show my face otherwise. I spoke to Evans on my way here.'

She found Rex propped up in bed, hoisting a glass of wine to his lips. About his shoulders rested a housecoat of iridescent satin, in hues of peacock, black, and rose. The fringed tassel of the tie was being applied to his lips, in lieu of a napkin. 'Oh, Miss McCormack,' he exclaimed, peering behind her shoulder to see if, by any chance, Jane was hiding there. 'Dashed rig to run into. How am I to duel with Foxey in this state?'

'The doctor says you will soon be up and about.'

'Don't know about that. Think I may have to batten myself on you for a couple of weeks,' he said happily, and snuggled down into the sheets. 'Er – if Miss Proctor is wondering, I can receive visitors. Didn't take no laudanum. Couple of glasses of ale will put me to sleep right and tight, Or wine.'

'I hope you are not suffering too much. So very unfortunate.'

'Little pain . . . heh heh. Well, well – all been very kind. Very kind indeed. Won't be a bit of bother to you. Roper will take care of me. I like steak for breakfast, with fried murphies. Roper knows just how I like 'em. If Miss Proctor enquires, you can tell her I am fine. Ain't going to stick my fork in the wall by a long shot. Will she be coming up?'

'Certainly she will,' Holly assured him. 'Dewar is downstairs at the moment.'

'Don't want *him* back up here jawing at me. How was I to

know the man is a Bedlamite? Nobody told me not to take the short cut. Least you could do is warn a body if there's a murderer loose. Mind, if I'd known what ailed old Evans, I'd have spoken to Dewar myself. Not allowed to shoot all these years because Dewar wouldn't lease him a measly five acres. Enough to drive a man mad, not being able to use your pops. Don't blame him in the least. Would have done the same thing myself, I dare say.'

'Is there anything you want? A book perhaps, or something to eat?'

'No books! Might manage to put away a leg of chicken and a bit of cake. A few pieces of toast – a dish of preserves wouldn't go amiss.'

'It is early yet. A long evening to get in before you will be ready for sleep. Are you sure you wouldn't like something to read?'

'Maybe Miss Proctor would like to read to me,' he said hopefully.

'Perhaps later,' Holly replied, though she had not the least assurance Jane would comply.

A few hints that Miss Proctor might like to have a hand of piquet or a game of jackstraws were all met with the reminder that she was with Dewar. Rex's pink face took on the expression known by his friends as his 'wise face,' which is to say he pursed his lips and narrowed his eyes, indicating deep thought. 'Tell you what,' he said, 'send Dewar up. Want to speak to him. Urgent.'

Holly relayed the message through Roper, who had been given the adjoining room. The simple ruse worked very well. When Dewar entered at the door a moment later, Jane was with him. 'What is it you want, Rex?' Dewar asked,

Rex's eyes and thoughts were all for Jane. He ignored the question, while a simple-minded smile settled on his face. 'I see how it is,' Dewar said to Holly, and went to join her.

Jane advanced to the bed and enquired for Homberly's comfort. The precise nature of any remarks exchanged between them was not overheard, but soon Jane was hopping out of the door to go after jackstraws. 'Shall I toss this *malade imaginaire* into my carriage and relieve you of him?' Dewar asked Holly, but with a tolerant smile at the victim.

'The doctor says he is not to be moved for a few days.'

'What a compliant doctor he is. *Entre nous*, I think we know the more serious ailment is heart-related.'

'Easy for you to say,' Rex charged, lending an ear. 'You ain't the one with his – body full of shot. Dashed uncomfortable. Especially getting it pried out. Near passed out with the pain.'

'You should have had some laudanum,' Holly told him. 'It would have eased the pain of the operation and made sleep easier afterwards. You are too stoical, Mr Homberly.'

'Ain't chicken-hearted anyway,' Rex told his cousin. 'Be back in the saddle in jig time – week or so,' he altered his diagnosis, as Jane entered with the jackstraws. Dewar drew a chair to the bedside for her, and the two were soon engrossed in a noisy game.

'Do you share my feeling that we are *de trop* here, Miss McCormack?' Dewar asked.

'Certainly not. I must act the chaperon, but if you would like to join Lady Proctor below. . . .'

'No!' he said, very emphatically.

There was no danger of mistaking this reply for a compliment to herself. It had very much the tone of opting for the lesser of two evils. 'No, I would like to hear my lecture now, if you please, and have it done with. You forgot to say "I told you so" downstairs. I blame the unusual reticence on your aunt's presence. You will be able to read me a much more satisfactory scold here. Come now,' he prompted. 'If I had done as you suggested this morning Rex would not have this unparalleled opportunity to pester Jane. He is delighted with his misfortune, which must take the wind out of your sail somewhat.'

'It could have been serious,' she answered.

'So it could. Only think if Evans had filled Rex's sword-wielding arm with buckshot, or happened to hit the horse in error. That is a very fine animal Rex rides.'

'You treat it lightly, which seems to be your customary manner of conducting what one would think should be serious affairs.'

'This is more like it,' Dewar congratulated her, and settled in, quite as comfortably as Rex, for a coze. 'I had intended speaking to my steward about the matter tomorrow. Odd he had not attended to it himself, but he misunderstood the situation. I shall ring a resounding peal over him. Meanwhile, I have assured Evans he will be leased the requisite acres, and he is now free to shoot us all quite legally. Foolish Game Laws. They were drawn up centuries ago. Well, I hope Tybalt's indisposition does not hamper our rehearsals too severely.'

Mr Homberly's merry laughing and flirting had soon dried his throat. Roper was requested to bring the company wine. 'My own,' he mentioned to the ladies, lest they thought it overweaning of him to offer them their own wine. 'Roper brought a couple of bottles in my cases.'

'I wonder where he got it,' Dewar asked innocently, as he examined the bottles from his own cellars.

After chewing it up, Homberly proclaimed it to be 'A thoroughbred. Not a saucy bone in its body. Yessir, a very well-behaved wine indeed.'

'What does that mean?' Jane asked.

'It is better not to enquire too minutely,' Dewar told her.

Holly asked Roper to fetch her sewing, as she wished to finish the shirts before the costumes made their demands on her. Seeing was difficult in the lamplight, but she hesitated to put on her spectacles with Dewar at her side, watching every stitch.

For an hour the invalid was entertained, then it was time for Dewar to take his leave. 'Don't cosset him,' he warned the ladies, 'or you'll have a tenant for life.'

'We shan't pay him a bit of heed,' Holly assured Rex. 'I'll have some food sent up for you now, before you retire, Mr Homberly. A leg of chicken and some cake, I think you mentioned.'

'Very nice of you. Little toast and preserves too – peaches for choice.'

'We wouldn't want him to fade away to a cartload,' Dewar mentioned, as the ladies bade him farewell.

CHAPTER 11

$\mathcal{I}$t was not necessary for the minor players to appear at every rehearsal. With only a small part, Holly decided to remain home the next morning and finish Sir Egbert's bookkeeping. She had some premonition Dewar would return that evening, and wished to be free to join the party in the invalid's room. She did not examine her reasons for this very closely. It was unusual to have interesting guests at Stonecroft, or even in the village. When they were present it was natural to want to be with them, was the rather vague way she considered it. She had finished the books by noon and, after luncheon, she took her shirts to Mr Homberly's room to lighten the tedium of a long day in bed for him. She did not think, as she set the spectacles on her nose, that she had desisted from this act when Dewar was present. Her eyes were tired from the books, she said, when Homberly mentioned her wearing them.

'Didn't know you needed specs, Miss McCormack,' he said, with a sympathetic glance. 'Pity. Ruin a girl's looks. Course you ain't a young girl any longer.'

'I'm not so old. I'm only twenty-six,' she said, threading her needle.

'Eh? Said you was thirty-nine.'

'I was joking, of course! Don't tell me you believed it!' she exclaimed, in real chagrin.

'Course not,' he answered readily. 'Certainly didn't look a day over thirty anyway, till you put them specs on.'

'Thank you. Did you pass a comfortable night?'

'Very. The chicken was dandy. Could have handled two legs. Bowl of smash wouldn't have gone amiss either. Cake was nice – a good big piece.'

'What exactly is smash?' she asked him.

'Why, turnips boiled and smashed up.'

'I'll see if Cook has any turnips,' she promised. For an hour they talked the greatest foolishness. Then she went to get wine for them, and was introduced into the intricacies of chewing and finding descriptive phrases to indicate her expertise. Mr Homberly had long since run out of materials and people to compare the wine to, and had switched to his own area of interest, horses.

'Don't like to run down your uncle's cellars, Miss McCormack, but this brew is a very commoner,' he said sadly 'Next thing to a job horse.'

'A very jade,' she agreed. She induced him to practice his few play lines by lavishing praise on his execution. This done, he sent Roper off for cards, and introduced her to the fine art of spotting a Captain Sharp, bent on cheating her at cards. As this diversion had all the charm of novelty, she promised she would return for another lesson. 'Meanwhile I shall just finish up these few shirts.'

'What is that you're always working at?' he asked, and she explained her task.

'Feel dashed sorry for orphans. Tell you what, Miss Holly, I mean to help you.' She had become Holly during the visit, and occasionally Miss Holly.

'Do you know how to sew?' she asked, only a little surprised, for nothing about this bizarre gentleman could shock her.

'Sew? Not in the least. Don't know one end of a needle from t'other. That is to say – know one's sharp – well, know t'other has a hole in it if it comes to that. Know quite a bit about needles, really, but don't know how to use them. No, I'd like to help the little orphans out. Give them a treat. Some sugarplums, or what have you. Plumcake would be nice, or ices. Except the ices would go down better in the summer.'

'If you want to help, Mr Homberly. . . .'

'Call me Rex. My friends do.'

'Yes, Rex – there is a better way to help.'

'Anything you say. Up to a pony. Can spare twenty-five pounds very easily.'

'That is generous of you!'

'Ain't poor. Own an abbey. Don't have a title of course, but own an abbey, with lots of lands and cows and all that. Worth a good penny.' This was said in hopes of her relaying it to Jane.

'If you are speaking of such a large sum I would like your permission to spend it all on one child.'

'That so? That's a lot of sugarplums,' he pointed out. 'For one fella, I mean. Make him sick as a dog.'

'I didn't mean to buy treats. There is one boy who is crippled. He was born with a deformed foot. Our local doctor is trying to help him. He has put a contraption on the boy – screwed his leg into a wooden frame, which is very painful for Billie. Bill McAuley is his name. It doesn't seem to be doing a bit of good. I would like to have a London surgeon come down and examine Billie. May I use your money for that?'

Rex surreptitiously wiped a tear from the corner of his eye. He was too overcome to speak for a moment. 'You're a very nice girl,' he said, and sniffled. ' 'Pon my word, a very kind-hearted girl. I'll arrange the money as soon as I'm up and about. For that matter, might as well get up, if Miss Proctor is going to be at the play practices all the time.'

'She'll soon be home.'

'She ever say anything about me?'

It was hard to tell him she never said anything complimentary or romantic, but at least Jane was not mean. She had never spoken ill of him. It was wrong, on the other hand, to encourage him in what was surely a hopeless passion. 'Jane is to go to London in the spring, Rex. I don't think she would be allowed by her parents to make any connection before that time.'

'Know they want a title for her. Lady Dewar said as much. Don't think she'll get Dewar, but then he certainly does admire her. Always saying she's a perfect Juliet, very sweet – all that. Forever singing her praises.'

'She is very sweet.'

'You're nice too,' Rex said, and smiled wanly. When Jane was too busy to drop in on him later that afternoon, but went instead into the village to visit a cousin, Holly began to seem even nicer. She was certainly a remarkably good-natured, generous girl, and had a sense of humour too. Without the spectacles, she was seen to be not a bad-looking girl. Every glass of wine or ale, sporting magazine, bowl of nuts, or plate of toast brought increased her beauty. A solicitous enquiry for his 'wounds' lent her an appealing aura. Till Jane popped in for two minutes before dinner, Holly was fast becoming an incomparable, but the two minutes reversed the decision.

By the time Dewar arrived that evening at eight-thirty, Rex was back in love with Juliet. She had got him a bag of sweets in the village, which was about as strong a declaration as he needed to feel she was his. She had offered voluntarily to fetch the jackstraws too, obviously smitten with him. He could not quite deduce the reason that she deserted him shortly after Dewar entered the room, unless she was trying to make him jealous. Just got up and walked away, with her sticks scattered all over the counterpane. And he had been letting her win too. Dashed hard to lie stock-still, so as not to disturb them. He lay with his ears stretched to over-hear her speech to Dewar. It was hardly of a nature to incite him to blind jealousy.

'We got home from the Abbey in half an hour, now that we are allowed to take the short cut,' was all she said. 'Evans was at the window, and actually smiled at us. It's the first time I have *ever* seen him smile.'

'I have seen him dance,' Dewar replied. 'He leapt from the floor and clicked his heels in the air when I took the new lease for him to sign. He sat in the middle of enough guns to stock an army, oiling and priming them up for action.'

Juliet laughed, while Dewar smiled at her fondly, admiring her young beauty. Holly's first thought was for Rex. Regarding him, she noticed his jealous distress, The other two began discussing some new interpretation of the play.

'Let me take Jane's hand and finish the game with you,' Holly offered, going to the bedside. Her fingers had been made dexterous by long stitchery. She neatly extricated a stick that had been wedged at a precarious angle under a whole pile of sticks.

'How'd you do that!' Rex challenged. 'That's impossible!'

'Like this,' she answered, repeating her coup with another jack-straw.

'By Jove, Holly, you're a witch!' he shouted, startled out of his pique by her accomplishment.

Dewar looked up, startled at such plain speaking. 'Holly is a very dab at spillikins, Mr Homberly,' Jane warned him.

'Only fair,' Holly asserted. 'Rex beat me all hollow at piquet this afternoon, now I shall get my own back from him. I think we must place a wager on this game, and let me win back the monkey I owe you from cards this afternoon. Is it a monkey I owe you, Rex, or a pony?'

'Only a pony. Told you, Holly, a pony's twenty-five pounds, a monkey is five hundred. That is, unless you're playing with a Hun. To them, it's five pounds, or sometimes fifty, depending on. . . . Anyway, it's five hundred pounds here, and you don't want to be betting a monkey if it's a pony you mean.'

'Holly, you were surely not gambling for such stakes!' Jane asked.

'Only in fun. We don't actually pay, but it is more fun if you bet, Rex says.'

'Tell you what, Holly, I'll give the blunt to your orphans if I lose. But we'll be playing for shillings, not pounds.'

'I cannot afford even shillings.'

'You won't have to. You're beating the trousers off me.'

'Agreed!' she declared, lifting yet another impossible straw free.

'That moved!' Rex charged, narrowing his eyes and leaning forward.

'It only moved because you jiggled your leg. If you would lie still I could get every stick out. I've got the hard ones already.'

'By the living jingo, I didn't move my leg. Not a muscle.'

'You twitched.'

'Did not.'

'You did so.'

'You calling me a liar?' he asked.

'Yes.'

' 'Fraid I must call you out then. Challenge you to a duel.'

'Afraid I must refuse.'

'Well, you ain't no gentleman, Holly.'

'And you, sir, are no lady. Oh, go on then, take a turn.'

An inadvertent twitch sent every straw on the counterpane flying, making extrication so easy for his adversary that the game was over.

Dewar and Jane, hovering at their shoulders, hinted they would not refuse an offer to join the game. 'Get your own straws,' Rex said bluntly. 'Know what you're up to, Dew. You want to take on Holly. She's playing with me.'

'We are clearly not wanted,' Jane said, with a little laugh.

This reminded Rex that the lady, at least, was wanted very much indeed but, unfortunately, she came with the gentleman, so that no headway was made in his romance before Roper shooed the ladies out the door prior to preparing his master for bed.

'You have billeted yourself on the Proctors long enough,' Dewar decreed. 'I'll send a carriage for you tomorrow morning.'

Rex looked at him long and hard, with his blue eyes protruding from his face. 'Maybe you're right,' he said.

'I am. Jane will be at the Abbey. You can do nothing to further your suit here all day, and we can both come over in the evening if you wish.'

'No need for you to put yourself out, Dew. Can manage as well without you. Better, in fact.'

'I can relieve you of Miss McCormack's attention a little – make it easier for you in that way.'

'Not sure I want to be relieved of it. Fact is, half in love with both the ladies. Jane's prettier; Holly's nicer. A very nice girl, Holly. I know she likes me, Dew. That's why I'm in a bit of a pickle, wondering if I should leave. Mean to say, shouldn't lead her on if I don't mean to have her and, when Jane is here, I don't think I do. She's very sweet on me, Holly. It pains to let me know she's only twenty-six. Lying actually, I believe. Admitted before she was older, but today she lowered it, after she found out I was twenty-seven myself. And she rushed Jane up older than herself – all a hum. Must be. Not a wrinkle or a crease anywhere on her phiz.'

'Jane is seventeen. Holly was obviously roasting you.'

'Possible. You must have noticed though how she's always hovering over me, looking after me. Very nice; I like it. Sat talking to me all day, and playing cards, and fetching me ale and wine. Well – stayed away from the play practice just to be with me. You must have noticed how she elbowed Jane aside to take her place at jackstraws. Little things like that. Always throwing her hanky at me. It was her idea that I stay here in the first place, now I think about it. Had an eye on me from day one.'

'She is kind. I think you misconstrue her intentions, however.'

'I don't. I mentioned Jane this afternoon, and she was at pains to let me know the parents ain't in favour of an early match. Cut my hopes right down. She's definitely casting her cap at me, and what I must decide is whether I mean to have her or not. What do you think, Dew?'

'I think you are mad.'

'She ain't that bad! Believe I aim too high to set my sights on Jane. Altmore is after her. Foxey running mad for her – not that he'd have a look-in any more than myself. *You're* sweet on her, and. . . .'

'I hope you didn't say that to anyone in this house!'

'Course not. May have let it slip to Holly, but . . .'

'I'm taking you home tonight!' Dewar said, with a grim face.

'Not tonight. I'm tired, Dew. Holly is sending me up a bowl of smash and two chicken legs. Noticed something else too,' he added, smothering a yawn. 'She didn't wear her specs tonight. Had them on this afternoon. Told her they was ugly, and she didn't wear them tonight, to please me. Didn't wear the old brown shawl either. Had herself dolled up in a newer one. Not a bad-looking woman, do you think, Dew?'

'She is passably attractive. Her voice is good.'

'Lovely voice. Very soothing,' Rex said and, closing his eyes, smiled fatuously. A soft, snorting sound told his guest he had succumbed to a brief nap, so Dewar left, frowning in confusion.

His mother was still up when he returned home, just finishing a game of cards with her crony, Sir Laurence Digby. After he had left, she turned to her son. 'Don't tell me I am actually to have five minutes of your time all to myself! To what do I owe this unusual honour?'

'To circumstances, Mama. I'm worried about Rex. He has taken the half-cocked notion Holly McCormack is setting her cap at him. Do you think it possible?'

'I shouldn't think so. I always took Holly for a sane woman. Maybe she's saner than I think. It would be a good match for her. Rex is well off, and would hardly be a demanding husband.'

'But he's so. . . .' He hunched his elegant shoulders and threw up his hands. 'What would they possibly have in common? A woman who is half shrew, and a man who is three-quarters a fool.'

'Oh but a fool of a man needs a shrew for a wife. Two fools would deal badly together. Holly is not a shrew exactly. She is accustomed to taking an interest in the villagers because of her late father's being a clergyman, you know.'

'I have reason to know she takes a keen interest in the welfare of the villagers.'

'What has she been needling you about, eh?' the dame asked astutely.

He smiled at her. 'The things you should have needled me

about. The orphanage; Evans.'

'I should have done, should I? It comes as news to me. I under-stood Roots is your overseer when you are away, which is to say ninety-nine per cent of the time.'

'What else wants doing in the village? I am becoming a little tired of having my knuckles rapped every time I talk to that woman. She makes me feel like a truant.'

'Give her a good setdown.'

'Easier said than done. She has the knack of being right, you see.'

'How unattractive of her. How does the play go on?'

'Fine,' he answered, in a distracted manner. 'Just fine.'

'You sound bored with it already.'

'I am, a little. Things will improve when Swithin arrives. He'll liven us up.'

CHAPTER 12

There was something very much wrong with the play. Dewar had never been entirely happy with Rex as Tybalt, but at least his role was small. The greater error had been in casting Foxey in the much more important role of Mercutio. Foxey played truant so often, especially when Rex was not there to duel with him, that he was virtually a stranger to half the cast. When he came, he still read his speeches, with no attempt at committing them to memory. After Rex's return, the two of them spent their time mooning over Juliet. Dewar had to read them a thundering scold, with the upshot that Foxey tossed aside his book and declared he was 'fagged to death with the whole dull thing.' One of the leading characters! In desperation, Dewar went to Jane to seek her help. She sat with Holly, reciting her lines while her cousin held the book to prompt her.

'Foxworth has resigned. You must do something. Talk to him, Juliet,' he begged.

'Quit? You cannot mean he is going to disappoint us!' Jane exclaimed.

'Precisely. Only you can help us. He will come around if you ask him.'

'Oh, I shall!' she said, hopping up at once to go after him.

'Casting Mr Foxworth in the role of Mercutio was not good judgement in the first instance,' Holly said.

'I know it well. He was staying here at the Abbey, and volunteered for the role. I let him have it before I remembered what an important character Mercutio is in the play. If I had anyone to replace him, I'd let him go.'

'There is a Mr Prendergast in the village who would make an admirable Mercutio. He works for Mr Raymond, but something might be arranged. . . .'

'A bit late for that.'

'Foxworth hasn't begun his lines yet. My friend could learn them faster.'

'Is your friend likely to resign his position to take part in an amateur theatrical production?' Dewar asked, rather ironically.

'If he were secure of another position at the play's end, he would,' she replied, with a significant look Dewar was coming to mistrust.

'Meaning?'

'It was generally understood Mr Prendergast would take over the school when he came down from university, to replace old Parsons. The position with Raymond is temporary.'

'Parsons has not spoken to me of retiring.'

'He never will, Lord Dewar. He is a bachelor who lives alone, but for one servant who looks after him. He would be moped to death if he quit work but, really, he is too ancient to continue.'

'That seems a hard trick to play him, after some forty years of faithful service.'

'Some sedentary, useful position could be found for him in the village – the circulating library perhaps.'

'I don't think it will be necessary,' Dewar replied, looking across the room, where Foxworth was receiving a copy of the play from Jane, and smiling blissfully. 'I think our problem is solved.'

'One problem. That leaves the more important one of the school requiring a competent teacher, and Mr Prendergast requiring a decent position so he can afford. . . .' She stopped short as Jane and Foxworth advanced towards them.

'All right then, I'll stay in your play,' Foxworth declared magnanimously. 'But only because Jane asks it.'

'He has promised me he will begin to memorize his lines,' Jane added.

'Jane is going to take them from me,' Foxworth said, smiling at her. 'We'd better get right at it,' he added, when he saw Rex hastening across the hall.

'Don't hear nobody offering to take my lines,' Rex sulked when he was told the story.

'I will be happy to take them from you,' Holly offered, out of pity.

'Kind of you,' he said, only partly mollified. 'Reminds me – money for your orphan. Sent a draft off. Should have it soon.' He ambled off, deciding to listen to Foxey and Jane instead of reciting his own lines.

Dewar turned to Holly, his brows raised. '*Your* orphans? Does he by any chance mean my orphans?'

'The orphans at St Alton's. Rex has kindly offered to help with the expense of. . . .'

'I do not require outside help! When I want you to stand on a corner with a cup begging, or to importune my guests, I will be sure to tell you, ma'am,' he said in a hard voice, his eyes flashing.

'You misunderstand the matter. Rex offered.'

'I can imagine what urged him to make the offer! You have been complaining of my neglect.'

'I have not!'

'Do you expect me to believe he offered money, out of the blue, for a group of youngsters he has never heard of, unless you spoke to him of the matter?'

'I didn't ask him for money. And if I had, it is none of your business.'

'St Alton's is my orphanage! I gave Johnson the additional funds two weeks ago.'

'We in the village have always helped. . . .'

'It is one thing for the local ladies to volunteer their time, something else entirely for them to badger guests under my roof for money.'

'It seems to me you are more concerned for your reputation as a host than for the welfare of the orphans. Have you taken any steps to help Billie McAuley?'

'You will not accept money from my guests,' he declared, and stalked off to discover from his mother who Billie McAuley might be.

Lord Dewar sent around a brief notice cancelling rehearsals the next day, and urged his actors to use the time to study their lines. A considerable part of their time was also spent discussing what had caused the cancellation, till Mr Johnson called on Lady Proctor to confide that Billie McAuley had been swept off to London in Lord Dewar's own private coach, with His Lordship accompanying him. Soon Lady Dewar was announced, followed shortly by Mr Foxworth and Mr Homberly, come to quote their lines to the ladies of Stonecroft. Rex, however, took such an interest in seeing Foxey recite that he sat at his elbow during the whole visit, without once glancing at his own book.

'This was a very sudden decision on Dewar's part, was it not?' Lady Proctor asked, her eyes skimming her guest's ramshackle toilette. Under her shawl she wore what strongly resembled a gentleman's waistcoat, an ancient one of straw-coloured brocade, lavishly trimmed with bright embroidery. It looked vaguely familiar, as having once adorned the body of her late husband, who had been in his grave for a decade.

'Aye, I believe I can take credit for it. He mentioned the lad to me yesterday, and I told him of Billie's clubfoot. But Johnson may have dropped him the hint, or it is not likely he would have known the boy's name at all, or that he had any trouble.'

Miss McCormack said not a word. She felt an emotion that was hard to decipher. Embarrassment formed some part of it, self-justification some other, and there was, as well, a good deal of gratification. 'A nice warm house you keep, Elsa,' the dowager rambled on. 'I hardly need my waistcoat. The Abbey is so draughty I put it on to keep the chill from my back. You ought to try it. An excellent contraption. If you can keep your back and neck warm, the rest takes care of itself. And the feet, of course,' she added, easing her toes out of an oversized pair of boots.

'How do the corns go on?' Holly asked.

'They always bother me in the damp. But my nephew, Swithin Idle, will soon be here, and he is as good as a doctor. He always quacks me when he comes to us.'

'Dewar mentioned he was to give us a hand with the costumes,' Holly said, hoping for a few more details of this intriguing gentleman.

'We had a letter from him this morning. He was detained, but I daresay Dewar will put a bug in his ear while he is in the city. Likely as not that's the real reason he went, and only took McAuley along while he was going.'

Gratification fell away from Holly. 'I hope he stopped to see Dr John before he left, to get Billie's history,' she said.

'No, he didn't mention it. Speaking of the doctor reminds me, Holly – that Folkstone pudding. I am bored to death with it, and refuse to eat the custard that comes recommended so highly. You must find me a new receipt. Oh, and while I am here, you wouldn't happen to have the receipt for that cold medicine you gave me last winter? I could taste the rum and white wine in it, and lemon juice. What was it gave that ugly colour?'

'That would be the liquorice, ma'am. There is also linseed and raisins and soft water. I'll get my book upstairs.'

'There's a good gel.' As soon as Holly left, Lady Dewar turned to her hostess. 'Seems your niece is planning to nab herself a beau,' she said archly.

'Holly nab a beau? That is news to me. Why, we scarcely see Mr Johnson except at the rehearsals, though he was here earlier this morning.'

'Johnson? Peagoose! It is Rex Homberly I meant. Dewar says she means to have him. Is there any truth in it, eh? You can tell me. Mum's the word. I shan't say a thing to tease her. We'll let her go and join the youngsters when she comes back with my receipt.'

This was done, but the most hopeful watcher would have been

hard pressed to observe any coquettishness on the young lady's part, or any interest on the gentleman's. When, after a few moments, Homberly did address a remark to Holly, however, Lady Proctor felt a pang of dismay. 'I wish you will not encourage her in this notion,' she said to her caller. 'I depend totally on Holly to keep house for me when I take Jane to London. I expect Sir Egbert must go up to London soon and find a house to let for us. Where would you recommend as a good location, Lady Dewar?'

'Belgrave Square,' was the prompt reply, to set her as far as possible from the Dewar mansion on Grosvenor Square. 'You could not do better than Belgrave Square,' she said firmly.

Lady Dewar was bone-selfish, but she was human enough to like some people better than others, and she infinitely preferred Holly to her aunt. She began to feel Elsa Proctor was using the girl badly, to scotch her chance at making a good match. Before she left, she said to Holly, 'Pay no mind to your aunt. I think you, and Homberly should suit very well. Very well indeed.' A nod and a wink in Homberly's direction accompanied the speech.

'What?' Holly asked, not quite able to believe it.

'Sly puss. *I* see what you are about. I shall sing your praises to him at every opportunity. He will do much better for you than for Jane. And if you can't bring *him* up to scratch, I shall put in a word with my nephew, Swithin Idle, though I doubt you two should suit in the least.'

'Oh, please, I wish you will not!' Holly exclaimed, blushing.

'Ninnyhammer! Why should they make a servant of you?' Lady Proctor had arisen to join them on their way to the door, and the private coze was over, but it cast Holly into a daze of which Rex Homberly made up no part. She was very curious indeed to meet Sir Swithin Idle, however.

Before leaving, Rex found a moment alone with her. 'About that pony I promised you, Holly, Dew says I ain't to give it, but I have it here. No need for him to know. He's seeing to the little crippled fellow himself, but you can buy sugarplums for the others with the blunt.' He chucked it into her hands as he spoke, with a blush at his generosity, or perhaps his duplicity at displeasing his host.

'You had better not, if he dislikes it,' she demurred, hardly knowing what was the proper course to take.

'Have to. Gambling debt. Gentleman must pay up his gambling debts. Buy 'em the sugarplums. Was young myself once. Like a sugarplum very well still.' He had withdrawn his hand, leaving the money behind.

'I shall give it to Mr Johnson as a donation, and let him decide,' she said, seeking an honourable out.

'Good idea, but I hope he don't go buying prayer books or Bibles.'

He very likely would, too, but the donation had become so troublesome she would accept even that. When all the company had left, she went to her room to put the donation away, her mind full of the transactions of the morning. Perhaps it was ill-bred of her to have taken the money. Certainly it had cast Dewar into a great pucker, but it was only pride that bothered him, having it said he did not attend to his obligations. He never would have attended to them without her pestering him. Probably would not have taken Billie to London either, were it not for wanting to hasten Sir Swithin Idle to the Abbey. She was very curious to see this cousin whom Dewar considered so important.

CHAPTER 13

*D*ewar's day in London stretched into two, with no further instructions from him regarding what his players were to do in his absence. Foxworth came a second time to rehearse with Jane, but there was no appreciable improvement in his recitations. The conversation had a way of turning from Mercutio on the least provocation. With the Season in London to look forward to, Jane was excusably eager to learn what treats were in store for her. Homberly would no sooner promise to take her to Vauxhall to watch the lanterns being smashed on the closing night than it would occur to Foxey she must not be deprived of hearing a trial for some good crime at Old Bailey and, with luck, she might witness a hanging too.

'Looney bin in Lambeth Field. Must go to Bedlam,' Homberly added.

'Newgate. You can get in there too if you know the right people,' Foxey promised.

'I'll wager you know just the right people,' Holly offered, as she tackled the second-last orphan shirt.

'Yessir, by Jupiter, I can slip you in with no trouble at all. Bridewell too.'

'You make me wish I were going with you,' Holly said, smiling at their gallant nonsense.

'Why, ain't you going, Holly?' Rex asked.

'No, I am to keep house here in the family's absence.'

'Handy,' was Foxworth's thought on the matter.

'Demmed pity,' Rex averred, with a guilty idea that if there were any justice in the world he would be in love with Holly but, unfortunately, there was none.

'What about the routs and balls?' Jane asked, distressed at the nature of the dos mentioned. 'And the Queen's Drawing Room?'

'You have to go to them too,' Rex admitted sadly. 'Pity, but it's expected.'

'And the opera, and for rides and drives in the Park, but you needn't waste much of your time at that slow stuff,' Foxey advised her.

While these two mentors outlined the glories of a season as they saw it, the knocker sounded, and Dewar was shown in, hot from London. His first glance, an extremely hostile one, was for Holly. He quickly looked around to greet her aunt and the others but, as soon as his social duty was done, he returned his smouldering gaze to Miss McCormack, then strode purposefully to her group.

'What's new in town, Dew?' Foxworth asked.

'Where's Swithin?' Rex enquired.

'Nothing. He'll be here tomorrow,' he answered, looking from one to the other as he spoke. 'Juliet,' he said, with a smile and a bow to Jane, 'I trust you are keeping these two birds' beaks to the grindstone. I have something to discuss with Miss McCormack.' He held out a peremptory hand, drawing her first to her feet, then off to a sofa set a little apart from the others, while she swallowed nervously, to consider what he might have to say.

'You know where I have been, and why?' he demanded.

'Yes, your mother was here yesterday. What had the doctor to say about Billie's leg?'

'A good deal to say about that wooden frame Dr John had screwed on to the poor boy. If he hadn't got it off soon, Billie would be hopelessly crippled for life. I want to thank you for bringing it to my attention.'

She waved the thanks aside. 'Can anything be done for him?'

'He will never be perfectly normal with respect to walking.

Some slight limp will always be with him, but Dr Halford – I took
him to Sir Henry Halford – has hopes for a good improvement
over the months. Hot packs, massage, exercise – Billie will have
to stay at the clinic for half a year.'

'All alone? Oh, the poor boy!' she exclaimed, picturing the shy
Billie alone amidst strangers, in a strange city.

'You wanted him cured!' Dewar charged angrily.

'Of course! Naturally I did, but he must be dreadfully lonesome.
Could he not have these treatments at the orphanage, where he
knows everyone. Dr John could oversee. . . .'

'It is that quack of a Dr John who is responsible for the half of
his problem. No notion how the condition should have been
treated, and not the sense to have recommended him to a specialist.'

Holly took a deep breath and counted to ten, with no real alle-
viation of her temper. 'Dr John does not claim to be a specialist,'
she began hotly. 'He has three times to my knowledge recommended to Johnson that professional special help be brought in
for the boy. When it was not done, he undertook on his own time
to read up on the matter, and did his best to help. If his best was
not good enough. . . .'

'His best was a damned catastrophe. An infection was setting
in. Luckily, it was caught at the beginning, before a real tragedy
occurred. It could have resulted in losing the leg.'

'Well it would not, for I have spoken to Dr John recently, and
he said he would have to take the frame off for that very reason.
He may not be learned in that special field, but he is a very good
general doctor. He is no quack. He at least cares, which is more
than can be said for *some* people.'

'It is impossible to care about something or someone you know
nothing about,' he pointed out.

'It is your duty to know!'

'I hire people to attend to those duties. Johnson ought to have
told me. He is in charge of the orphanage. In fact, he ought to
have attended to it himself, long ago. Money was not *that* scarce.'

His defence was presented firmly but, in his own heart, he felt derelict and, of course, guilt coloured his temper.

'Yes, he ought to have done something about it – told you, at least. But, as he did not, I daresay he did not tell you a few other things either. Billie is very shy.'

'I know that. I accompanied him to London. He hadn't a word to say for himself, literally, for ten miles.'

'Well then, you can see how uncomfortable he will be there, amidst strangers. Surely Dr John could carry out the treatment if the London specialist gave him instructions.'

'I wouldn't trust Dr John with a dog.'

'That is grossly unfair. I tell you he is a good, conscientious doctor.'

'My mother puts little faith in him.'

'Your mother, if you will pardon my frank speaking, dislikes any cure that does not appeal to her appetite. Her illness has become a hobby for her. You meant well to take Billie to London, but you would have done better to consult first with Dr John, to discover Billie's past history, and it would have been better to take John with you to consult with Sir Henry, to learn what should be done to treat the boy here at home where he would be comfortable. He is so shy he will not dare to tell them in London if he is suffering or – or anything.'

'You might have told me sooner!' he said angrily, scarcely able to keep his voice down to a dull shout.

'I didn't know what you meant to do, or I would have told you. Dr John's feelings will be hurt too. You meant well – the impulse was kind, no doubt, but it might have been done in a more thoughtful manner. Dr John would have been so flattered to go, and how he would have loved to meet Dr Halford! He reads all his extracts.'

'Billie needs a specialist's care, particularly for the immediate future, till that swelling has subsided. If it is possible to move him later, it will be done,' he said in a cold, flat voice.

Holly felt an inexplicable urge to laugh. It was hard to understand why he was so extraordinarily angry. And, as he was in such a temper, why did he knuckle under to every suggestion? Johnson always described him as 'very obliging' to be sure and, as it was true, why had no one imposed on him sooner? She studied his profile silently as he stared across the room, trying to read his thoughts. 'That would be nice,' she said. He spared her one brief glare from the corner of his eye. 'Thank you. I mean – not that it is my place – only I'm sure Billie did not think to thank you.'

His last view of Billie had been of a white, frightened face, with tears gathering in the eyes. Thanks, he thought, were not the words Billie would have uttered, if he could have spoken. It was hard on the child to have left him alone. The damned woman was right, as usual. Shaking all this aside, he asked, 'How is the play coming along in my absence? Is Foxworth shaping up at all, under Juliet's tutelage?'

'Not noticeably,' she confessed. A look toward the group told him the folly of having Jane act as coach.

'That was a bad notion on my part. She is too much distraction. I would have done better to put you in charge. I wonder you did not undertake to supervise them on your own.'

She swiftly tallied the number of insults he had combined in one thoughtless statement. She was not attractive enough to distract gentlemen; she was rude and overbearing; and the tone of the words must surely add a special insult of their own. 'You overestimate my talents. I would not care to be responsible for such an impossible job. Mr Prendergast. . . .'

'You began to tell me of Mr Prendergast on a former occasion. A friend of yours, is he?'

'Yes, a local gentleman. His family has a small estate nearby. When you put him through university, it was generally assumed you meant him to take over the school.'

'*I* put him through university?' he asked, with a blank look.

'So he says. I cannot think he would have any reason to lie about it.'

'It seems it is not only my neglect I am unaware of, but my philanthropy as well. You are much interested in Mr Prendergast's case, I think?'

'Everyone takes an interest in Mr Prendergast's case. He is our village romantic,' she explained. 'He is young and handsome, you know – the classic case of a poor gentleman working hard to make something of himself. As Mr Foxworth is totally uninterested in the play, and Mr Prendergast really very eager to participate. . . .'

Some slight stiffening of Dewar's body brought her speech to a halt. 'I do hope you have not given Mr Prendergast any false hopes with regard to the role of either Mercutio or schoolmaster,' Dewar said, in his imperious manner.

'Oh no. He realizes very well all the blessings are yours to bestow, milord, when you eventually get round to it.'

'Good, I'm glad he does,' he answered curtly, then excused himself to go and speak to Juliet.

Homberly did not mind jostling elbows with Foxey, but when Dewar added himself to the girl's circle he retired to the less demanding company of Holly. 'See Dew is in a great pucker. Told him about the pony for the sugarplums, did you?'

'No, he is in a pucker about something else this time, Rex,' she answered, and laughed.

'Been thinking about what you said, Holly. About your not going to London. Pity.'

'I shan't mind. I never expected to go, you see, and my hopes are not built up.'

'Still – your aunt going. Jane going. Seems to me it wouldn't take much trouble to slip you into the carriage as well.'

'I will be needed here to look after the house. It is rather nice to feel needed, you know.'

'Demmed shame.'

When Lady Proctor saw Rex sitting with her niece, she moved to forestall his falling in love. 'Holly, my dear,' she called across the room, 'would you mind just taking a run upstairs to see if the boys are ready for bed? Nurse was to send them down to say good night to me. It is high time they were in bed. If they are, pray do not have them rooted out.'

Rex scowled into his lap to see Holly sent off like a dashed servant. Something ought to be done about it, by Jove, and he wished he could think of something other than offering for her. His own sister was to make her bows, but he had some little fear his mama would not appreciate having a spinster whom she did not know added to the presentation. When Holly returned, her aunt promptly sent her off again, to see if Sir Egbert could not join the company in the saloon. How was she to bring Lord Dewar up to scratch, if Sir Egbert insisted in staying in his study all night long, as though he were still Squire Proctor, with no social duties? On Holly's second trip, Lord Dewar as well scowled.

Sir Egbert came when he was summoned, but his notion of social intercourse was to sit with his wife and niece. There was no conversation with the others till the tea tray was brought in. 'Your mama mentioned Sir Swithin Idle is to join your party soon,' Lady Proctor said to Dewar.

'Yes, I spoke to him on my way home from London. He is to come tomorrow.'

'Will he be in your play?'

'Not as an actor. He will be concerned with the production. He has often performed in the past but, as he comes so late this time, he will not take any role.'

Listening, Holly was struck with inspiration. She would not push Mr Prendergast forward again. Sir Swithin must be Mercutio.

When Sir Egbert, hinted into courtesy by a speaking glance from his spouse, enquired of Dewar how his swine were coming along, the conversation turned to this rustic topic, which perhaps had something to do with the celerity with which the tea was drunk up, and the guests rose to take their leave.

'Boor!' was Lady Proctor's condemning word to her husband. 'I hope you can speak of something other than swine and manure when we go to London. I don't know how I am expected to get your daughter a *parti* when her papa must insult every gentleman who comes into the house.'

'No one but that dandy of a Dewar would take it as an insult to discuss farming,' he defended, and left, wondering what he should have spoken of. Elsa had informed him on another occasion it was wrong to speak of money. He raised swine to make money. What else was there to talk about?

CHAPTER 14

The next day, at rehearsal, it was made clear to everyone that Foxey was not pulling his weight. Every scene in which Mercutio had a part was held up by his lack of preparation. The others were no longer using their books but, even with his text in his hand, Foxey could not perform satisfactorily. He could scarcely read the words, let alone memorize them, or pronounce them with any force or expression. He frowned into his text, stumbling out the obscure phrases. ' "O that she were an open *et cetera*, thou a pop'rin pear!" Now really, Dew, what the deuce does this drivel mean? Imagine Shakespeare sunk to saying *et cetera* – thought he was supposed to know all the words. I refuse to learn this muck.'

When he was not on stage, he was causing a commotion in the pit, duelling with Tybalt, pestering Juliet, and generally upsetting the organization. When the cast took a break for tea, a group of the mature dames got together to discuss the matter. 'I am surprised Dewar does not replace him,' Miss Hall said.

Several of the dames cast a meaningful glance on Holly. She shook her head firmly. 'I have already hinted and been snubbed. I think his cousin, who is to arrive today, may do for the part.'

'Ah, very likely that is what he has in mind,' the ladies agreed, happy to have a solution without having to confront Dewar over it. He was very agreeable and obliging, to be sure, but everyone has a fault, and wanting – in fact insisting – that everything be done his own way was undeniably Dewar's imperfection. Mrs Abercrombie, though she did not mention it, could hardly fail to notice that her stage had been lowered not inches, but three feet. The Misses Hall, too, had not been entirely happy to have their orange trees pulled out of their warm conservatory and hauled to the Abbey in the cold, to see how they would look in the orchard scene. And as to the mead! A battle had nearly been precipitated over that point. Welsh nectar would have been ever so much easier (and cheaper) without adding any anachronism to the feast, but it was mead Dewar insisted upon, and was to have, while the Bartletts had the trouble of making it. No open hostility was allowed to be seen, but in the privacy of certain saloons there were a few uncomplimentary remarks exchanged.

'How is the fermentation coming on?' Dewar asked Mrs Bartlett as he passed amongst his slaves during one of the tea breaks. This was done daily, to keep them in line.

'Excellent. It will be ready on time for the play,' was her answer, with no hint of displeasure.

'Your trees got back to the conservatory in good form, I trust?' he asked the Hall ladies.

'Oh yes – a few leaves lost in the shipping, and the cold blast of air was not at all – but they are intact,' Miss Hall assured him.

'I see you have added a white flag to the flagstaff for our afternoon performance, Mrs Abercrombie. Excellent. A very Elizabethan touch. We shall require a black one for the evening. The orphans, you know, are to be treated to our dress rehearsal in the afternoon, with the evening performance for the villagers. It will be a busy day for us.'

Smiles and agreement all around. Not a word of complaint was uttered by any of his helpers.

'Not sewing today, I see,' he remarked to Holly, who sat with the matrons. 'Glad you are finished the shirts. Swithin will be here tonight with his drawings for the play costumes.'

'I hope he is not delayed again,' she replied, thinking he would be hard pressed to learn Mercutio's part.

'He won't. Mama has asked your aunt to bring the family here for dinner, to meet him. I was to take him to visit you, but this will do as well. Your aunt has already accepted, on the family's behalf. It will be more useful for us all to meet here, where the stage is erected. I am curious to hear Swithin's pronouncement on it. I hope he is pleased.'

'You place a good deal of value on his opinion, I take it?' she asked, her own opinion of Sir Swithin rising higher by the moment. For Dewar to give any intimation of deferring to anyone was an unusual turn.

'His judgement is infallible in such affairs. I used to argue with him when first we began working together on a few efforts, but have learned to trust his instincts.'

'I look forward to meeting him.'

'He looks forward to making your acquaintance as well, ma'am,' he answered, then turned to the next lady, leaving his companion pleasantly titillated. He had spoken to Sir Swithin of her and, whatever he had said, it must have been complimentary, as the cousin wanted to meet her.

Holly did not normally take much pains with her toilette. She had a good blue silk gown in which she had been appearing at formal public dos for the past two years. It was well made, without aspiring to any rarefied heights of fashion. As it was being saved for the Christmas ball held annually at the Assembly Hall, she had no thought of removing it from camphor yet. No, she would wear her green sarsenet, with her good white shawl to add a touch of fashion. Her hair was carefully pinned up, so that no loose mouse tail would slip its anchor and go tumbling down her back. In honour of Sir Swithin, she wore her mother's pearl brooch, and felt she had done all that humankind could expect in the way of embellishment.

Lady Proctor saw the evening as one of vital importance. It was the first time the Proctor menage had been invited to dine at the Abbey *en famille*. She and Sir Egbert had thrice, over the years, formed part of a large party, the invitations coming late enough that there was some question as to which couple had hedged off at the last moment. This was quite different. Certainly it was a compliment to Jane, and therefore Jane must be shown to best advantage. Her white formal gowns under preparation for her presentation were much too grand for the occasion, but her new rose silk, her mama thought, would do admirably. Pearls around the neck would add elegance without sophistication. It would not do for her to be too sophisticated, as Dewar so frequently mentioned her youth, sweetness, and innocence. Actually, it was Juliet's virtue, as manifested in Jane, that inspired his compliments. He hardly seemed to know where the one girl left off and the other began. Lady Proctor, not wishing to rival her daughter, contented herself with a brown velvet gown, devoid of fringes, ribbons, lace, or any trimming, its severity lightened only by her topaz and diamond necklace. This avoiding of her customary 'elegance' showed her to better advantage than her usual costume. Her niece told her she looked 'all the crack,' and even Sir Egbert, no connoisseur, said she would be the prettiest gel there.

She may have been the prettiest in her husband's view, but there was no doubt her daughter took the palm in everyone else's opinion. Rex and Foxey lay in wait for Jane's entrance, and flung themselves forward to greet her when she came in. Even before her wrap was off, Rex was admiring her gown.

'That's her pelisse, ninny,' Foxey told him.

'I know it. See a gown underneath. Pink. Very nice pink.'

Miss McCormack's pelisse was removed without a word. She, likewise, was shown into the saloon without being annoyed with compliments. Once there, Lady Dewar ran an eye over her and said, 'All rigged up, eh Holly? That'll turn Homberly's head.'

Dewar greeted them all, then cut Jane out from the pack and within two minutes was sitting with her, while Foxey and Rex complained to Altmore that, by Jove, if they'd known this was how he meant to behave, they'd have stayed at the inn and taken their mutton there. It was for Altmore to do the pretty with Miss

McCormack. He was less obvious than the other bucks in his pursuit of Jane, but even he had no control over his eyes, which slid off to the corner every few minutes. Some conversation must be made and, with an amused shake of her head, Holly said to him, 'Has Dewar said anything about replacing Foxworth as Mercutio? It will be impossible to put the play on with him, don't you think?'

'He hasn't said anything, but he must realize Foxey is hopeless.'

'We were wondering if his other cousin – the one who is to arrive this evening – might be persuaded to fill in.'

'Who, Swithin?' Altmore asked, with a startled look at her. 'Good God, no! Where did you get that idea?' Then he laughed as if he would choke.

Holly's eagerness to see this cousin grew, and continued to grow throughout the dinner, during which several references were made to Swithin, but of so varied a nature that no firm conjecture could be made as to his physical appearance. She was still in a bewildered state when the gentlemen joined the ladies after dinner. Rex, who loved his wine equally as much as he loved Jane, solved the matter of choosing between them with his usual simple expediency. He picked up his glass and a decanter and took them into the saloon, thus securing the choice spot by Jane's side. Holly sat with her, and learned that she was not the only one whose interest had been piqued by the many references to Sir Swithin. Jane too was on tenterhooks to see him.

'A robust, hearty rascal, this,' Rex said, looking at Jane over his wineglass.

'And how tall is he?' Jane asked.

'Eh? Tall? What the deuce. . . . I am talking about the wine, Jane. A robust fellow, this claret. Got a deal of bottom.'

'*We* are talking about Sir Swithin,' Jane told him, with an amused shake of her curls.

'Ain't robust. Ain't hearty either. Ain't much of a rascal, come to that.'

'Yes, but what *is* he like?' Holly asked impatiently.

'Won't care for him,' Rex told her. This was the only piece of opinion they could get from him. Dewar and Foxworth were not slow in following Rex into the saloon, and they too pulled up chairs in a semi-circle around Jane, causing Lady Proctor to smile in satisfaction as she cast a meaningful nod in Sir Egbert's direction. Observing it, Lady Dewar felt a pronounced desire to shake her son till his teeth rattled. Dangling after the chit, and putting ideas in the mama's head. As soon as Dewar was seated, Jane turned to repeat her question to him.

'Judge for yourself. Here he is now,' Dewar answered, nodding toward the doorway. With her pulse racing, Holly too turned to follow the direction of his glance. An uncontrolled little ripple of laughter escaped, before her fingers flew to her lips to stifle it.

Sir Swithin Idle twittered in, a symphony in golden hues, looking very much like an overgrown canary, and sounding rather like one too, with his clear, fluty voice chirping a medley of extravagant phrases to Lady Dewar at the doorway. His jacket was of gold brocade, his waistcoat a shade darker, his inexpressibles lighter, his bird-like twigs of legs encased in white silk stockings. His hair was a soft cap of tawny curlets, which had been allowed to grow longer than was the fashion in nonartistic circles, and which Holly suspected was set up in papers every night, like a lady's. No one had ever actually seen Swithin apply rouge to his cheeks or lips, but they bore a suspiciously high colour Six of his ten fingers were bedizened with rings, only the thumb and index finger of each hand escaping adornment. He carried a gold-edged quizzing glass which he held aloft at a dainty angle, and occasionally tapped against his chin.

Rex Homberly made an inchoate sound in his throat, denoting deep disgust, and Foxworth said, 'Damn, Dewar, I hope you didn't ask that painted popinjay to spend the whole visit here.'

'God made it, let it pass for a man,' Dewar replied, with a slightly disdainful smile as he looked from Swithin to his companions.

'Dashed man-milliner.' Rex scolded.

'Occasionally,' Dewar agreed, 'but, for the nonce, he is to be our man-modiste, and create the costumes for our drama.'

'Ain't getting *me* into no yaller jackets,' Foxey warned.

'Nor breeches either,' Rex seconded, though in fact he often wore yellow breeches.

In a soft aside to Holly, Jane said, 'My, isn't he pretty? I love his curls.'

Before answer could be made, Swithin was kissing his fingers to Lady Dewar and mincing across the room towards them. He drew to a stop in front of Jane, and took up a pose with one hand lifting the quizzing glass to examine her, the other placed on his hip. His left leg bore all the weight of his slender body; the right was daintily crossed over it, the toe pointed forward, just touching the floor. Holly found herself waiting eagerly to distinguish the first words uttered by Swithin.

'Quite right, Dewar, my dear boy,' he chirped languidly, his gaze never wavering from Jane. 'She is Juliet. Stand up and give us a pirouette, dear, and let us see you all around.'

Jane obediently arose and turned in a circle slowly, looking back over her shoulder with a questioning face as she did so. 'Exquisite! It will be a delight to dress you,' he declared, lowering the quizzing glass and gesturing dramatically with both arms outflung.

'Land that caper merchant a facer for two pennies,' Rex mumbled under his breath, while Foxey said he'd do it for free.

'Who else have we got assembled here?' Swithin ran on, always in his high, grating voice, with something a trifle querulous in it, as he peered through his glass. 'Altmore – ah, the perennial Romeo. Dear boy, you must be fagged to death, playing the juvenile hero forever. Foxworth – Homberly – hmm. Attendant lords, scene-swellers, one does sincerely hope. And you,' the glass turned to Holly. '. . . Nurse to Juliet?' he asked, raising his brows and looking so extremely silly with his lips pursed that Holly could scarcely keep from smiling.

'I am playing Lady Capulet,' she managed to say.

'Ah, yes – the golden voice! Had I heard you speak sooner, I would have known. Dewar, old chap, dead on, as usual. A golden-voiced warbler. She will make us a superb Lady Macbeth one of these days. Or, if she is half so ill-natured as you say, she would make a divine Shrew. A *Shakespearean* shrew, to be tamed. A Kate!' he told her, as she glared first at him, then spared one flash for Dewar. 'Oh my, such dangerous orbs! I come to comprehend the phrase "a killing glance", which always sounded so overdone before.'

Dewar stepped forward rather quickly as Holly drew in her breath to attack. 'Everyone – I want you to meet my cousin, Sir Swithin Idle. And I shall make my guests known to you too, Swithin.'

'Only stage names, I do implore, Coz. An excess of names is too wearying after a day of travel. And what's in a name after all? I am no saint, I promise you, though I was born on July fifteenth and bear the bishop's name. All a hum. I shall reserve all my faculties for the task before me. I have brought you *bales* of the most exquisite material with me for costumes.'

With an embarrassed smile at the Proctors, Dewar managed to insert their names very quickly. Swithin looked at them, said nothing, then turned back to his own thoughts. 'We must look the materials over *ensemble*, you and I, Coz. I await your opinion of them. A *stupendous* spider gauze with iridescent threads in blue and green and shimmery, for Juliet's party. Oh, I adore it – and a fairly satisfactory lutestring. One would not have thought it possible to wear lutestring, would one, but the colour, you will agree I know, is unexceptionable. A brocade for Lady Montague, stiff and formal. You will want that quality in her gown.

'For Nurse, you will want a plain striped cotton, with a white apron and cap, and I think I shall give her dirty fingernails. A nice common touch, a sort of symbolic suggestion of the earth, as she is an earthy wench. She suggests bigamy, you know, to Juliet.'

'A striped cotton and white apron sounds very English,' Holly said, 'and very modern.'

'Yes, Kate, we are doing the play in contemporary dress, as

Shakespeare himself did – in contemporary English dress, that is,'
Swithin told her. 'I believe I forgot to tell you that, Dew, old chap.
As you are returning to the true flavour in your casting – faultless,
by the by, from what I have seen – I am on thorns to see your
thrust stage – ah – as I was saying when I interrupted myself –
mmm, yes. I have decided to use contemporary dress. *C'est tout.'*

While his listeners raised a vociferous protest, with even Jane
adding a shy demur to this notion, Dewar stood thinking, biting
the interior of his cheeks to aid concentration. 'I like it, Swithin,'
he said, when the outrage had died down. 'I like it excessively. An
excellent idea. I am so glad you are here. There are dozens of
details I have been wanting to talk to you about.'

'We'll burn the midnight oil, dear boy. I shall *adore* it.'

'Ain't getting *me* into no modern outfits,' Homberly said, with
a defiant glare at Swithin.

'Please yourself, Rex,' Swithin said in a dismissing way. 'We
shall contrive to carry on *sans* your portly presence. Tell me – have
you ever given any thought to a Cumberland corset for that
unsightly protuberance you are growing?' he asked, with a
seething examination of Rex's stomach.

'Ain't a scarecrow, anyway!' Rex retaliated.

'Dashed right!' Foxey supported him.

'I make sure the two of you together couldn't scare a humming-
bird, less a crow,' Swithin agreed, then he turned back to Dewar.
'My good man, do you *really* propose to put these two ruffians on
stage? *Do* tell me in what roles you have cast them. Falstaff I could
envisage, or Caliban, but in "Romeo and Juliet". . . . '

'Tybalt and Mercutio,' Dewar replied, with a wondering glance
to the ungainly pair.

'*Mon Dieu!*' Swithin shook his curls in wonderment, then
proceeded to settle the question in his own way. 'You have
decided on a spot of comic relief. I envisaged the duel scenes as
some of the more glorious moments of the drama. I cannot quite
see them as farce, but you are a genius, Dew. No question of
that. I know you have some reason for this seemingly inexplica-

ble piece of casting.'

Rex had been observing the newcomer darkly, and finally gave vent to his thoughts. 'Ain't no dashed comic relief! Dashed insult.'

'Certainly is!' Foxey agreed.

'Why do you two belligerent gladiators not go out into the hall-way and run each other through, hmm?' Swithin asked with an amiable smile.

It proved an entirely acceptable suggestion. 'First sensible word you've said yet,' Rex told him haughtily, and stomped out, after lunging at Foxey with his outstretched arm which, fortunately, did not yet hold a sword.

'I am *most* curious to see what you have done with the duelling scenes,' Swithin said after the two had charged out the door. 'I *do* hope those two are not let loose on stage with halberds or polearms. There won't be a shred of scenery left standing.'

'No, they use rapiers,' Dewar told him.

'Even an épée, as we are being contemporary – but no. The point makes itself. The épée calls for restraint, formality. You will try to get the bravura effect of the Italian school. Don't despair, Dew. I shall work out some choreography for them. Foxworth is probably capable of a simple thrust, and Rex of a parry. It is only to teach them the fine points of feint and riposte. No doubt it can be done, but have you forgotten Mercutio must also *speak*? What an indomitable optimist you are!'

'We *are* having a little difficulty on that score,' Dewar admitted.

'Not surprising. But, of more interest – the costumes. I had the inspiration of contemporary dress en route here from Heron Hall. I stopped at home to deliver Mama a new *chapeau*, very feathery and hideous. She adores it. I have lit on a few dramatic innova-tions, and I want your utterly frank opinion, Dew. Pray do not spare me. We must be *brutal*, for Art's sake. Juliet – our lovely Juliet – is to be dressed in the beginning as a child. I adore it myself. Start her out with her hair down and her skirts up a little, for she is only thirteen at the time. It will set the seal absolutely on her age, create just the effect you want, of a child's innocence being violated prematurely. And this Juliet you have found! She could play a child superbly. You did not praise her nearly enough, though you hardly spoke of anything else in London. Now tell me – what do you think of it?'

'I like it,' Dewar admitted, looking intently at Jane. 'Yes, with that golden hair down and a girlish bow in it perhaps, with ribbons trailing down the back . . . the skirts just slightly pulled up to show a few inches of ankle.'

'Mama won't like it,' Jane said, and felt very much that she did not like it either.

'Mama will love it, *ma petite chère*,' Swithin disagreed, so pleasantly that it sounded like a compliment.

'Just for the first scene,' Dewar pointed out.

'So, Dewar, what other originalities have you come up with?' Swithin demanded.

'The thrust stage, as I mentioned earlier. We are to have madrigals sung before the play, and Miss McCormack has added her mite. We mean to have the servant girls go through the aisles with oranges.'

'How entirely Nell Gwynnish! Excellent!' Idle exclaimed. 'When may I see your pretty, witty Nells? Actually, that would have been *the* touch for your Restoration comedy a few years back, *n'est-ce pas*? We should have met this Kate sooner. You won't mind if I call you Kate, dear?' he asked Holly, who obviously minded very much. 'I shall design *ravissant* mobcaps for the orange wenches, and peasant blouses *très décolleté* to show plenty of snow white bosom. I hope your wenches are well-endowed?'

'Adequate,' Dewar assured him, while Holly's mind quickly scanned the servants to determine which girls he spoke of.

Swithin nodded in satisfaction, then heaved a deep sigh. 'Do you know, I am quite fatigued with so much cleverness? I shall sit these weary bones down on a sofa, and would relish something restorative, Dew. I am feeling peckish – tea and toast fingers, unbuttered, will suffice. I must chat with your mama. How adorably quaint she is. When one has no looks and no elegance, one is wise to be as gothically unfashionable as possible. At least she is *something* then, and not a mere nonentity. Whose reach-me-downs is *Tante Hélène* wearing tonight? Your late papa was used to favour that flowered waistcoat last century, if memory serves. How charmingly it suits her.' He walked daintily off, while Dewar called for tea and toast for his guest, then returned to the ladies.

'An interesting fellow, Swithin. Don't you agree?' he asked.

'Remarkable,' Jane said in a failing voice.

'Quite casts you into the shade,' Holly told him with a mocking smile. 'He has you beat in both elegance and conversation, I think. To say nothing of original dramatic ideas.'

'I do not consider Swithin to be cast in the same mould as myself,' he answered swiftly, in a repressive voice.

'Oh, no indeed! He is *much* fancier. A sort of deluxe version of Lord Dewar, the cover heavily trimmed in gold.'

'You wretch! You perfectly vile woman!' he said, some expression between a laugh and a frown on his face as he looked across the room to Swithin. His cousin sat on the sofa holding aloft a pretty teacup, his little finger crooked aloft, one thin yellow knee crossed over the other, his little black patent slipper jiggling. Dewar took a deep breath and said, 'I do *not* curl my hair, or wear a dozen rings, or lisp, or speak half in French!'

'No, I said he was fancier. Merely, you are similar, not identical. Besides, you are much taller.'

'Holly is roasting you, Lord Dewar,' Jane said in a placating way. 'I like Swithin. He is so droll.'

'He is certainly very comic,' Holly agreed.

'You are not so astute as I had thought, Miss McCormack,' Dewar said. 'You heard his philosophy mentioned with regard to Mama. When one has no natural distinction, one must go one's length in some direction to avoid being a nonentity. Swithin elected to play the fop, and he does it to the top of his bent. He has good ideas and is clever for all that. I like him enormously.'

'So do I,' Jane agreed. 'And so does Holly, really. It is only that she is vexed because he called her a shrew.'

'That was one of his more extravagant compliments,' Dewar informed them. 'Kate is not only a shrew, but also "Young, beauteous, brought up as best becomes a gentlewoman," according to the play. You may be sure Idle is aware of it.'

'That is not the aspect of Kate's character that comes first to mind, however,' Holly said.

'True, but Swithin can hardly know yet of your less appealing qualities.'

'Only what you were kind enough to tell him. Never mind, he'll learn soon enough.'

'Not much doubt of that. But a word of caution. Tread softly, Kate.' There was an anticipatory smile on his lips as they went to join Swithin and Lady Dewar.

There was suddenly a loud bang in the hallway, followed by the unmistakable reverberation of breaking porcelain, as a very valuable Bustelli Nymph hit the floor, to be broken into a dozen pieces as it bounced along the marble. Everyone hastened to the hallway to view the damage. 'My Julia! You've broken my Bustelli figurine!' Dewar shouted in dismay.

With a glance to the table from which it had fallen, Swithin picked up a Meissen goat, done all in white, and frowned at it. 'Pity it couldn't have been this instead,' he remarked, and placed it close to the table's edge.

'Accident!' Foxworth said sheepishly. 'Tell you what, Dewar. I'll replace it.'

'It is irreplaceable. Go and duel somewhere else. Try the barn.'

'Thought of that,' Rex said. 'Didn't want to butcher a cow by accident. 'Course you could eat it. Not a dead loss. Let's stop, Foxey. That was my round. Owe me a pony.' Upon catching sight of Jane, he remembered he was in love with her, and set his sword against the wall, where it promptly clattered noisily to the floor. He gave it an angry scowl, turned on his heel, and ignored it.

'Take me to see your stage while we are on our feet,' Swithin suggested to Dewar. He placed his hand on Dewar's arm, as a lady would, and the two of them strolled off. 'I am most curious to see how you have handled the proscenium,' Swithin was overheard to say, as they rounded the corner.

'Dear boy!' Foxey said, in a mocking soprano voice to Rex, 'Allow me to offer you my arm to view the proscenium.'

Rex tottered forward on tiptoes and accepted the arm. The rest of the audience tried, with varying success, to contain their grins as they returned to the saloon.

Foxworth seemed suddenly a much less horrid Mercutio than he had previously. With a little shrug of disappointment, Holly turned back to the saloon with the others.

CHAPTER 15

$\mathcal{T}$he first quarter hour of the next morning's rehearsal was given over to acquainting the players with the director's new assistant, and the assistant with the accomplishments and contributions of each member.

'Madame Abercrombie,' Idle lisped. 'The *wizard* who contrived this delightful replica of an Elizabethan stage for us. I must consult with you later, dear, on a little project I have simmering on the back of my mind. I know all this star-crossed lovers' tragedy will cast me into deepest dismals, and shall revitalize my flagging spirits with a dashing Aristophanes comedy. Broad farce, bawdy jokes. *Lysistrata*, perhaps, done as a parody of Lady Hertford's running the country. We shall delve into the obscurities of Grecian staging *ensemble*, madame.'

'How nice. Lovely,' she answered, dazed, but knowing she had been complimented.

'The graces of the garden!' he chirped, as Dewar presented him to the Hall sisters. 'How I have looked forward to meeting you. My *rosa mundi* has wilted on me – just curled up its dear little petals and shrivelled – in my rose garden at Heron Hall. I shall kidnap you and carry you off to cure it. Dew tells me you are both enchantresses. He threatens to adopt one; I shall kidnap the other, I promise you. Which one is mine, Dew?'

'Shall we flip a coin?' he asked, with a wink at the ladies, who tittered in shocked delight.

Idle's greeting of each member was in the same vein. Extravagant in the extreme, but good-natured, assigning to the ladies more expertise than they possessed, which is never taken amiss. A month before, they would not have known what to make of such a man, but Dewar's coming had prepared them somewhat. Idle was a caricature of Dewar, a Dewar exaggerated to a hilarious degree and wearing a more elaborate jacket. Mrs Abercrombie would write off for a book on Grecian staging, the Misses Hall would take up their French grammar to facilitate translation of their book, and life would go on, its pace a little increased, its flavour a little richer.

Rehearsals were begun, but did not go beyond the first act. Mercutio's first speech, 'Nay, gentle Romeo, we must have you dance' was delivered, 'Come on, Altmore, give us a step.' Idle cringed, screwed up his eyes, held his hands to his ears and howled in pain.

'Really, dear boy,' he said to Dewar, when he had recovered, 'you mentioned *commedia dell'arte*, but this is absurd.'

'I realize he must be replaced, but in the meanwhile the play has kept him from killing all my game. And dogs. I shall send off for Boo Withers today. He has the part by heart, from having performed it at Chatworth, you know.'

'Impossible! *Cher* Boo is incommunicado. Locked up on his yacht at Dover, ready to dart for France if he is run to earth. He met Cuthbert in a duel over a courtesan. Cuthbert's pistol exploded in his face, and Boo is taking credit for a hit. Quite a comedy, really. It ought to be dramatized. Such a lack of refinement, fighting over a lightskirt. One ought only to duel over cards and ladies. I shall read them both a lecture when next we meet. So then, it looks as if you must don buskins and save the play, Coz.'

'Only as a last resort. Miss McCormack has some friend who might do.'

'Miss McCormack? Oh, the austere lady who thinks we are both mad. Any suggestion she makes is bound to be eminently rational and uninspired. We are in little position to cavil. Or are we? Yes, to be sure, we are. Otto Wenger is free, and so desperate for entertainment he even mentioned attending a few sessions of Parliament. I shall send off a message at once.'

'Good, tell him it is urgent.'

'Consider it done. Meanwhile, let this Mercutio get on with more abusing of our patience, and the Bard's English.'

Otto arrived the next evening. In days gone by, the arrival of an eligible stranger in Harknell would have been a major event. At this exciting period, Otto was an anticlimax. He was neither dandy nor dilettante but only a bored baron, whose days were filled by seeking amusement from whatever corner it issued. Despite his name, Otto spoke no German, but the presence of an Otto in their midst inclined Idle to *ein bisschen* of *Deutsch*. Wenger was of medium stature, with brown hair and eyes and a large nose. He made a satisfactory Mercutio, no better or worse than Mr Prendergast would have done.

Sir Swithin continued taking a very active part in the direction and production of the play. His suggestions were not always sensible, but they were always interesting. It was his notion to add a few Italian songs to the opening musical. This was at odds with the costuming and general decor but, as he pointed out, the play was set in Verona and there was no point in ignoring Italy entirely. They were not to become slavish about it.

'I play the flageolet rather well,' he admitted unblushingly. 'I shall render a few airs – 'In Dulci Jubilo', perhaps, passing amongst the audience with the orange wenches as *un musico ambulante*, in the Italian street-style. I shall design myself something bucolic and quattrocentoish to wear. A loose, long shirt, gathered at the waist, with flowing sleeves – perhaps a few laurels in my hair. Long silk stockings. . . .' His pink face fell into a meditative expression.

'Why not make it a skirt?' Foxworth muttered to Rex, who growled in agreement. Miss Proctor was paying scanty attention to either of them since Sir Swithin's coming. Her gentle nature responded well to the many compliments of Sir Swithin. Lord Dewar would occasionally express some impatience with her voice, which she could not always remember to project, or her memory work, which was difficult to perfect, but Sir Swithin defended her.

'A little louder, Juliet,' Dewar called from the pit.

'We don't want to miss a word of your sweet voice,' Swithin added. 'Just a little louder, fair Juliet. You are doing splendidly,' then, aside to Dewar, he continued, 'The girl is half angel, I swear.'

The costumes were finally begun, to Holly's relief. 'Wonderful, clever Kate will be in charge,' Swithin said, with a hopeful eye to her. He was a little foolish, but by no means stupid. He realized well enough Miss McCormack was, of all the ladies, the least enchanted with him. No amount of flattery helped the matter either. It had quite the reverse effect. 'How fortunate we are to have so many skilled ladies at our disposal.'

'I am not particularly skilled, but I can sew a straight seam as well as the next one. Let us get on with it.'

'It should present no difficulty,' Dewar said. 'As agreed, we are to have contemporary English costumes. The local modiste can do the brute work, if you will take charge and see that it gets done. In fact, there is no reason the cast cannot wear some of their own clothes.'

'That enchanting gown Juliet wore the first night I saw her, for instance,' Idle mentioned. 'Rose it was – a gentle, mallow rose. We shall want the spider gauze for the famous balcony scene. Something to sparkle in the moonlight – it has glitter to be worn on the underskirt. The rose might be an interesting choice for her to die in. The ambiguity of lively rose will heighten the pathos of her death while still half an infant. Blue is too obvious, don't you agree, Dew?'

'A good idea.'

'For Lady Capulet, we will want something a trifle more dashing than she customarily wears,' Idle went on, subjecting Holly to a close examination. 'She is a lady of some consequence, and we wish her youth to be stressed to heighten the awareness of Juliet being scarcely in her teens. We don't want you to suggest advanced age, my dearest Kate, but only maturity. No need to swathe yourself in bombazine or hide the fact that you have still a figure.'

Holly shot a hostile look at him, to be met with a suave smile. 'Or so one assumes,' he added, peering in vain at her shawl. 'We shall get you out of blankets and confirm the point one day soon. Pray do not glare at me, Kate. I meant no offence. Some of my dearest friends dress like beggars. *Ma chère Tante Hélène, par exemple*, never wears a thing less than ten years old, and prefers it to have been worn by someone else for at least five of the ten. We are not all birds of paradise.'

'No indeed, but some of us certainly are,' she replied, with a disparaging eye at his jacket.

'True. We come in all shades of feathers. Some sparrows, and the rare few like yourself, who are nightingales, delighting us with the unexpectedness of a golden voice issuing from a plain – er, *unassuming* exterior.'

'What do you think of a turban for Lady Montague, Idle?' Dewar asked, hoping to switch the subject before Holly turned violent.

The execution of the two directors' various ideas to enhance the spectacle required considerable skill, ingenuity, and hard work. Between gowns to be sewn, scenery painted, prompters to help out with speeches, and a dozen other odd tasks, the whole company was kept hopping. No one hopped as hard as Holly. She was more accustomed to being put upon than the married ladies, which perhaps accounted for it. She worked quickly, quietly, without expecting praise at every turn. Then too, her part in the drama was not large, and her lines and execution both perfected, so that anyone could fill in for her when need be.

There was the matter of outfits for the orange-wenches – wicker baskets for their wares, which Swithin thought ought to be decorated with orange blossoms to enhance the show. The Hall sisters could not oblige with any strain of orange blossom that would remain fresh under such rough usage. It was for Kate to find artificial blooms and attach them to the basket handles.

'It will cost two pounds for enough artificial flowers to do the baskets,' she told Dewar, horrified at the expense. 'They only have silk, and those are very dear.'

'Did you have them put it on my bill at the shop?' he asked.

'No indeed. I did not buy them at all. It is too expensive.'

'What a clutch-fisted manager of properties you are! Buy them. And before you prepare a lecture on thrift, I shall assign you another task. Decide whether the flowers should be gifts for the orange-girls after the play, or put into our properties trunk to hold for another production.'

'It would be a nice gesture to give them to the girls,' she decided.

'It was my intention. I thought I might have to do it behind your back.'

'As money is clearly no object, I shall venture another idea that has occurred to me. It is about my cousins, Peter and Paul. Jane's brothers,' she identified further, as he did not appear to recognize the names, despite having met them more than once.

'Has she got brothers? How strange she never mentions them.'

'She has got them all the same. Nine and ten years old, and very irate at being left out of all the fun. I have read mention of boys selling nuts in the shell at the plays in Shakespeare's day. At least, the book said the folks liked Falstaff so well they stopped cracking nuts, so I suppose they must have bought them there. I was wondering whether Peter and Paul could not be given the role. There would be no expense in it. Someone in our group will provide the nuts free of cost. It would be only for the afternoon performance, as their mother would not approve of their being up all night.'

'Yes, do see to it. If anyone else has small children who want to participate, they could hand out the ton of sugar-plums Mr Homberly's contribution to my orphans has bought,' he replied, regarding her closely while she looked, trying to read his expression.

'He insisted . . .' she said, with an embarrassed little smile. 'I gave the money to Johnson to do as he. . . .'

'And forgot to warn him not to tell me. I am shocked at your having overlooked a detail. In future, I would appreciate your coming to *me* if my boys require anything.'

'I'll do that, while you are amongst us.'

'Do I read an inference that I do not spend enough time amongst my people?'

'Why no, sir. If you read that into my speech, it must be your conscience intruding,' she said innocently, then rushed on to other points, rather quickly. 'Tell me, who is to be the Chorus? Who will read the Prologue? You have not rehearsed anyone for it, have you?'

'I dislike the idea of a Chorus. The thing is unintelligible when read by more than one person. If your friend, Mr Prendergast, wishes to have some part in the production, perhaps you would like to invite him to do it.'

'Oh, how nice! I was hoping I could convince you to ask him.'

He looked at her closely. 'Mr Prendergast must be a skilled speaker for you to be so anxious to include him in the presentation.'

'It is not that. This will give him an excuse to attend your party afterwards. I hated to think he must miss it, for he is about the only gentleman in town who had no excuse to come. The ladies who have been slaving for you all these weeks can bring their husbands and families, but Mr Prendergast had no invitation and was feeling very left out.'

'I shouldn't think it necessary for me to tell you to invite your particular friends. Pray feel free to ask anyone that I, in my abysmal ignorance of the village people, have overlooked. As a matter of fact, I am rather curious to have a look at your Mr Prendergast.'

'There is something he would like to say to you as well,' she answered mysteriously.

'What is that? You have gone this far; you might as well tell me the whole. Come, while I am in a good mood,' he urged, but his mood did not seem particularly good to her.

'He would prefer to speak to you himself, but I shall just give a little hint. It is impossible for a man to get married when he is only acting as a clerk for a solicitor. He works for Mr Raymond, you perhaps remember.'

'We are speaking of the school, is that it?'

'I have said more than enough.'

'You are wise not to try my patience,' he agreed, and turned his attention back to the stage.

Mr Johnson was seldom absent from rehearsals. He took a keen interest in all matters pertaining to the play. It was he who suggested a transparent curtain be used as a backdrop to add romance to certain scenes.

'A brilliant notion!' Sir Swithin praised. 'It could create a sort of visual leitmotif, an indication to the audience, if you like, that they are to set their hearts to romance for what is to ensue, when we have Romeo and Juliet in their love scenes. The thing could easily be done. A large sheet of calico with a light behind, and the scene painted with transparent dyes. I shall design it *moi-même*, and all these clever, wonderful people will paint, under my direction, while you, dear boy,' he turned to Dewar, 'can put a bit of polish on those local performers who are to give us the *après-drame* – the tumblers, jugglers, dancing dogs, etc. *Do*, I beg of you, take the bear out of my hair as well, or Rex will destroy my creation. Bound to put a foot through it, you know.'

'A little hiatus is not a bad idea,' Dewar agreed. 'I am saturated, stale with this unrelieved play-acting. New ideas are bound to occur with a change of pace. I shan't spend the day supervising the jugglers, however. I have something to attend to in London. I shall be gone two days, I expect.'

'Excellent,' Idle said. 'In that case, take Foxworth as well.'

Holly had not forgotten Billie McAuley, still alone in London, despite her two mentions to Mr Johnson that his face would be familiar to the orphan, and he could be spared for one day to go and deliver him home. Before Dewar left, she found an opportunity to accost him.

'As you are going to London . . .' she began.

'That's why I'm going.'

'I beg your pardon?'

'You were about to remind me Billie is still there alone. I had a note from Sir Henry today that he is progressing satisfactorily, and can now be brought home. I asked him to notify me.'

'Oh,' was all she had to say.

'Saved myself a lecture, did I not?' he asked, smiling. 'Sorry to rob you of one of life's little pleasures, Lady Capulet.'

'You misread my character, sir. I do not get any pleasure from lecturing people. Indeed, it is a pleasure to see you acting so properly without reminding.'

'For a change,' he added, with an ironic little smile. 'You must not take the notion I am totally reformed only because I am about to make my second trip on the orphan's behalf.'

'The first trip was not wholly on his behalf, I think. Your mother mentioned your going to the city to urge Sir Swithin to join us.'

'No, I went to deliver Billie, but always believe in killing two birds with one stone. The second bird on this occasion is that the fountain for my dairy is completed. I am to approve it before it is removed from the sculptor's studio. Do you have any other commissions I might perform for you while there? Don't be shy to put them forward. Any smallpox victims wanting a cure, lepers, lunatics for Bedlam, or miscreants for Newgate? I already have the pleasure of carrying Rex and Foxworth, so a few more passengers will not be the least bother.'

'Oh, is Rex leaving? I had not heard it.'

'He will be returning. I cannot risk his capturing Juliet's heart during my absence. Idle feels he might be a menace to the transparency as well.'

'Well, as you are going, Sir Egbert is dreading the trip to hire a house for the season. I don't suppose. . . .'

'Good. I'm glad you don't suppose I have turned house-hiring agent in what we jokingly call my "free moments." '

'No, no. It is only that, since you are going and have one spare seat, you might offer Sir Egbert a drive. It would be neighbourly, and it seems such an extravagance to go with a seat empty.'

'I daresay you would consider it an extravagance as well for Sir Egbert to put up at an hotel when a neighbour has a house with a room standing empty.'

'I was not going to suggest that, though it certainly would be. . . .'

'Yes – neighbourly. It comes to seem a shame for Sir Egbert to go to the bother of hiring a house, when I have one in London already.'

'You needn't be sarcastic! You are the one who suggested it – about offering him a seat, I mean.'

'Is *that* what I suggested? Well, well, I am certainly becoming a pattern card of consideration. By all means, ask your uncle if he would like to share my carriage, but I mean to be back within two days.'

'Could a house be rented in that time?'

'If your uncle is not overly nice in his demands, it could.'

'Oh, Sir Egbert is not at all nice, and my aunt has already selected the location. Belgrave Square, as your mama suggested to her, so it might be done in a day.'

'*Mama* suggested?' he asked, smiling quizzically.

'Yes, is it not a good location?'

'It strikes me as an excellent location,' he answered. 'Mama too becomes thoughtful in her dotage.'

'That is not a nice way to speak of your mother.'

'It must be the company I am keeping. I was shocked to hear you state so baldly that Sir Egbert is not at all nice. A discussion on the care and feeding of swine should provide a diversion on the trip. I am always open to new ideas.'

'I don't think you will get any to your liking from my uncle. His pigstyes are not at all fancy, Dewar. No tiles, no fountains. . . .'

'No curtains, no Persian carpets, no china and silver-plate. . . . Poor devils. Tell me, Miss McCormack, do you take me for an utter fool?'

She looked at him a moment, considering the matter with deliberation. 'No, not an *utter* fool,' she allowed, with a little choke of laughter. 'Sir Swithin is an utter fool; you are only half a fool.'

'Good day, ma'am,' he answered, after inhaling a long, slow breath. 'I shall take my leave, before you inform me what the other half is.' She began to speak, but he held up a peremptory hand. 'No! Pray, do not. Say no more. It would be unfitting for me to beat a lady. The other half, in my own view, is a gentleman.'

'There is just one more *tiny* favour,' she said, with a doubtful look.

'There are some who don't know where to stop. Go ahead then. What is it?'

'My uncle would be so very flattered if you asked him yourself, rather than having me do it.'

Dewar frowned, more displeased at this request than the rest. 'Yes, but I am not at all sure I wish to flatter him to *that* extent,' he said, with a reluctant voice. 'Oh, very well, I'll do it.'

A broad smile spread across Holly's face. 'Do you know, I come to think Mr Johnson is right about you. You really are very obliging, when you are handled properly.'

He stood watching her, a bemused look in his eyes. 'Dare I ask what you have found to be the proper way to handle me?'

'Carefully, Lord Dewar. Very carefully.'

'One trembles to think *this* is careful treatment!' He turned abruptly on his heel and walked away, smiling. The throaty sound of her laughter followed him. A wonderful voice the woman had, but what words she used it for!

CHAPTER 16

'*Gudgeon!*' Lady Dewar shouted when her son revealed he was to drive Sir Egbert to London with him. 'How am I expected to keep that woman in her place when you spend your days running after the chit telling her how pretty she is, your nights in her saloon, and now take her papa to the city in your carriage? You might as well offer them the use of our house for the Season and have done with it.'

'Strangely enough, the lady did not suggest it,' he said.

'It was *her* suggestion you take Sir Egbert with you, was it?'

'Certainly it was. It would not have occurred to me in a decade of Sundays.'

'Encroaching creature! I shall hint you are on the verge of making someone an offer if she says a word to me. She thinks, since she is become Lady Proctor, she may choose who she likes for her gel. I begin to regret I ever hinted to Holly that Rex would do for her, for he would have served to keep Jane away from you.'

Dewar said not a word about which lady had dunned him for the drive. 'Holly has no interest in Rex. There is a Prendergast gentleman she speaks of. . . .'

'I never heard anything of a romance in that quarter. Not that Elsa Proctor would allow it. She is bone-selfish, and means to use Holly as her housekeeper while she sports it around London. Quite a shame the way she has kept that girl from making a match all these years.' Lady Dewar had never before given the matter two minutes' consideration, but was only looking for some ill to say of the woman, to vent her spleen. 'They dress poor Holly like a servant.'

'Swithin mentioned only the other day her resemblance to yourself in that respect, Mama,' he quizzed her.

'Did he indeed, the two-faced rogue! He always compliments me on your father's waistcoats. It shows in your manner when you have been associating with Idle. You become even more than usually satirical. As to my wardrobe, you may be sure I did not dress for comfort before I was married. I powdered my hair, wore corsets and gowns cut so low I was forever freezing to death, like everyone else. Now that your father is gone, however, there is no point in dressing up only to please the likes of you and Swithin Idle. You two are fine enough to uphold the family's reputation for elegance.'

'Shall I order you any new waistcoats while I am in London, love?' he asked, undismayed by her attack. 'Hessian boots, beaver hats, pantaloons? Very warm on a cold winter's evening, the pantaloons.'

'One could wear them under a skirt, I daresay,' she said, creasing her brow in interest.

'They would do wonders for that figure of yours too. It wants a little expanding,' he said, with a teasing smile at her wide girth.

'I have two pleasures in life, Chubbie. Eating and sleeping. Don't think to deprive me of either of them.'

'You cut me to the quick, to think I add nothing to your simple pleasures. What did I do to inherit a sensuous mother?'

'Watch your language! If you want to bring me something from London, bring me home a daughter-in-law. A *lady*, one who is out of short dresses, if you please, and not into long words like that Hazelton woman you had home last time you were here. Spouting French and Italian and I don't know what else.'

'English was the other language, Mama. About this daughter-in-law, have you any preference for a blonde or a brunette? Any other requirement at all but that she be old and ignorant? Ugly, perhaps. . . .'

'Yes, you want to make sure she has a good thick hide, or she will not be able to stick it long with you. Go away now. Send Digby to me. I want to play cards.'

'How sharper than a serpent's tooth it is, to have a thankless mother,' he replied, and sauntered out the door.

At Stonecroft, the matter of Dewar's unprecedented offer to Sir Egbert was also under discussion. It was seen as not only a sign but a wonder. 'Very condescending of him,' Lady Proctor decreed. 'An outstanding display of preference for Jane. Quite out of the blue too, the offer. I wonder he did not mention it to me or to Jane, but just popped down here by himself and asked you. I daresay he will take the opportunity of privacy the trip affords to speak of *other matters*,' she said coyly, with a hopeful glance to Jane.

'Aye, he mentioned he would like to hear more about my new breed of swine,' Sir Egbert answered. Holly, who was in some confusion as to the misinterpretation being placed on Dewar's offer, smiled to herself at this speech. This was why he had been reluctant to speak to Sir Egbert himself!

'Don't you *dare* to prose his ear off with those Berkshire sows you have bought, Egbert. Remember your position in society.'

'It is news to me if a knight can't raise hogs, demmed good ones too.'

'If you dare to utter one word about those sows. . . .'

'Heh heh, only teasing you, my pet.'

Lady Proctor pushed her daughter and Holly upstairs to allow privacy for a discussion of dowry, just in case the matter should arise en route to London. Holly had not the heart to tell them Rex and Foxworth would also be in the carriage. In fact, when the gentlemen called the next morning for Sir Egbert, the plan had been changed somewhat. Rex had his own carriage and was giving a lift to Foxworth. These two gallant wooers did not trust Dewar alone in the house. They went into Stonecroft with him to ask Jane six times each if they could get her anything while they were in London, and to remind her they would be back in two days. They strongly recommended the corner of Conduit and

Bruton Streets, and Glasshouse and Bond Streets, respectively, as being the best abode for her, these locations putting her on their own doorstep.

While this was going forth, Dewar turned aside to Holly. 'Your thrifty heart will dislike the use of two carriages, but there is a reason for it. Dr John goes with us to speak to Sir Henry and, of course, Billie will have to be brought back as well. A full load for the return trip at least.'

'What an excellent idea to take Dr John!'

'Rather vain of you to say so. It is your own. I never hesitate to steal a good idea from any source. As I have been so very obliging in this matter, I hope my asking a favour of you during my absence will not go amiss.'

'I will be happy to help you, if I can.'

'I know of no one who could do it better. Will you keep an eye on the production while I am away? Swithin is admirable but, like all creative geniuses, he needs a firm guiding hand. You won't let him set the play to music while I am gone, or bring in some *deus ex machina* ending to turn it into a comedy? He has the feeling, which I own I share, that, up till the end of the first act or so, William Shakespeare set out to write a comedy in *Romeo and Juliet* but wandered astray.'

'I shall do my poor best, but Swithin is not totally biddable by anyone.'

'Very true, but only last night he said he was scared to death of Kate McCormack. Now, when he has gone to all the pains of learning your last name, it confers a greater distinction than you realize. He doesn't know mine, and if he did not dislike it so much I daresay he wouldn't know his own. Even Shakespeare, you must have noticed, is always referred to as William. A lady who can frighten Idle is capable of anything.'

'Very well then, I shall frown and scold him into obedience, and be called Shrew for my trouble.'

'We *artistes* require a shrew, to keep at least one of our toes on the ground. Delinquent owners of estates could use one as well.

Could I presume on your charity to oversee my steward as well, in my absence?' he asked, with a lazy smile.

'My ill temper cuts no ice with Roots, Dewar. If he decides to turn your stables into a pleasure dome while you are away, you must not hold me responsible. But then I place the blame – er, credit? – in the wrong dish, to accuse Roots of the renovations in the dairy.'

'I believe I shall take my leave before we come to cuffs, ma'am. I had hoped to leave with your blessings this time.'

'*Vaya con dios*,' she answered. 'Swithin taught me the phrase. He has promised to teach me a few curses in German as well. All German sounds like the grossest profanity to me, but he assures me *gemutlichkeit* means something pleasant. I forget what.'

'Good lord! When did you have time to set up a flirtation with him? Idle only encumbers ladies with a smattering of foreign tongues when he is planning to fall in love with them. I might have known when he learned your last name!'

'If he ever learns my first one, I shall run for cover.'

'Tell Mr Prendergast on him,' he suggested, with a questioning look, as though waiting for some reaction.

She flushed in confusion, for it was clear Dewar thought Prendergast was her beau, yet to explicitly deny it would seem an overreaction. Lady Proctor disliked the whole tenor of the conversation very much, and had soon interrupted to turn Dewar's attention to herself. The gentlemen were finally heading to the door, with all the ladies of the house going after them to the roadway to wave them off.

'Well, my dear, we shall just stay home today and have a little rest,' Lady Proctor decided, when they were alone. 'There is no point dashing off to the Abbey when Dewar is not to be there.'

'We planned to help Swithin paint the transparent curtain, Mama,' Jane pointed out.

'I most particularly told Dewar I would help,' Holly added.

'I noticed you were at pains to attract his attention, Holly,' Lady Proctor answered in a strained voice. 'Rather forward behaviour.

Sir Egbert hardly knew what to make of it. I daresay he is trying to explain it to Dewar this very moment. There are plenty to help with the painting. Jane needs the time to learn her part and, if you have nothing better to do, Holly, you might help me get the mud stains off the bottom of my wool skirt. You were always good at that.'

There was never any point arguing with Aunt Elsa. She had decided the family were to remain home, and that was that. Holly was not in the least sorry when the door knocker sounded and Mr Johnson was shown in, looking for his ride to the Abbey – but with a piece of news, and a suggestion to occupy Holly's day in a more exciting fashion than cleaning her aunt's clothing.

'Poor old Parsons is ill. In his bed with the gout,' Johnson said, as he was shown in. 'I shall have to dismiss the school today. Miss McCormack will not be able to fill in for him, with the play to see to. I have left the oldest student, Humphries, in charge till I see whether I can find anyone in the village to take over. I thought Prendergast might be able to, but Raymond is away and he is pretty well occupied.'

'We are not going to the Abbey today, Mr Johnson,' Lady Proctor told him, 'so you can take the school yourself.'

'I?' he asked, astonished. 'You forget we are working on my transparency. I must be there. If you are not going, I'll hasten along to Abercrombie's, and see if I can ride with Abbie,' he said, and turned to leave without even taking a seat. At the doorway, he stopped and turned back. 'If you are not going, then Miss McCormack can take over the school, as she has done in the past. Just for the day, till I can make some other arrangement. I fear Parsons is out for a couple of weeks. Will you go, Miss McCormack?'

Holly enjoyed her occasional day at the schoolhouse. She liked the slim recompense as well as anything. 'If my aunt can spare me?' she asked, looking for guidance to her aunt.

'Run along. You won't want the carriage. Jane and I may need it to go to the village this afternoon.'

The school was not an unwalkable distance. Holly skipped upstairs for her pelisse, with only a little wince of regret that she must miss the goings-on at the Abbey. Even with Dewar and some of the others away, it would have been a busy, agreeable day. In fact, she experienced a stab of guilt as she hastened her steps toward the school. She had been neglecting all her charity duties of late. Outside of finishing the orphans' shirts, she had done nothing in that line. She had visited no sick persons, mended no prayer books, prepared no treats or diversions for the poor. She had become a hedonist, like all the others. Her father would be ashamed of her. But she would make up for it now. She would replace Parsons till some qualified man could be found for the spot. With a smile just a hair short of smugness, she thought it would not be long till Prendergast was appointed. Especially at this time, when her presence at the Abbey was, if not absolutely necessary, at least desired. Mr Raymond would require a replacement for Prendergast as well, but that was a position anyone could fill – a matter of copying letters and filing them. A waste of a graduate's time to be so menially employed.

To her utter amazement, Sir Swithin awaited her in his carriage when she emerged from the schoolhouse in the afternoon. 'Kate, you traitor!' was his emphatic greeting. 'You were supposed to help me!'

This was shouted from the carriage window, then he opened the door and stepped out, to send the children grinning amongst themselves to see such a sight. He wore a ground-length coat with sixteen collars, each of a different shade of blue, ranging from a pale sky blue on top to navy on the bottom. The coat was navy, with nacre buttons, large and uniquely shaped, like kidneys. He wore no curled beaver hat, but a confection of his own design that fitted snugly about the ears, designed to protect these delicate vessels, which were prone to aches if exposed to winter's blasts. It resembled a helmet, and was done in deep blue velvet. He looked so absurd Holly was hard pressed to contain her own mirth.

'Oh, Sir Swithin!' she gasped, then could contain it no longer.

A throaty little gurgle erupted, to be stifled with her fingers.

'It is almost worth appearing ridiculous, to hear that golden echo,' he declaimed, handing her into the carriage, and stepping lightly in after her. 'Here, dear, put this sable rug over your knees. The bricks still retain some traces of heat, I trust. I have been waiting a quarter of an hour for you. I sent my carriage to Stonecroft to collect you this morning, and heard the news. How *could* you disappoint us? I have battled all this day to complete the transparent curtain, *sans* luck. The dyes clouded – they *must* be transparent, you know. Then those appallingly stupid women sewed them on to the frame crooked so that the crenellations of the castle outline slope like a stable roof. Pots of dye spilled. I swear the very cream for tea curdled in the cup without you there to attend us, Kate.'

'Mr Parsons is ill, and there was no one to take over the school,' she explained briefly.

'Let the world slide, Kate. Such good advice that Shakespeare stole it from Heywood, who doubtlessly stole it from the Greeks. Don't take the cares of the whole world on your slim shoulders. Just the play is enough weight for them.'

'When it comes to a choice between reality and make-believe, Sir Swithin, there is no question in my mind which takes precedence.'

'Not the least in my own mind either. Make-believe must be given the right-of-way. Our imaginations are what separate us from the wild beasties. Cats and dogs tend their young and teach them what they must know. Only we humans are able to indulge our fancies. I consider it a moral duty to exercise my imaginative faculties. No, do not object. Only open your lips to say "Yes." I have already spoken to your aunt. Tomorrow you come to the Abbey and rescue us from chaos. It is arranged.'

'Then it will have to be disarranged. I return to the school tomorrow.'

'Kate, this very wide streak of stubbornness – I dislike it. I *admire* it tremendously, but I do not like it. We'll send the prosing preacher down to knock the students' heads together. *You* will return where you belong.'

'Mr Johnson might have something to say about that.'

'He has already said the school must be closed, but I am not at all sure Dew would like that. He approves of education.'

'Lord Dewar will be back tomorrow evening. For one more day, I shall attend the school. If he wishes to make some other arrangement then, I will be very happy to return to the dye pots,' she told him, and was not budged an inch from her decision, despite three quotations from Shakespeare, one from the Bible, and one from Goethe, in German, that neither of them understood.

Another day of chaos ensued at the Abbey. At four in the afternoon, Lord Dewar returned from London, leaving Sir Egbert off at Stonecroft to describe the house hired to his wife, while Dewar continued home. His first act was to go along to his refectory hall to see how the dramatic arrangements had progressed in his absence.

Swithin ran up to him. 'Dew – dear boy – catastrophe has struck!'

Looking at the dye-splattered scene before him, Dewar's heart sank. 'I might have known! I told Kate to watch over things. What has happened?'

'She has *betrayed* us. Gone off these two days schoolmarming, while we sink into total chaos. There was never such a mess since the scene of creation.'

'What are you talking about?'

'Your schoolmaster is struck down with an ague. Why did I not think to *cure* him? My wits are gone begging. But there – I am in love. Yes, you may well stare! It struck me equally by surprise. After she left, I found a pleasing image of herself behind that wanders in my soul. Dorimant, was it not, in *The Man of Mode* who uttered the wonderful phrase? I find a pleasing image of Kate, bringing order to this – *disaster!*' He pointed a patent toe at a welter of dye pots, poles of wood, and rumpled calico. Tossing his bejewelled fingers into the air, he declared, '*C'est impossible. C'est tout à fait impossible!* This would not have occurred had my Kate been here.'

'*Your* Kate?' Dewar asked, blinking. 'This is a new turn.'

'Yes, I am amazed at myself, for having succumbed to the charms of a perfectly average female – *sans* looks, *sans* elegance, *sans argent* I fear. *Sans* everything. Who would have thought it of me? There is *character* in the woman, Dew. One would have thought that would have been enough to discourage me, but it has quite the reverse effect. I am not at all happy about it, to tell the truth. I am frightened to death of her. She is so *strong*, with the moral stamina of a Puritan. I hope she doesn't make me go to Parliament and become a worthy. I made sure it would be Juliet – or even Lady Montague. A married lady is such a nice *safe* object of affection, *n'est-ce-pas* But I do run on. I shall let you congratulate me now, and express your amazement.'

'Does Holly know?'

'Holly who? Good gracious, is *that* her name? I think Holly is bad luck. I'm sure I heard it somewhere. She *is* bad luck, a very shrew. Laughed at my stunning new greatcoat with the buttons carved to my own design. She is above the fripperies of fashion herself. I dote on her very dowdiness. She is a splended heroine, Dew, a Boadicea donning armour to do battle. Boadicea deserves a better literary fate than she got at Fletcher's hands. Shall we write her her own tragedy?'

'Shall we put on this damned play first?' Dewar asked angrily.

'I suppose we must but, to tell the truth, my heart is not in it. I want a play where Kate is heroine. Meanwhile, you must find a tutor for your school and bring her back here. A Prendergast person, someone mentioned, is the heir apparent to the seat of your school. Get him, at once! *Tout de suite.*'

Dew regarded him a long moment, then spoke. 'Dear boy, if you really wish me to spike your gun. . . . The day I appoint Prendergast, he is in a position to wed Kate.'

'Marry *him*, a schoolmaster? A driller of children? A near-peasant who works for his daily bread? Good God – she would love it. So very worthy. What is to be done?'

'We haven't much choice in the matter.'

'None. She will *make* us hire him.'

'When it must be done, 'tis best done with grace.'

'Is that Shakespeare, Dew?'

'No, it is Despair, Swithin.'

'You feel for me in my dilemma. I appreciate it. We have always been close friends, true epicures. I shall go with you to see the Prendergast. I expect he is very large, and doubtlessly ugly. I may triumph over him yet. I have some – *charm*, have I not, Dew? Some evanescent quality that attracts women? Ladies do seem to like me.'

'You are different. Therein lies your charm. One never knows quite what to expect from you.'

'Yes, falling in love with Kate, *par exemple*. That surprised even me. She has coerced my passions. Colley Cibber – so under-rated today – invented the phrase. Kate has gone him one better. She has mauled my heart, ravaged my brain, and I am not at all sure she won't end up cutting my hair as well. But I shall adore being changed by her, I think. Once a fellow becomes predictable, he is a dull old dog, good for nothing but work. Prendergast will be predictable. He will wear low collars and short hair and admire Samuel Johnson. I hate him already.'

'He probably drives a gig and wears muddy boots,' Dewar added.

'Are you joking me, Dew? Too cruel.'

'I am feeling rather cruel. By all means, let us go and see Mr Prendergast.'

The meeting was brief. Not fifteen minutes after entering his rooms, the two gentlemen exited, wearing defeated faces. 'He is not so ugly as I had hoped,' Swithin said, disconsolate. 'His jacket too – quite unexceptionable. Not Weston, nor even Stultz, but a creditable imitation.'

'Hung on a very creditable pair of shoulders,' Dewar added.

'His face – quite like the Apollo Belvedere. You must have noticed the resemblance, the lapidary quality of that profile. Yet the lips sensuous, as if they were alive. Well, they are alive, aren't they? He would have made an admirable Mercutio, by the by.'

'Oh no, he is Romeo. He seems a rational creature as well.'

'Downright intelligent. And, if we say one more word in his praise, I shall expire of jealousy. I *hate* Mr Prendergast! The way his eyes lit up when you told him the salary. I swear I could sense him dividing it into parcels of household money, twenty-five pounds for the hire of a cottage, twenty-five for food. Kate will feed him mutton and potatoes and mend his jackets. Ah well,' he added, beginning to rise from his fit of the dismals, 'she will likewise get the transparency dyed and hung.'

'We had. better stop at Stonecroft and tell her about Prendergast.'

'You know my *chemise* – the one I wear to play the *musico ambulante*, Dew. I had it dyed a pretty saffron shade, but am beginning to think I shall revert to the violet shades of half-mourning I wore when my dog died. If Kate spurns me, that is. I shall have it dyed a windy indigo colour. I do wish I had violet-coloured eyes to match. My violet period was probably my favourite – sartorially speaking, that is, for of course my heart was broken.'

'Would you mind awfully to shut up, Swithin? You do get very silly at times.'

'Am I being a frightful bore! How dreadful. Don't hesitate to tell me. I hate to be a bore.'

CHAPTER 17

The remainder of Mr Prendergast's afternoon on that day was a busy one. His first item of business was to inform Mr Raymond he wished to leave as soon as was convenient. Hard on the heels of this was the matter of getting his own younger brother installed in his place as Raymond's clerk. As well as permitting his own immediate transfer to the school, this would provide his family some additional income. He dashed the note off home with a happy heart, wishing to settle all details before going to his fiancée with the wonderful news. After a jubilant dinner with her family, he left early, for he wished to see Miss McCormack and thank her in person for her efforts on his behalf. He learned during the interview with Dewar that she had suggested him for the post. He was in Lady Proctor's saloon when the group from the Abbey arrived.

Dewar was vexed to see Holly was already informed of the news. Swithin was considerably annoyed to see her sitting with the competition, both of them smiling in triumph. He must conquer her by his consummate charm. Let her see how infinitely superior he was to Prendergast, in all but appearance. He would be urbane, witty, original. He would counter Prendergast's dull common sense with magnificent flights of fancy and poetry. He would be utterly scintillating and irresistible. Having come courting, he was outfitted carefully with this end in mind, in garments vaguely rose in hue, with deep brown accents in waistcoat. Holly, he noticed, wore a drab shawl over a drab gown and, having been surprised by Prendergast's early visit, had not had time to repair her coiffure. A tail of hair hung forlornly behind her left ear.

'I have just been telling Miss McCormack of my appointment,' Prendergast said, after the gentlemen were in. He had arisen at Dewar's entry, and towered half a head above Swithin, who advanced mincingly toward him.

'*Naturellement*,' Swithin drawled, drawing out a handkerchief to fall in graceful folds from his dazzling fingers. 'It is no surprise to her, I think.'

'A very pleasant surprise,' she answered, smiling to Dewar, who nodded briefly and took up a seat between Jane and her mother. Swithin perched daintily on the edge of a petit point chair and crossed his legs.

'Tell me, Prendergast,' he began, 'how soon can it be arranged for you to take up your duties at the school? We require our Kate back at the play. Things fall apart without her.'

'She keeps us all running smoothly,' Prendergast answered, with a warm smile in her direction. 'I expect to be free by the first of next week. As you find Miss McCormack indispensable, I daresay the students could be suborned to take a holiday on Friday. Perhaps on the weekend I could attend a rehearsal myself. I am eager to see the stage. I hear a great deal about it from the ladies.'

'Ah yes, we must hear you recite your bit at the beginning,' Swithin said.

'And my Prologue to Act II,' Prendergast reminded him. 'That sonnet is one of my favourites – an eloquent plea for young love.'

Swithin sneered at him, but with such an inconsequential face the expression was difficult to read. Prendergast thought he was going to sneeze as he brandished his handkerchief still. 'It is a subject dear to my heart at the present time,' he added, smiling to Holly, who had just heard of his approaching nuptials.

Dewar glanced toward them. 'Tell me, milord,' Prendergast went on, 'have you informed Parsons yet that he is retired? I planned to visit him tonight, and would not wish to mention it if he is unaware of the fact.'

'No, I haven't told him yet.'

'Oh dear, it is well you asked the question!' Holly exclaimed. 'What a dreadful way for him to discover he is unemployed. What are your plans for him, Lord Dewar?'

'I have no alternative employment in mind for a septuagenarian,' he answered. He saw at once that Miss McCormack was again displeased with him.

'The days will be very long for him, cooped up in two rooms. He is used to being busy,' she pointed out.

'He is too old to work.'

'Yes, real work is beyond him, but some sinecure must be found,' she answered.

'In any case, I shall say nothing till you have spoken to him,' Prendergast said, arising to hasten his steps back to his beloved, and happy to be able to delay the visit to Parsons. He took a polite leave, with once more special thanks to Miss McCormack and Dewar.

Eager to win favour with Holly, Swithin began to mention a series of unlikely occupations for Parsons. 'He might be my penman for the new *drame* I am creating,' he said, looking to see how she was impressed by this plan. She felt the tail of hair tickle her ear, and reached to put it up, totally ignoring his remark. 'A tragedy based on Boadicea,' he went on. 'You may imagine what led me to that subject:' His little yellow eyes were sparkling with passion.

'Who is Boadicea?' she asked.

He smiled fondly. 'The historical figure I refer to, but I use her, of course, as a vehicle for a living female whom I much admire, as William subtly hinted at a parallel to Elizabeth in his *Julius Caesar*. It is not an original idea to use history as a parable for the present.'

'What living character do you refer to?' she asked, mildly curious, no more.

'Naughty girl!' he chided, batting his handkerchief. A delicate odour of lavender assaulted her nostrils.

Sir Swithin's conversation was not always as proper as it might have been and, as she feared she had wandered into impropriety with the question, she let it drop. 'What would Mr Parsons's duties be in all this?' she asked.

'He could act as my scribe. My calligraphy is beautiful – quite a work of art but, unfortunately, it is illegible. I use a style adapted from the illuminated manuscripts of the medieval age. Lady Halton was so impressed with a note I sent her last year that she mistook it for an *objet d'art* and framed it. It was writ on parchment during my medieval period. It was not at all important – only an apology, in verse, for not being able to attend a levée she had called me to.'

'It is thoughtful of you to suggest it, Swithin, but that would be only a very temporary employment, for the while you remain here,' she said.

'Dear lady, I am so *enchanté* here that I may stay on indefinitely.'

'You may think so,' Dewar announced from across the room, from which location he had been listening to the conversation with an ironic smile on his face.

'He jests,' Swithin told Holly. 'Dewar adores my company. Our souls march in harmony – well, dally along in harmony, let us say. But your point is well made, Kate. We must find Parsons a permanent *coin* in which to await eternity. The scriptorium at the Abbey suggests itself as the ideal spot. A schoolmaster must feel at home surrounded by the marks of his profession – books, pens, ink pots. You could use him to make a fair copy of that pandect on the *drame* you have been compiling these ten years, Dew. How does it progress, by the by?'

'Slowly. I am revising the Elizabethan period at the present.'

'Don't overwrite it, dear boy, and let all those lovely visions be lost in revisions.'

'That sounds like a good post for Parsons,' Holly said.

Dewar nodded his head in acquiescence. 'Shall I speak to him then?' he asked.

'It is hardly for me to say!' she said, feeling she was being roasted for taking so lively an interest in his doings.

'Very true, but somehow you always *do* say, and it would make things easier if I knew what you want done at the beginning,' Dewar said, with an innocent stare.

There was an interruption as Homberly and Foxworth were shown in, not entirely sober. Falling on to a chair in the middle of the room, Rex said to Jane, 'Dewar tell you?'

'He has been telling us about Mr Parsons's retirement,' Jane answered.

'Eh? Ain't talking about a dashed parson. Me and Foxey have decided to wear our horse's outfit for the romps after the play, after all. Ain't going to be a bear. Somebody else can be a bear. The pelt would fit you, Swithin.'

'It would fit, but it would not *suit*, silly boy.'

'True. Got a point there,' Foxey mumbled. 'Idle can't growl. Can hardly talk.'

'Hardly talk?' Rex shouted. 'Never shuts up. Worst clapperjaw I ever met.'

'Don't talk right. He chirps, but he couldn't growl worth a tinker's curse.'

'Methinks Mr Prendergast would feel quite at home in the bearskin,' Swithin suggested.

'I'm sure he would enjoy to do it!' Jane said at once.

'Oh yes, he has a great sense of fun,' Holly agreed.

Before Swithin could enter on any more insults, Rex lurched to his feet to secure a chair closer to Jane, and engaged her in some conversation. Dewar quietly arose and joined Swithin and Holly on the other side of the fireplace. She was curious to hear the details of the trip from him. 'How is Billie?' she asked. 'Does he show any improvement yet?'

'A little. It will be a gradual process. Dr John has his instructions for the treatment. The boy's spirits are considerably improved.'

'I am so glad. My uncle is very happy with the house he hired. And I am very happy with Mr Prendergast's appointment,' she told him, with an approving smile.

'We will all be happy to have you back with us at the Abbey. After keeping all my promises to you, I have a few words to say on *your* behaviour, ma'am. You were left in charge of the stage properties. May I know why you so cavalierly abandoned your duty?'

'I abandoned my duty? No, sir, I must take exception to that. It was *your* tardiness in dealing with Parsons's retirement that made my presence at the school necessary. You did leave me some latitude in the matter of attending to your duties in your absence, if you will recall. I made sure you would be more concerned for the instruction of the children than the amusement of the villagers.'

'You mistake my priorities.'

'Amusement always comes first, does it? Sir Swithin has already outlined your pleasure principle to me. You must forgive me if I cannot agree with it. I see pleasure as a privilege, earned by first attending to one's duty. The boys require an education; we do not actually need the frivolity of a play.'

'Mankind does not actually require anything to subsist but a cave and a slingshot. As society progresses toward civilization, more and more refinements are considered necessary.'

'Yes, we know what rarefied heights that philosophy reached in France only recently, where Louis was so civilized he bankrupted the nation to provide his luxuries. But you refer, in your own case, only to such refinements as Delft tiles and fountains in your dairy, I collect? Were you happy with the fountain, milord?' she asked icily.

'Not completely. I had the shepherd's nose recarved. The modeling left something to be desired. That was not the refinement to which I referred, however. As far as that goes, a fine and stately home in good repair is part of my people's heritage. They will not live in it, but they like to know it is there, to visit on public day, and to point out to visitors. They appreciate it; it gives them a feeling of being civilized.

'You cannot be civilized till you can read and write.'

Swithin, wishing to join the talk, said, 'Actually, Kate, that is a misconception. The delights of reading a good sonnet or play are not negligible, but. . . .'

'The delights of a play are negligible to those who go hungry.' She stopped then, as she was speaking in anger, and implying as well something that was not quite pertinent. So far as she knew, there were actually no starving people in the neighbourhood.

'Pray continue. You have my complete attention,' Dewar said, regarding her with one brow raised to a dangerous level, his nostrils pinched. 'We have got the path put through Evans's place, we have tended to the orphanage and the roof, and to Billie McAuley; we have got the school a new master and Miss McCormack's friend a post. What else remains to be done? We grasshoppers on the lawn of life occasionally give a thought to duty.'

'When you have the welfare of so many in your keeping, you should give more than an occasional thought to it. But it was my intention to thank you this evening, Dewar, not deliver yet another scold. And so I thank you.'

'You are welcome – may I now know which of my people are *starving?*'

'None. You have performed well recently. I suppose you have earned a few hops on life's lawn.'

Swithin sighed peevishly. 'If we must be insects, let it be dragonflies, with beautiful iridescent wings. Or butterflies, flitting through life, sipping nectar where we may.'

'An apt simile,' Holly agreed.

'I have a certain talent for a simile. And you, dear Kate, will be the ant at the picnic of our life. Life for some certain few transcends the everyday business of earning bread. I am of those few, and so is my dear coz. You are not cut out for it, but you will partake of it on your own level, sewing costumes for us.'

'Never again!' she said, in a steely voice.

'You must. The arts are vital. Someone must write the poetry for others to read and enjoy, and to use as a gauge – an interpretation, if you like, of life's mysteries. Only think if dear William had not written his plays. The world, you must own, would be a poorer place. Who cares if he was a little inconsiderate of his wife – leaving her his second-best bed was a gratuitous insult, and unworthy of him, but we must forgive such a man all. And since the glorious plays have been writ, they must be kept alive by performances. It is fallen to the lot of the more sensitive spirits – Dew, myself, our little group – to fulfill this function. Cultural envoys to society at large, you might say. A species of genius, really,' he finished up.

'I understood a genius to be involved in original work,' she parried.

'You have been reading French, Kate! How clever of you. I take credit to myself for enlarging your horizons. Genius was perhaps too grand a word, but how boring life would be if we never flattered ourselves.'

'Not much danger of that!' Foxworth said.

Homberly was in some danger of falling asleep, and Foxey becoming obstreperous. Dewar decided to take them home before they became even worse nuisances.

'You will be at the Abbey tomorrow, Kate?' Swithin confirmed.

'Yes, if Dewar will notify the students in some manner that school is cancelled for one day.'

A slight inclination of his head was the only reply he made before saying his good evenings to everyone.

As they drove home, Swithin whined gently, 'She is a hard woman to satisfy. She will keep me on my toes.'

'You overlook Mr Prendergast.'

'She does not love him. Did you not observe the pretty smile on her lips when we entered the saloon? Much brighter than she wore with him.'

'I noticed.'

'But a very daunting woman. She can shrivel a man's confidence in two seconds. I found myself comparing her to an *ant*, imagine! How degrading, and it was not what I meant at all. The fact is, Dew, I begin to wonder about myself. Do we do right to fritter life away in idle pleasures? When you asked her who was starving, I had an overwhelming urge to say "Let them eat cake," and that would have been an unforgivable levity in her eyes. I think – oh, dear boy, you will never believe it – I think, after the play, I am going to Heron Hall to spend some months attending to estate business. The very thought appalls, but Kate must not find my affairs untended, or she will find me morally inferior, as she so obviously does you. Are you listening to me?'

'I'm trying not to. I wish you would be quiet.'

'Too cruel,' Idle lisped, and fell into sulks.

CHAPTER 18

*a*t times, it seemed impossible the play would ever be ready for performance in mid-December. There were the usual number of unlooked-for vexations. The weather turned unpleasantly harsh, causing many of the chaperons to remain home, and the actors to complain as they stood about the draughty refectory hall trying to keep warm at the flames from the two fireplaces. The Misses Hall's oranges were not ripening at a rate to ensure maturity in time for distribution. Rex continued muttering his lines, rubbing his ear and then his belly in consternation, and displaying none of the swash-buckling manner his role called for. Foxey, though he was now reduced to a minuscule part, was never present for it, but out marauding through Dewar's coverts. Otto Wenger proved not so familiar with the role of Mercutio, after two years, as one might have hoped. Mr Johnson developed a declamatory style not at all in keeping with the sedate, natural effect Dewar was striving for. The actors complained at being able to wear nothing more exciting than their everyday gowns, and took to adding bows, feathers, and glitter on their own, again ruining the overall effect strived for. Worst of all, the star of the production, Juliet, was not coming up to scratch.

With the best will in the world and a really staggering amount of work, Jane could not remember all her lines. Her dog-eared book sat at her elbow from breakfast through lunch, dinner, and her nightly cocoa. She became so weary with Juliet that she actually broke down and cried one day at rehearsals. Fortunately, this occurred on a day when her mother was not at the Abbey. The outburst made a strong impression on everyone, particularly the gentlemen. A hushed silence fell over the group, while their eyes, full of accusation, turned as one toward Dewar, the immediate cause of her tears. He had reminded her with some impatience that the play was to be performed in slightly more than two weeks and, if she was ever to put any expression into her speeches, she really must memorize them at once. Fatigue, frustration, anger, and embarrassment welled up inside the girl. She wanted to shout at Dewar, but in the end it was a great heaving sob that came out, then she turned and bolted from the stage, out the back door of the refectory hall, to disappear into some small room to recover her composure.

'Shabby behaviour!' the flower ladies declared. They were firm supporters of Dewar in any and all affairs.

'Dashed tyrant!' Homberly charged, and was supported by Foxey.

'Bloody dictator. Won't stand for this,' Foxworth added, and sat down.

'Too cruel,' Swithin mumbled, but there was some confusion as to whom he accused of cruelty. He was sitting with Kate in a corner at the time, holding up the tail of his saffron shirt while she stitched some lace on the cuffs. Not what one would expect to see on a shepherd's shirt, Kate thought, but he assured her that if *he* were a shepherd he would sell his last sheep to buy lace.

'I had better go to her,' Holly said, and ran off to follow her cousin. She soon became lost in a maze of rooms and corridors. She was about to return to the refectory when she heard from a doorway beyond the sniffles of a lady in distress. She hastened forward, then stopped. Dewar had arrived before her, and was drying Jane's tears, with an arm around her shoulders. His words were unintelligible, but the tone – gentle, consoling, loving – was having the required effect on Jane. The sniffles were her final display of temper. She lifted her pretty, tear-stained face and smiled shyly.

While Holly stood stock-still, watching but unwatched, Dewar said, 'Forgive me, love. I'm a beast, and I am very sorry.' Then he reached down and kissed Jane lightly on the lips.

Holly slipped away back to the hall, feeling upset and guilty for having seen what was not intended for her to see. When Jane came back, her hand was tucked into Dewar's arm. His treatment of his leading lady was more gentle from that time onwards, and Jane's performance markedly better. Dewar's attention to Juliet during the ensuing days was little short of lover-like. All the ladies were gossiping, lifting their brows, and wondering amongst themselves when the announcement would be made. Swithin, with his alacrity for similes, declared Lady Proctor was as pleased as an Ascot Cup winner.

'Methinks she gloats prematurely,' he said to Holly. It was his invariable custom to stick to her like a burr. She made not the least effort to be pleasant to him. In fact, the more he stuck, and bothered her with his high-flown nonsense, the harder she tried to shake him off. He blossomed into ever greater blooms of rhetoric, complimenting her on her 'character' in wearing the plainest gowns she owned when not even he could devise a compliment on her wardrobe.

'We shall see, I have watched Coz fall in love an even dozen times. He always falls in love with his leading lady. It would not do to suggest he does it on purpose to screw them up to a good performance. Indeed, it would be unfair. You improve my character, Kate. Its being unfair would not have prevented my saying it a month ago, so long as it was clever. I tell you everything. It is a sure sign a man is in love, don't you think, when he can't keep any secrets from a lady?'

'I expect it is only the sign of an indiscreet nature,' she answered, with a great lack of interest.

'You are the cruellest she alive,' he smiled fondly.

'Thank you, Swithin. Tell me, what does your cousin do *after* the performance? With regard to the lady he has been making love to during it, I mean?'

'He usually leaves the vicinity as soon as possible. Dashes off to the next production, or exhibition, or party. The lady cries willow for a week, then forgets him.'

'Where do you two dilettantes go after this particular production?'

'Odd Dew has not said anything. It is unlike him to have nothing in mind. He mentioned doing a Molière thing, but our English audiences are too lazy to appreciate a play done in French. The fault of having nothing lined up may well be my own. I mentioned going to Heron Hall – my home – for a period of quietude and work. *Work*, Kate.'

'The drama of Boadicea?'

'Ah, no. That will be pleasure, sheer self-indulgence. I refer to accounting,' he shuddered. 'Speaking to bailiffs, looking at wet fields, admiring animals of a domestic nature.'

Occasionally Lady Dewar bestirred herself to join the players. 'Dear *Tante Hélène*, do join us,' Swithin offered, drawing up a chair for her. 'We were just discussing your son, and what he means to do after Christmas. Has he said anything to you?'

'Gracious, no. I am only his mother. He doesn't tell *me* anything. What have you jacks-of-all-trades in mind to amuse yourselves?'

'Jacques-of-all-arts would be more to the point, *Tante*. We are innocent of trades and labour.'

'Parsons was here this morning, coughing all over me. He has had a miraculous recovery from whatever ailed him. I will be lucky if I don't come down with a wretched cold. He said something about Dewar writing a book.'

'The pandect,' Swithin nodded. 'Work will not be resumed on it immediately, I think. He has been touching up the Elizabethan bits while they are fresh in his head. New work will require a change of scene, and of lady.'

'What happened to the Grover gel he was seeing earlier?'

'Someone or other married her. She was a totally uninteresting female. She would not have done for your *fils* at all, dear *Tante*.'

'I begin to wonder if he will ever find anyone to do for him for more than a month at a time,' she confessed, with a little worried look at Jane.

'He will never find such a rock, an utter foundation, as his papa found in you, and that is what Dew really needs, I expect. We flighty *artistes* seek an earth mother, in our deepest heart of hearts. We do not want a female competing with us in beauty and elegance and charm. We want the centre of the stage for ourselves. Some nice, plain, sensible girl.' He did not add 'like Kate,' though his glance included her in passing. Then he turned his interest to the stage, where he was soon taking exception to Homberly's nonchalant meandering on to the boards.

'Good God, Tybalt is supposed to be a hot-headed, swaggering, reckless buck. Only look how Rex is turning him into a puppy. Homberly, dear boy, I say!' he shouted, and darted off.

'Oh these play actors!' Lady Dewar sighed, rolling up her eyes in disgust at his departing form. 'And my own son every bit as bad. He would like to wear the patches of a Harlequin, I suspect, if he did not have to wear his title instead. He delights to act up in that theatrical way, and is always a deal worse when he is with Swithin. They urge each other on, only Dewar don't dare to pull it with me, or I call him Chubbie to bring him into line. He hates it. He knows *I* am not taken in by his role of worldly player. There is no doing anything with Swithin. *He* is past redeeming, but I sometimes entertain the slim hope that the right woman might do something with Chubbie. Your cousin, though she is a pretty little ninny, is not the one. He is at the top of his bent to act the role with her, so I know he does not really care for her.'

Holly listened closely, then turned her attention to the stage, where Swithin had taken the rapier in his own hand to demonstrate a riposte to Rex. 'Come, we shall practice elsewhere, and let our Director get on with Juliet's scene,' Swithin said.

'Juliet, my pretty,' Dewar said, 'a little more from the lungs, if you please, and not quite so much awareness of your tragedy. Don't act as though you know the play's ending. A little-girl-lost sort of quality is what I am looking for, not Mrs Siddons. Just be yourself, pet.' Then he stopped and looked back over his shoulder toward the rear of the hall.

'Holly, can you come here a minute?'

She went towards the stage. 'Would you mind walking to the far door and telling me if you can hear her? This throwing-the-voice business always sends her into her tragic vein. It would be better if she could use her normal tone. Do you mind?'

'No.' She went to do it. In a few moments, he joined her there to test for himself what volume and timbre Juliet was achieving.

'We have our choice – a melodramatic bellow or a perfectly inaudible whisper. Which is it to be?' he asked.

'It is important to hear the words, don't you think? And really, Dewar, I doubt our local audience will be so critical as you fear. They would appreciate a good rant. They can hear Jane *talk* anytime. They want to hear her *act*.'

'A percipient comment, but the audience will not be composed entirely of neighbours. I have friends coming from London, fellow enthusiasts who are curious to see what I am doing.'

'It won't be so bad. You'll see,' she consoled him.

'So *bad*? My dear girl, we are not competing with *bad* amateur productions. We are competing with the *best*.'

'Which do you consider the best?'

'Why,' he said, considering, 'I think my own production of it when I was still a student in Cambridge ranks as high as any I can remember. An entirely different play from this one. I used all men, in the Shakespearean tradition, with a good deal of ranting and raving. A fine production, of its sort. Sir Harold Peacock made an exquisite Juliet. But not so beautiful as Jane,' he finished up, with a long, appreciative look at the stage. 'One wonders who Shakespeare had in mind, *n'est-ce pas?* Certainly not his wife. There is intriguing research to be done on the Bard's life.'

'Why don't you undertake it, as an addition to your pandect,

Chubbie?' she asked with a gurgle of laughter, then escaped before he had recovered.

Jane's feelings for Dewar were not formally known. She was pleased and flattered at his attention, as any young girl would be. Whether there was more to it than that, Holly had not enquired, and her cousin had not said. Jane seemed equally happy with the attentions of Rex and Foxey. Dewar's true feelings were also in some doubt.

At the next opportunity that offered, Holly asked him, 'What will you do after the play has been presented, Dewar?'

The look he cast on her was full of suspicion. 'What have I neglected to do now? I am not so conceited as to think you care for my plans, and you have no small talk, ergo you have some thoroughly unpleasant task cut out for me.'

'No, I am not so presumptuous. . . .'

'Yes, you are,' he interrupted swiftly. 'What is it? Has friend Prendergast decided we require a new school? Is that it?'

'You must speak to him on that score. I have not seen him since he was appointed schoolmaster.'

'What!'

'He is very busy. Besides his new position, he is planning to marry, you know. Or perhaps you did not, but he has long been engaged to Miss Peabody, and they are now looking about for a cottage.'

'But I thought *you*. . . . Good lord!' His eyes darted to Swithin.

'What did you think?' she asked, with some rather strong idea of the answer already.

'Oh – nothing. Swithin will be happy to hear it. He took the notion he had a rival in Prendergast.'

She bestowed an eloquent, silent, expressive stare on him. 'Swithin is without rival in his own particular sphere. Unless perhaps you. . . .' She stopped, as he adopted a menacing aspect. After an exchange of challenging looks, she cleared her throat and said, 'You did not say what you plan to do after Christmas. Will you be helping Swithin with his Boadicea *drame*, or. . . .'

'No. We are not twins, as you seem to think. We have each our own interests, which sometimes overlap. I have been giving some thought to music. A nice balance of interests is what I seek. Something modern, or at least not Elizabethan. On the other hand, there is the whole field of theology that I have hardly touched these last several years. Johnson has brought a few items to my attention, and I have not had time to look into them.' His voice became artificial-sounding to her ears as he continued. 'Or I might revert to my old interest of painting, do some research into the Byzantine school, for instance.'

'The Byzantine school! How interesting!' she said, in a drawling imitation of his accents. 'Pity you had not thought to have a Byzantine mosaic put in your dairy pavilion, Chubbie.'

'You have been talking to Mama!' he charged.

'I confess. And she is perfectly correct. Your old name has brought you right down to earth. Odd to think of your being a chubby baby. So very un-Byzantine. They always make the babies look like little midget adults, don't you think? I should have thought you were that sort of infant, born with a book and sceptre in your fingers. You must look into the reason for these child-men when you are researching the Byzantine school,' she said, then turned quickly and escaped before he could retaliate.

He looked after her as she hitched a thoroughly dilapidated old shawl around her shoulders and sauntered off to seek a spot near the grate, for she had caught a cold. He continued looking, worrying the inside of his jaw, all unaware of Swithin creeping up on him.

'You are amazed at my choice,' Swithin said, following his gaze. 'A case of succumbing to kindness in a woman, and not her beauteous looks.'

'Kindness? There is not a charitable bone in the woman's body. She is an unmitigated shrew.'

'That too. A kind shrew. I adore paradoxes. I adore my Kate. Will you stand best man at our nuptials, Dew? I must begin to work on the arrangements. I will want a monumental celebration.'

'What – has she accepted you?' Dewar asked, with a sudden, convulsive leaning-forward of his body.

'I startled you. *Do* forgive. No, I have not yet proposed. I thought to propose in verse – one of my illustrated parchments. It will make an interesting heirloom for our children.'

'A superb notion,' Dewar smiled, relaxing. 'I have some gold ink in from Russia. You will want to try it.'

CHAPTER 19

$\mathcal{T}$he doubts of the penultimate week regarding the play's ever being ready in time turned to a certainty it would not, in the final week. 'It's hopeless!' Dewar proclaimed, throwing up his hands. 'It cannot be done. We'll have to cancel. This mess will make us a laughing stock amongst our friends from London.'

Swithin said nothing, but Holly felt such a rage well up within her there was no holding it back. All the trips to the Abbey, all the learning of lines, all the amassing of properties, the hours of rehearsing, the endless mass of sewing, the excitement and anticipation of the villagers – all to be tossed aside as of no value because Dewar felt his reputation in London might suffer from a slight lack of perfection. Taking a deep breath, she turned on him, arms akimbo. 'I trust you are not serious!'

'You know it is impossible. You were against it from the start,' he pointed out.

'Yes, I was. I thought it a colossal waste of time and money, both of which could have been put to better use. As the time and money have been spent, however, and the whole village been led to believe they are to see a play, it would be – *criminal* to disappoint them. A gentleman would not do such a selfish thing.'

'*This* gentleman would,' he replied coldly.

'I have never seen such a display of childish impetuosity. You are vain, selfish, proud, egotistical. . . .'

'Got a devil of a temper too,' Rex warned her in a low aside.

Dewar's eyes glittered dangerously. There was a tense silence in the hall as one and all awaited his outburst. To their relief, he said only 'Bah!' or something that sounded like it, then stalked off, leaving them to wonder whether this was the end of all their work. Swithin said, 'Well done, Kate. Mind you, it was not at all necessary. Dew didn't mean it. Had no thought in the world of not putting on the play. He's asked two dozen friends from the city to see it. He usually threatens not to go on with it at some point during the final stages. Tempers become frayed. Your own as well, I daresay.'

'Feel like a broody hen myself,' Rex admitted. ''Nuff to give anyone the jitters, being cooped up in a dashed freezing room for weeks on end.'

'What oft was thought, but ne'er so poorly expressed,' Swithin agreed. He assured the onlookers that work would resume as soon as Dewar had calmed down, and they must all just allow themselves to go limp and rest for a few moments. 'You too, Kate,' he said, adjusting her shawl more closely round her neck. 'I worry about that cold you have caught. I have decocted some drops for you. Take sparingly, they are very strong. Liquorice and sugar, linseed, raisins, a *soupçon* of rum and vinegar, the whole to be shaken gently before taking. If the cough is in danger of invading the chest tonight, you must dip a flannel in boiling water, sprinkle with turpentine, and apply to the chest. I have found it wonderfully effective in the past. I saved dear Prinny from a lung inflammation with it. I am dashing off for my own greatcoat this instant. I swear the grates in this great frigid hall defy legend, and produce smoke without fire. The coldest smoke ever generated anywhere,' he shivered. 'I shall find something warmer for your shoulders as well.'

'I'm not cold,' she told him. She felt decidedly warm inside still from her confrontation with Dewar, and rather foolish as well, if it had all been unnecessary. But then, how was one to know? And he could not be allowed to stop the play at this late date.

Swithin encountered Lady Dewar as he roamed the rooms looking for a pretty shawl for Holly. Informed of his errand, she gave him instead another of her late husband's waist-coats for the girl, explaining that Holly would not mind what she looked like. 'For she's a nice sensible gel and would rather be comfortable than fancy.'

'How true. She is above mere finery. I shall just top off her cough medicine with a dash of cinnamon from this little pounce box I always carry about with me, and make her take some. You were happy with the aperient I made up, *Chère Tante*?'

'It gave me a wonderful relief, Swithin. Leave me the receipt. It don't gripe like Scots. Don't gripe in the least, but is very effective.'

In the ensuing days, Holly appeared at the rehearsal in Lady Dewar's husband's waistcoat, green with yellow stripes, which was perfectly effective in keeping the chilly blasts from her back without unduly encumbering her arms and hands. An aroma, not entirely appetizing, of linseed and liquorice hung about her, for she had frequent recourse to her medicine. Her nose was red, and her eyes tended to moistness. Concerned for her health, Swithin made her wear a pair of jean slippers that extended nearly to the knees, specially made to his own design for keeping the draughts of Heron Hall at bay in the winter months.

After recovering from his fit of pique, Dewar attempted an apology a few days later. 'Things are going a little better now, I think,' he said, as his wandering eyes took in her various layers of protection against the cold. 'I had truly no intention of cancelling the play. The artistic temperament, you know – hot-headed.'

'Lucky head! It is the only hot thing in this room.'

'Two fireplaces are not sufficient to heat it. The Abbey was used to be a religious place. Perhaps it was a part of their penance to freeze during meals.'

'I am surprised your improving hand has not been busy here to install more adequate heating. The new Rumford fireplace, for instance, would be all the crack.'

'I shall make a note of that. A new wrinkle, for you to be urging me to tend to my own comfort. It is usually the unfortunate poor you are looking after.'

'Yes, quite a dab at making orphan shirts. Shall I sew you up one, till you get your new fireplaces?'

'Not necessary. I too am wearing my waistcoat. Very handsome, incidentally,' he said, with a playful look at her borrowed garment.

'Your father had good taste,' she agreed, glancing down at it.

'You didn't think I had inherited it from my mama, did you? I have a waistcoat upstairs with rosebuds that might suit you better. No, on second thoughts, you will spill that vile medicine on it, as I notice you have done to Papa's.'

'Swithin made a syrup for me. So kind of him. And let me borrow his slippers too. He's really rather sweet, when you get past his foolishness. Get to know him better, I mean.'

'Yes,' Dewar said, very briefly, almost as though he disliked to acknowledge it. 'I believe I mentioned to you some time ago that he was an excellent fellow, in his own way.' Then he quickly changed the subject. 'À propos de rien, my fountain has arrived from London for the dairy. Would you care to see it?'

'We can't leave now, in the middle of rehearsal,' she said, surprised at the suggestion.

'I'll call a tea break. It won't take long.'

'I imagine some of the others would like to see it too,' she suggested, looking toward Jane.

'Oh no. You are the only one who derided my idea. I want *you* to see how nicely it has turned out,' he replied, taking her elbow, and walking her rather quickly towards the door. 'Have some tea served. We'll be back soon,' he said to Altmore in passing.

'Where are you going?' Altmore asked.

'Out.'

'You were very curt with him,' Holly chided.

'I am vain, selfish, proud, and egotistical, remember? Also rude, and with an excellent memory. A thoroughly bad article when you come down to it. I have performed one unselfish act of late, however. I have got Billie a Bath chair. Ordered it while we were in London, so that he need not be completely immobilized while he is recuperating. He adores it. Rents it out to the others at a penny a ride while he is not using it. A budding entrepreneur, that one. He let me take a scoot down the hallway without cost. Fun. Old age will not be without its rewards.'

'Have you actually been to the orphanage then?' she asked.

'I have, and without your prodding me, too. I went over to discuss Christmas preparations with Johnson and the people there. Your shirts were wonderfully well received,' he said, with a quizzing smile. 'You will want a coat to go outside. No need to send for your own. Here's something belonging to the backhouse boy that you will like. Fustian – nice and warm.' After helping her into it, he pulled the collar up about her ears, looked at her for a moment, said 'Waif,' and held the side door open for her to exit.

'Aren't you wearing a coat?'

'It won't bother me. My hot head will keep me warm,' he answered. The two of them hurried at a brisk pace across the space that separated the thatched dairy from the main building.

'Oh, how pretty!' she exclaimed when he opened the door to let her enter. It was like entering a bucolic scene from a picture, so harmoniously was all arranged. A dozen girls in blue, their hair bound in a knob atop their heads, with a pert white cap serving to ornament it, were busy at their tasks. Some were squeezing butter; some scoured pails; the majority of them stood around the large stone table skimming. A rather simple marble statue of a shepherd, nearly life size, was at its centre, raised on a pedestal, from which fresh water flowed down to the table beneath. The table was rimmed, with a drain at the centre to prevent overflow. The skimming pans were washed from beneath with the water. The dairy was clean and tidy, with nothing foolishly elaborate. The shelves were marble, as opposed to the stone in Sir Egbert's dairy. The girls were all outfitted in the same uniform instead of the more customary assortment generally seen. The Delft tiles had been affixed to the wall, lending a simple, picturesque charm without being overly ornate.

'It is no longer dreary and depressing to the dairy girls,' he mentioned, glancing around. 'But, of course, the real reason for the renovation is that I was struck with the whim for a Dutch dairy, and I deny myself nothing,' he added, with a playful sideways glance to his companion. 'The fountain is of less importance in winter than it will be in summer. Then its cooling and freshening effect will be appreciated.'

'It is not at all what I expected,' she said.

'You expected my fountain to be some Italianate monstrosity of writhing gargoyles and nude nymphs? There's a leveller for me. My one redeeming feature, you see, is that I have impeccable taste.'

'It doesn't seem much of a renovation for twenty-five hundred pounds,' she said, recalling Mr Altmore's conversation on the subject.

'The greater part of the sum is for a new cheese barn, yet to come. Five hundred for the tiles, and another five for the rest that has been done so far, if you are keeping count for me,' he said, then turned aside to speak to the dairymaids, making some enquiries about their work.

With a curious eye, Holly observed them. They were young, pretty, smiling self-consciously and occasionally giggling at the presence amongst them of their employer. Dewar, always the innovator, was soon adjusting pots and trays on shelves, and suggesting that curtains would be quaint.

'How is the play going, Miss McCormack?' one of the girls asked shyly.

'It is coming along nicely.'

'We're looking forward to it. Lord Dewar says we are all to see it. Half in the afternoon with the orphans, and half at night with the village folks. I never thought to see Shakespeare performed,' she finished, with a happy sigh. 'Is it true Miss Jane dies?'

'Yes, it is a tragedy, you see.'

'Tootles will cheer us up after with his juggling. We are looking forward to it so.' After this brief speech, she curtsied prettily, and returned to her tasks.

'Are you girls warm enough out here?' Dewar asked before leaving. There was one movable grate in the room, which had elevated the temperature above that achieved in the refectory hall. They had no complaints.

'Better get your collar back up for the dash home,' he warned Holly. Once back within the Abbey, he said no more about the dairy or the statue. He went to have his tea, joining the matrons for the occasion, while Holly was left to wonder why she had been honoured by the little trip.

Activity increased to a feverish pace in the last few days. Holly thought, looking around the hall, that if a stranger entered the room he would think he had landed in Bedlam. There, sitting in a corner like an elf, his legs folded over each other, his slim body wrapped in his many-collared greatcoat, sat Swithin, practicing on his flageolet. He wore his helmet pulled well down around his ears. In another, Rex and Altmore lunged at each other with swords, while Foxey, in an effort to keep warm, had got too close to the fire in the grate and had accidentally ignited the tails of his coat. Dewar had finally given in to the arctic temperatures and was swathed in an elegant dark green garment with his initials embroidered on the pocket. It was, perhaps, a dressing gown, but was worn as a cape, with the arms not in the sleeves. He was to be seen on the stage directing, in the wings sorting out properties, and dashing through the hall harrying servants to do his bidding.

In the midst of the confusion, Holly was acting as prompter. The Misses Hall could be seen watering their orange trees, which had once again made the trip to the Abbey. Lady Dewar was occasionally on hand, complaining of the noise and cold. She had two new items added to her toilette. She was wrapped from head to toe in a blanket, topped with a turban erected for her by Swithin, with a piece of material hanging down her back, like a desert traveller, which was 'just the item' to ward off the breezes from her neck.

'All you need is a camel, and you are ready to join Lady Hester Stanhope amongst the Bedouins,' her son complimented her.

'At least I don't go into company in my dressing-gown.'

'No, love, you make do with the bed sheets. Why not bring your canopy down and be quite comfortable?'

'Maybe I will.'

Swithin began to notice, at about this time, that Dewar was spending more time with Holly than ever the exigencies of the play could account for. When he wanted an opinion about some reading of the play, an item of stage property, or even a cup of tea, he would appeal to Kate. Indeed, his sudden requirement for a prompter could be seen as a desire to keep her away from himself. Why must his Kate sit on the stage prompting when all the bothersome people had learned their parts quite by rote? At one of the many tea breaks, Swithin tucked his flageolet under his arm and ambled up to her. 'You know, Kate,' he said, 'methinks Dew does not approve of this match I have in mind. Don't stare! You know you have stolen my heart. I do believe our director is jealous.'

'Jealous!' she exclaimed, colouring up briskly.

'Yes, he is afraid of losing me. We have worked together repeatedly over the years. Quite an artistic history of Albion could be read from our association. We helped traverse the rocky path from dullness to Romanticism, in both literature and painting. To say nothing of our efforts in architecture and music, working together with excellent and, occasionally, even brilliant results. I wish you could have seen our *Medea*. In fact, I wish you could have *been* Medea. *Our Man of Mode* too was something quite out of the ordinary. But we shall not desert him. You will become a part of our group. Dewar need not fear I mean to desert him.'

'Don't talk foolishly, Swithin,' she answered. 'You know I have no intention of leaving Stonecroft. My aunt depends on me.'

'Ah, but so do I, my pet.'

Dewar strode briskly up to them. 'I need you, Kate,' he said. 'I have to talk to Bernier about the dinner arrangements for the night of the play, and want you to take Juliet's last scene from her.'

'What is on the menu, dear boy?' Swithin asked.

'Just something light between performances – a luncheon, with dinner served around midnight after the last performance. Ginestrata perhaps between, to fortify us. With, of course, toad-in-the-hole and black pudding for the gourmets, Rex and Foxey.'

'Ginestrata – excellent, I approve,' Swithin nodded. 'It is appropriate – a Renaissance receipt. We will want toast with it. The Madeira must be of the best, Dew, and I personally shall sprinkle the cinnamon, so that Bernier does not overdo it.'

'Yes, do that. Come along, love,' Dewar said, holding his hand out to Holly.

Endearments were sprinkled as heavily as French spices amongst this histrionic company. Jane was frequently called 'dear' or 'sweet' and it was not unknown for even the gentlemen to bestow a 'dear' on each other, but Holly could not recall that Dewar had ever so honoured her before. She looked at him, startled. Till that moment, he had not seemed to be aware of any departure from the norm but, as their eyes met, some conscious expression crept into his own. He did not blush, or smile in embarrassment, nor even allow his glance to waver. He just looked a moment longer than was comfortable, then said, 'Come,' again, and pulled her up by the hand.

'It is Juliet's final dagger scene that wants polishing. I am trying to prevent her from becoming Mrs Siddons. The actual words are few. I would like to convey the idea she rushes into suicide before she quite knows what she is about. An air of distraction, well short of grand heroics, is what I am striving for.'

Dewar had spoken of having to consult with Bernier but, when he reached the stage, he took up a seat to view once more Juliet's suicide. 'That bit of throwing the arms out is poor – overdone. It gives the impression she is going to topple over backwards, and she must fall forward to stop the fall with her hands, or she'll split her cranium open.' Then he raised his voice to advise Juliet. 'Don't let go of the dagger, Juliet. Hold on to it with both hands, and try sinking slowly to your knees, then falling over. Gracefully.'

'I'll run through it again, Dewar. You wish to speak to your chef,' Holly reminded him.

'No hurry. Let us see Juliet die again first. I have never quite understood this play, you know. I felt it so very contrived, unrealistic, almost un-Shakespearean. Jane's playing Juliet as an extremely young girl, hardly more than a child, gives me a clue as to its plausibility. I daresay a girl just into her teens might behave as foolishly as Juliet does. It was a lucky notion to stress her youth. Casting older ladies in the role befuddles the motivation, for the person playing the role becomes the character, temporarily. For the duration of the rehearsal and presentation, I mean. One cannot imagine a Miss McCormack, for instance, running herself through for loss of a husband.'

'Very true, particularly when she does not have one.'

'There is some possibility that situation may be rectified in the near future, if I am not mistaken?' He turned to look at her, making the words a question.

'You mean Swithin?'

'But of course. He wearies us to death o' nights with eulogies on your eyes, ears, nose, but, most particularly, your overwhelming personality. An offer is imminent. Will you have him?' he asked, in a bright, casual way, smiling pleasantly.

'No. I wish you could prevent his offering. I have hinted I could not possibly marry as often as he makes these absurd implications.'

'What is absurd about them? Swithin is eligible, and you are not otherwise attached, so far as I know. You mentioned very recently that you have come to appreciate his unique qualities.'

'There is a world of difference between appreciation and love.'

'The one will sometimes lead to the other.'

'This does not appear to be one of those times. Besides, my aunt depends on me to keep house for her in the spring.'

'He could be persuaded to wait till summer, if that is the real impediment.'

'No! I couldn't ever. . . .'

'Then it is an excuse, not a reason.'

'If you like. Oh, I *wish* he would not ask me. I cannot like to offend him after all his kindnesses, but. . . .'

'What is it you dislike? Is it the sort of life he leads? All this business of plays and pursuit of the aesthetic ideal? The *fripperiness* of his life, quite of a piece with my own, in fact? You must not let that dissuade you. He sees you as a sort of counterbalance to that side of his existence. He would not expect to change you, Kate. His only fear is that you will be at pains to change him more than he likes.'

'I have not the least desire to change him at all. He is fine as he is, but not as a husband for me.'

'Yes, but you have not told me *why*. Is it his style of life you dislike, or something more personal? His physical size, shape, whatever. . . .' He threw out one languorous hand to indicate the many shortcomings of Sir Swithin, while his bright grey eyes examined her minutely.

'I simply don't care for him enough. I *like* him; I could not love him in a million years.'

'You are a romantic. You mean to marry for love, then. I would not have suspected it from you. If you have definitely decided against the match, you had best prepare a firm refusal. He means to speak to you very soon, before he leaves, and we are only here for a few more days.' He turned his attention to Juliet and, after a few words with her, went at last to confer with Bernier on the ginestrata.

Holly remained behind watching Juliet perform, but her thoughts were not with the drama. How very uncomfortable it would be, having to refuse Sir Swithin. How very odd, too, that Dewar had undertaken to question her on the matter. Was Swithin correct in thinking Dewar did not approve of the match? He had seemed rather relieved, she thought, when she told him she meant to decline the offer. He was too well bred not to try to hide it, but some traces of satisfaction had been there. Yes, when he called her a romantic there had been satisfaction in his eyes. More than satisfaction; there had been approval. Oh, but she was a fool to be a romantic in her position. Marriage to Swithin would change her life dramatically – pitch her into the midst of exciting doings. If she were wise, she would accept. Soon the play would be over, and she would be sunk back into dullness, with Dewar and everyone gone. That she could return to her charity work gave not a shred of relief either. A premonition of regret was with her, as she sat, staring moodily as Juliet stabbed herself and died, most theatrically, falling into an ungainly lump on the floor.

CHAPTER 20

$\mathcal{T}$he day before the play was to be enacted, the players remained late at the Abbey, at work on the details. Bernier had prepared a feast for them, and spirits were high. Holly was placed at table between Rex and Swithin. In an effort to dampen the latter's ardour, Holly spent the greater part of her time attempting to discourse with Rex.

'So you ain't coming to London in the spring,' he said. 'Pity you must miss all the fun.' This cheerless beginning did nothing to improve her spirits. 'My sister's making her bows.'

'You have mentioned her.'

'Going to call on Jane. Daresay I won't have a look-in at all. Mean to say, all the beaux. . . .' He cast a glance around the table and uttered a deep sigh. 'What is this rot?' was his next speech, lifting a piece of meat on his fork. 'What they call a ragoot, I fear. Never guess it from this dish, but Dewar's got a good chef. Can whop up a dandy bubble and squeak. Don't taste like cabbage at all, the way he does it. Cooks very well, for a Frenchie.' He took consolation from his wineglass, urging Holly to do likewise.

'Give her a chew,' he advised. 'She's no duchess, but she ain't quite a commoner either.'

'This *ragoût à la Bourgignonne* – certainly not common,' Swithin pointed out, leaning forward to include himself in the conversation.

'Ragoot? Dash it, we're talking wine!' Rex countered. 'You

don't chew ragoot!'

'It *is* tender,' Holly said, in some little confusion.

'A very tender lady,' Rex agreed. 'Côtes du Rhône, I fancy, though I ain't sure I don't get a whiff of Provence in the bouquet. Bit of a half-breed, actually.'

'A young wine,' Swithin commented, discovering what matter was being discussed.

'Not an ape leader, certainly.'

As the plates were removed and the wine changed, Rex licked his lips in approval and said, 'This is more like. This one is a full-bodied wench.'

'The wine you are drinking should never make you regret the one you have finished,' Swithin pointed out, 'The order of wines decrees it.'

'No reason to regret it so long as my glass is full,' Rex agreed.

'You misconstrue my meaning. Wine should set off the meal, as the diamond does the ring, throwing its particular sparkle on each course.'

'Oh if it's diamonds you're talking, it's champagne you mean. Champagne is the diamond of wines, as Alvanley was saying a while ago,' Rex said, with a sage nod, then he tipped up his glass and sat, bleary-eyed, while Swithin at last got Holly to himself.

'We shall enjoy many such dinners as this together soon,' he began. 'This *ragoût* is a charm, and the snails *à la Bernier* to come are a miracle providing, of course, one has a taste for *escargots*. They are fed for a fortnight on milk – there is the secret. Bernier would not reveal it for worlds, but I have been spying about the sheds, and saw them in an earthenware pot, covered in milk. The mystery of the sauce I have still to unravel. There is lovage in it, and coriander, and rue – just a *soupçon*. Similar to the Roman style – *elæologarum*. We shall experiment at Heron Hall,' he promised, with one of his fond smiles that usually made her want to laugh, but tonight she felt a strong urge to cry instead. It did sound like such fun, to be doing all these silly, extravagant things.

'You know I will not be going to Heron Hall, Swithin,' she

replied automatically. Was she foolish to discourage Swithin? She glanced up, to see Dewar looking down the table toward her. He looked pensive, still and quiet, as though caught in the act of contemplation. He raised his eyebrows in greeting, lifted his glass to salute her, and drank. It was an odd moment, catching her by surprise, almost as though he knew what was in her mind. Dewar glanced to Swithin, then to Rex, then back at her, with a smile. The whole interlude was less than a minute, less than thirty seconds, but when she left the table, those were the only few seconds she recalled with any precision.

The ladies did not retire to the saloon after dinner, nor did the gentlemen remain for port. Dinner was late, and the guests returned home as soon as it was over. Lady Proctor, with a husband to be fed, had not remained past four in the afternoon. She had gone back to Stonecroft, taking her carriage with her. 'How are we to get home?' Holly asked Jane. 'I suppose Rex will take us if Mrs Abercrombie's carriage is filled.'

'Dewar is taking me home,' Jane replied.

'Oh! I can go with you, then.'

'I don't think so,' Jane said. 'We are dropping off the Halls, and that makes four in the carriage.'

'I can sit bobbin, if necessary.'

'Is Swithin not taking you? Dewar mentioned it.'

'No! You must let me go with you,' Holly said in alarm.

At that instant, Dewar came up to them, carrying Jane's pelisse. 'See if the flower ladies are ready, will you, pet?' he asked her. Turning to Holly, he said, 'Tonight's the night. Ready?'

'Did you arrange this? How *could* you!' she charged. 'You know my feelings.'

'Worse, I know *his*. Might as well get it over with. He means to have his say, and will end up declaring himself from the stage tomorrow if we don't let him do it now.'

'Whatever shall I say!' she exclaimed, in great agitation.

'Say *no*, Miss McCormack,' he suggested. 'That was your intention, was it not?'

'Yes, but. . . .'

'Swithin will recover. He always does.'

'What, does *he* make a habit of offering for someone every time a play is put on, too?'

'*Too?*' he asked suspiciously. 'Am I the other amorous fellow? I don't offer; I just flirt. I am only half a fool, remember? Swithin does not invariably offer either. He likes to surprise himself. He didn't offer for Juliet when we put it on at Cambridge, I know. Of course, Harry Peacock played Juliet, and he was a little on the burly side for Swithin. He hasn't made anyone an offer since August, to the best of my knowledge.'

'There is not much honour in it then, is there?'

'You would know better than I what gratification it gives you to be amongst his chosen few dozen. In any case, don't lose sleep over it. I want Juliet's mama in her best looks tomorrow. Is your costume ready?'

'Yes, you have seen my gown.'

'I have not seen it on you. Oh, here they are already,' he said, as Jane and the Halls approached. Holly thought there was some little annoyance in his tone. She was aware as well of a feeling of disappointment herself. It gave way to outright foreboding when Swithin was seen, following behind the ladies.

He was bundled into his special greatcoat and helmet, that added so much to his unprepossessing appearance. How could anyone take him seriously, even with a Heron Hall to his credit? A curl had slid or, more likely, been carefully pulled down from under his helmet, to sit pasted to the middle of his forehead. It reminded her of a nursery rhyme. 'When he was bad he was horrid.' She feared she was to have a perfectly horrid trip home. Already the others were going out the door, and Swithin was grasping her arm in a possessive manner. She could not but compare him to Dewar, preceding them. He was tall and erect, outfitted in the highest kick of fashion, to be sure, but well within the limits of taste. He was not garishly different, like Swithin.

Just at the doorway, Dewar stopped to hold the door wide for them, giving her a chance to compare their faces as well. 'Watch your behaviour, Swithin,' he said, with a joking smile. 'And you too, Kate.'

Dewar's carriage was waiting at the front door. As it pulled away, Swithin's came forward to take its place. With a heart rapidly sinking to her ankles, she climbed inside. He didn't even wait till the horses were off before grabbing her hands and smothering them in kisses.

'Please don't,' she said, pulling away. This only urged him on to greater excesses. His arms, that looked always so ineffectual, got a hold on her shoulders that was impossible to break, and he pulled her against him.

'I will speak!' he announced, in quite a mannish voice. 'You have trifled with me long enough, Kate.'

'*Trifled*? Indeed I have not!'

'Heart's delight! Then it is *not* a refusal. I knew in my deepest soul you could not be so cruel. You who have such concern for the poor and destitute could not treat me ill.'

'Swithin, I am not going to marry you,' she told him, pushing against his chest, and managing to wrench free from him.

'You must! My life and all my happiness depend on it. I have already planned our life together. I will change my ways for you, Kate. The master bedroom at the Hall is to be rehung in violet silk, so as not to overpower your retired colouring. You will give depth, meaning to my life, and I shall teach you to laugh and sing.'

'I know how to laugh and sing, Swithin, and you must discover a meaning for your life by yourself. I do not mean to marry, ever.'

He sulked and pouted for about fifteen seconds, then a smile, not at all happy, but resigned, noble, took possession of his face, making him look rather like a solemn rooster, but for the lack of a crest. 'A mutual vow of eternal celibacy!' he said, in a wondering voice, tinged with tragedy. 'What a superb idea!'

'Oh, indeed, I did not mean you must share my celibacy!' she said, startled at his rapid shift of ideas.

'Kate, my own Kate, you underestimate me. People *do*, only

because I am short. Napoleon too was a short man, but only look how he conquered the world. For a time. Nothing is forever. But our vow will be forever.'

'It was not precisely a *vow*,' she pointed out but, as she realized how his imagining it was one kept him away from her, she let him chatter on in this vein, knowing instinctively he was play-acting. She recognized the accents and, at times, the very words of Altmore's Romeo in his rants. She leapt from the carriage as soon as it reached Stonecroft. 'Don't trouble to get out, Swithin. You'll take cold.'

She darted up the steps, to meet Dewar coming down after delivering Jane home. In her haste, she had not seen his carriage making the turn behind the house.

'How did it go?' he asked merrily.

'Wretched!' She continued without stopping, till Dewar's arm caught her wrist and drew her back.

'Don't tell me he turned violent on you! Swithin is a tame man in a carriage.'

'How would you know?'

'Surely he didn't. . . . Just what happened?' he asked, startled out of his merriment.

'We have taken a vow of mutual celibacy, *eternal* celibacy at that!'

A slow smile formed on his lips as he glanced to Swithin's carriage, where his cousin's helmeted head projected from the window, waving a kiss to Kate. 'That won't last long,' he prophesized.

'It had best last till you get him away from here!' she said angrily, then pulled her wrist free and hastened into the house.

CHAPTER 21

a t last, the long-awaited day arrived. The momentous occasion was great enough to get Lady Proctor downstairs by nine o'clock. She had her own particular problems to attend to. Should she go to the Abbey at noon with the girls for the orphans' performance and remain through for the evening, or should she spend the afternoon preparing a toilette grand enough to impress the city visitors who were to attend in the evening? It was the sort of problem that did not come her way often. She was not of a mind to miss a single moment of Jane's glory but, on the other hand, she had no desire either to take a change of outfit with her and make her toilette at the Abbey without her woman, nor to make a hasty dash home between performances. Sloth won out. She would spend her afternoon in the hands of her woman and the local coiffeur, and entrust Jane's dressing to Holly.

'Do her hair the way we decided, Holly, with some of those silk orange blossoms entwined in it for the balcony scene. Dewar had a wedding on his mind when he bought orange blossoms. It is a certain giveaway of his feelings. And for dinner afterwards she is to wear the spider gauze outfit from the balcony scene, only unstiteh those curtain things Swithin had put on the sleeves to flutter in the breeze. They will be sure to drag in the soup or knock over a wineglass. Did I tell you what Dewar said to her last night when he brought her home? So very particular, his bringing her alone. He wished a few moments alone with her, you see. He did not come up to scratch as we had hoped, but he said he would call on us in London. He said most particularly too that his aunt would sponsor her at Almack's, the most distinguished club in London. We were concerned about getting her in. He is planning to take her up. That much is obvious.'

'Yes, I'll see to her hair and the outfit, Aunt. I wonder if I might borrow your pearls for the play? Swithin thinks that, as Lady Capulet, I should wear some jewels.'

'What a pity, my dear, I plan to wear the pearls myself. But I have an old string of fish-paste pearls in my box I used to wear before Bertie . . . before. Wear them and welcome. On the stage, no one will notice the difference.'

'Those are the ones I meant, Aunt! I was not asking to wear your real pearls.'

'Take the old ones and welcome. Keep them. They will look well with the nice black gown you are to wear. I should wear it to the dinner afterwards if I were you, Holly. It lends distinction. That was a good choice. Idle has a sharp eye in his head for fashion; I'll say that for him. He can spot elegance a mile away. An excellent idea, having my black silk cut down for you. In the normal way, a youngish girl could not wear black to a party, but this will be a good excuse. Why, you might be putting ideas in Mr Johnson's head,' she added recklessly.

In fact, it did flit across Johnson's mind that Miss McCormack would make a charming widow when he saw her outfitted in her new elegance. It was unusual to see her without a few layers of shawls around her shoulders that concealed her shape. The black gown was well cut. The pearls lent an unaccustomed touch of elegance, if they were not examined too closely to see that they were beginning to peel. The recalcitrant hair, too, had been done up in papers to give it body, so that it held its place fairly well. It was not the word 'widow' that occurred to Swithin when he saw his forsaking lady-love enter the refectory hall.

He had passed the greater part of a sleepless night adding dramatic touches to his future proceedings as a man pledged to a blighted love. He would wear black himself for a while. His violet period had been a success; this would be even more tragical. He would be weary, dispirited; utter long sighs and cast heart-broken gazes on Kate. He rather feared the friends coming from the city would jeer at him, but to see Kate look so elegant, really quite pretty, cheered him. He did not wish to appear more than usually ludicrous, and a pledge of eternal celibacy to a woman who was not even pretty might have that effect. Outsiders would not have time to discover all of Kate's marvelous qualities.

He had been pouring his delightful misery into Dewar's ears just before her arrival. Dew, the dear boy, was being even more than usually understanding, and suggesting exactly what Swithin wished to hear – that 'eternal' in such cases meant a month, six weeks at the outside. Kate began walking towards them to remind Dewar to raise the white flag to indicate the afternoon performance. She could not fail to notice that Swithin was regarding her with an unaccustomed ardour. 'Kate – stupendous!' he said, smiling sadly.

'You are admiring my aunt's pearls,' she said, embarrassed at the compliment, the more so as Dewar was looking on, trying to hide his amusement. 'They are false, I'm afraid.'

'No, I am admiring your aunt's niece,' Swithin countered. 'And what I am admiring in particular is not at all false.' This speech was accompanied by a searching examination of her anatomy.

'The flag should be raised, should it not?' she asked in a rush, to deflect any more compliments.

Rex came forward, eating an orange, to suggest that, by Jove, if these were meant as a treat it was a cruel prank to play on an orphan. He had tasted sweeter lemons. 'You look very fine today, Holly,' he said, regarding her critically. 'You ought to dress up more often. Take the shine out of them all. Where's Jane?'

When Jane drifted forward in a cloud of white, it was clear that she too took the shine out of them all. But there was little time for flirtation. With all the preparations to see to – the filling of the orange baskets; the final primping of their outfits; the movable heaters to increase the hall's temperature; the arrival of Mrs

Raymond's dancing dogs, who had to be taken outside till the play was over; the final running over of troublesome lines – these and a dozen other details kept everyone busy.

When, at last, the orphans were shown into the hall, an agreeable sort of fatigued excitement had been achieved. Mr Johnson pointed out to Holly that Billie McAuley was well enough to come with them. 'We have got him a Bath chair, you see. An excellent contraption.'

'How are you, Billie?' she asked.

'My legs don't hurt much now,' he replied. 'Lord Dewar says when I can walk he'll get me a pony.'

'Ha ha, one of Dewar's little jokes,' Johnson explained. 'When you can walk, you won't need a pony, McAuley.'

'I won't ever walk very well,' Billie pointed out, in a philosophical spirit. 'But Lord Byron has got a foot like me, and it doesn't stop him from riding or boxing or shooting or anything. Lord Dewar says he even dances sometimes, when only his friends are around, and he can swim like a fish. Anyway, I'd rather be like me than blind, like Milton. He was a poet, Miss McCormack.'

'I have heard of him,' she said, but she knew Billie would not have heard of him if Dewar had not taken the trouble to tell him, to buck up the boy's spirits. 'Here, we shall put you right in the front row, Billie.'

'I can make the chair go by myself. I have very strong arms,' he said proudly. With a great heave of the arms, and the fingers pushing the wheels, he could make it roll on a flat surface.

'Plucky little fellow,' Johnson said, looking after him. 'Still, it doesn't do to spoil him.'

'If *he* does not deserve a little spoiling, I don't know who does, Mr Johnson,' she answered.

'There is Dewar going to speak to him now. The boy's head will be turned with so much attention.'

Dewar's attention was not limited to Billie. He passed amongst the boys, making jokes with them, tousling heads, and even raising his fists with one stocky specimen for a playful bout of fisticuffs. 'Keep that right hand up,' he warned. 'You'll never be my bruiser if you can't learn to keep up your guard.'

'Abrams was used to be a bully till Dewar took him in line,' Johnson told her. 'He has promised to get him a spot in Jackson's Parlour in London when he is sixteen, to train him up for a bruiser, if he behaves himself. He places more faith in reward than punishment.'

'Can I see your prads, like you *promised*,' a thin, slightly wall-eyed urchin begged, when Dewar passed his way.

'Run along. You'd rather talk to the groom than hear the madrigals, I daresay. But be back here in half an hour for the play. Even a groom should know his Shakespeare.'

'When did Dewar become so familiar with the boys?' Holly asked Mr Johnson. 'He spent his days rehearsing the play.'

'He often takes a run over to the orphanage after dinner, or just before. I have frequently gone with him,' Johnson told her.

From the orphans, Dewar went on to tease the orange girls, to adjust their mob caps and compliment them on their curls. It struck Miss McCormack that he was very much at home amongst his people, for a man who only visited once in two years.

She had not thought *Romeo and Juliet* a play that would give much pleasure to children. Indeed, certain passages had been altered or deleted entirely for the young afternoon audience. How much enjoyment they actually took from the tragedy it was not possible to know, but the children certainly enjoyed the outing. The local school children were there as well. A temporary teacher might have been found for one day, to allow Prendergast to say his prologues, but an occasional dose of Shakespeare was deemed good for them. The youngsters, as well as that part of the audience composed of servants and merchants from the village, enjoyed the production exceedingly. The females of all ages pulled out their handkerchiefs at just the right places. They fumed with fury at old Capulet (Sir Laurence Digby) for forcing Juliet's hand into a match, shook their heads in disapproval of the old Nurse for suggesting bigamy, shrieked in thrilled horror when a sword found its mark in a duel scene and, in general, displayed the proper reactions to the scenes put before them. The occasional forgetting of a line or dropping of a rapier by Rex only added to their pleasure.

There was no denying the *après-drame* was the more successful portion of the entertainment for this particular audience. The dancing poodles, decked in pink ruffles and little pointed hats, were adored, and applauded till hands were red. The shrieks of mirth rose to the ceiling when Rex and Foxey donned their horse's suit and danced with the bear (Mr Altmore). The bear then balanced a large red ball on his nose, tossed it to the horse, at which time Foxey (still the front end of Dobbin) lifted one foot and kicked it into the audience. This spontaneous (possibly accidental) bit was so popular it was repeated thrice. The juggler kept his oranges in the air all at once and, for a few rare moments, also managed to twirl a hoop around one toe at the same time. Music, largely overpowered by shouts and laughter, was provided by the *ambulante musico*. When it was all over, individual meat pasties were served, with lemonade and those tarts and sweets that had fallen short of perfection and were not dainty enough in appearance to set before the evening guests. A pony's worth of sugar plums was the parting treat, not despised either, even by the adults.

It was a scene of merriment that was worth every minute of the effort, every stitch of the needle, every harrowing hour of the.rehearsal. It was magical enough to make even a slightly straitlaced spinster realize that pleasure was a positive good. This afternoon had given more enjoyment to everyone than a hundred woolen undershirts or a dozen bottles of hot soup. Holly knew it was a day that would linger long in the memories of the children and villagers. She would not soon forget it herself. It was an occasion, like a coronation in the city or a victory celebration after a large battle.

When the guests had departed, the cast were served a more elegant repast of ginestrata, toast, assorted fowls, ham, and side dishes. It was the first time any of them had been confronted with a table laden with victuals, but with no chairs for the diners.

'We are having an informal actors' meal,' Dewar told them. 'Take a plate and cutlery for yourself, and eat where you choose.' This movable feast was served in the morning parlour, where chairs lined the wall, while some overflow of people were required to either stand or wander into the next room, a small parlour that had the disadvantage of being away from the food but the counterbalancing advantage of having tables to hold one's plate. The oddness of the party lent it a hue of glamour. The bucks soon took advantage of unconfined seating to place themselves near to the prettiest girls, without having to make conversation with anyone they disliked. Juliet was surrounded by beaux, and Holly found herself herded into a corner by Swithin, who was too full of his new nobility to be hungry and thus forgot to offer Holly much food either. He looked at her with the eyes of a heart-broken spaniel, and an occasional wan smile that quite took away her appetite.

He would not be lured into his customary eloquence. Every mention of the play's success was greeted with a world-weary sigh. 'Excellent. Quite excellent,' was about all he would say, and that much was said with an effort.

Dewar moved amongst the company, being polite and praising their afternoon performance, with a few suggestions for the evening show still to come. Spotting Holly's predicament, he brought her a plate of sweets for dessert. 'It went well, don't you think?' he asked them both.

'Excellent,' Swithin sighed, then forced himself to add, 'I hope it does not augur a disaster this evening. When the dress rehearsal goes well, the performance is usually marred.'

'Everyone will be more nervous this evening with your company from London in the audience,' Holly mentioned. 'They should be arriving soon, should they not?'

'They have been trickling in this half hour. They are being shown to their rooms, and will be fed something before the play. I must go to them very soon. Try some *chantilly*, Holly. You must keep up your strength for tonight.' A little conspiratorial smile told her he sympathized with her in her predicament. As he walked away, she noticed that he was really very considerate. He thought of everyone, noticed the little problems that beset all his crew. He thought to compliment the flower ladies on the sour oranges, and even had a kind word for Jane's brothers, who had spilled a bowl of nuts on the floor. Most of all, he was attentive to his leading lady. How had he worked his way to her side when there were at least half a dozen bucks vying for her attention? Jane smiled softly at him. She looked, quite simply, ravishing. 'I forgot to put the orange blossoms in her hair!' Holly thought, with a pang of guilt.

Everyone felt, as soon as they returned to the refectory hall, that there was an increased tension in the air. Performing for orphans and school children was one thing, performing for a sophisticated London audience, accustomed to the professional works of Covent Garden and Drury Lane, was another. The flag had been changed from white to black, indicating an evening performance. Candles were lit along the wall brackets in the room, and the footlights were ready to be illuminated. The transparency was not yet in place, but it too would be used to greater effect in the evening performance.

When the gentry from the neighbourhood began arriving and taking their seats, the cast went behind the curtain to prepare for the great moment. Peeps from behind the curtain into the hall showed the city folks now taking up their places – dark-suited gentlemen with opera glasses, slickly barbered hair, and very white hands. And the ladies! There were real diamonds sparkling; there were ostrich feathers in their hair; there were turbans; and there was a good deal more of bare shoulder and bosom than had ever been seen before in Harknell. 'Indecent,' the Misses Hall called it. Even Mrs Raymond, frequently chided in the village as a bit of a dasher, thought it 'fast,' and wondered if she dare have her new spring gown re-cut to this style.

When, at last, the madrigals were sung and the curtain about to be lifted, the crowd stopped coughing and chatting. The director went to join his friends in the audience. Mr Prendergast cleared his throat nervously, straightened his cravat and strode out to initiate the play:

Two households, both alike in dignity,
In fair Verona . . .

he began, in a somewhat tremulous contralto voice. By the time he finished, 'our toil shall strive to mend' came out in his normal baritone. No lines – at least, no essential ones – were forgotten on that night. Rex Homberly did not drop his sword. Juliet achieved some semblance of the tone Dewar had been striving for the past weeks. The lamps had the desired effect on the transparency, causing a wonderful view that roused even city folks to a surprised 'ah!' when first it was revealed. At intermission, oranges and nuts were passed, and the *ambulante musico* strolled amongst them, sadly piping his flageolet, and wishing he had thought to have his lute shipped down from Heron Hall instead. A flageolet was not tragic enough for him now. It was an instrument for Pan, not fitting to Swithin's new mood. But, by slowing his tunes down to a dirge, he caught the essence of the mood he sought. Several of his friends asked him what ailed him in any case, and heard, at great length. The play recommenced and continued on its course, uninterrupted till the end, with only an awkward fall by Juliet at the climax to flaw perfection. She caught her toe in the hem of her skirt and tripped, landing with an unromantic thump.

But, when praise was being distributed afterwards, this was seen as a cunning device used by the director to heighten reality. 'Daresay that is what *would* actually happen,' said Mr Dickens, the manager of Drury Lane. 'The whole done with great originality, Dewar. You have excelled yourself. Ingenious to have used such a pretty set of youngsters for your cast. Your Juliet – superb! And her mother, Lady Capulet, played by an incomparable. There was a new twist. Who is she, by the by? The best voice I have heard in several years. I do not exclude our professional ladies either.'

'A local girl – lady. Not eligible for the London stage, but I have some plans to do a production of *Shrew* featuring her in the near future.'

'I don't believe I caught the name.'

'You wouldn't know her,' was the unsatisfactory answer.

Mrs Raymond enjoyed an hour-long flirtation with Lord Simon, the greatest rake in London, and a two-hour scold from her husband when he got her home. Foxey and Rex got pleasantly tipsy, and even Mr Altmore imbibed enough to become frolicsome and pursue Juliet with more ardour than usual. 'Exit, pursued by a bear,' Swithin sighed, when his costumed friend followed her from the room. 'Possibly the most famous stage direction in history, Kate. Shakespeare, of course.'

The Misses Hall, deceived as to the strength of mead, had three glasses each and were seen to perform a jig, with Mr Raymond clapping time.

An elaborate after-play dinner was served in the dining-hall, where care had been taken that every local should have the plea-sure of a city dining partner, to add to the night's stimulation. Lady Astonbury told Sir Egbert she was enchanted with his daughter, and the novel, dramatic heresy of casting such a youngster as Juliet. 'Oh, aye,' he agreed, wondering what the woman was talk-ing about, 'but she's a good gel for all that. To make her bows in spring, you know.'

Lord Simon, an amateur horticulturalist, listened with real inter-est to his companions, the flower ladies, and invited himself to view their conservatory the next day. The juxtaposition of Lady Proctor and Sir Crowell Stagland was less successful. He was stone-deaf, but he nodded his head very civilly, and occasionally gratified her by ogling her new gown, so she was not totally displeased with him. The inhabitants of Harknell had never had such a day, nor such a night, and still it was not over. There were musicians come down from London as well to perform for an impromptu dancing party after dinner.

Bereft of Jane's company (she was a definite success with the London smarts), Rex and Foxey took the ill-conceived idea of donning their horse suit to try the waltz, and so disturbed a maid bearing drinks that she spilt the whole tray. Swithin's vow of celibacy did not deter him from spending every minute at his lady's side. With all the ruses at her command, Holly could not shake him off. As his friends had by this time some awareness of his state, they were not cruel enough to deprive him of her company, so that she was left nearly all alone with him, while the most eligible men she had ever seen danced with everyone else.

As morning hovered near, however, Mr Johnson did accost her for a dance and, once she got away from Swithin, she contrived to remain away for as long as she could. She darted behind the wall of people that stood at the room's edge to hide from him, and walked into Lord Dewar.

'Slipped the leash at last, have you?' he asked. 'We shall have a waltz, before Othello gets a rope out to haul you back to the bed of nails. Were you ever so bethumped with awful, inappropriate metaphors, I wonder? It must be the mead taking its toll.'

'You sound like Rex,' she laughed.

'*I* do it with a better grace, but he does it more natural. A misquotation for every occasion. It saves thinking. I have spotted Swithin loitering at the far end of the room. If we can waltz in tight circles at this end, we may escape detection. Come.' He took her hand and led her to the floor.

Dewar was certainly not foxed. He was not unsteady on his feet, or uncertain in his pronunciation. Holly took the idea all the same that he had had more mead than was good for him. His smile was wider than usual, and his speech, normally rather elegant, was more careless than she was accustomed to hearing. A little flush was on his cheeks. As they danced, his arm also began to tighten around her waist quite noticeably. 'It has been quite a day, hasn't it?' he asked, smiling down at her.

'It's been a wonderful day.'

'In fact, it's been quite a visit.'

'It will seem very dull when you are gone. When all of you are gone, I mean. Swithin and Rex and Foxey – everyone.'

'Cautious Miss McCaution! Tch, tch, I had high hopes for half a second you were going to forget yourself and say you would miss me. But you must not despair at all of us leaving. I shall find Swithin a new heart-breaker and come back for more lectures.'

As she glanced around the room, Holly could see there was no shortage of heart-breakers in their lives. Elegant, laughing ladies, their smiles flashing as brightly as their jewels, were present in distressing numbers. This was the sort of company these city gentlemen were accustomed to. The marvel of it was that Swithin could ever have fancied himself in love with her. It was the novelty perhaps that appealed to him, and the propinquity. 'It should not prove very difficult,' she answered.

'I give him a month at the outside. Of course, it is a new role for him. He may enjoy to play the ascetic and give it a longer run. But, then, I am given to understand you are firmly committed till the end of the Season, in any case – to mind the house at Stonecroft, so it cannot make much difference. Summer will be soon enough for *your* new role.'

'Are you really going to put on *The Taming of the Shrew?*' she asked hopefully, for it had been spoken of.

'It is one of the projects I am considering, but only if you will promise to be the shrew. But for the present moment my project is to evade Swithin till this set of waltzes is finished.'

It took some lively footwork, but it was accomplished. 'Now I shall return you to your keeper,' he said. 'The best place for you. The *safest* place I mean.'

'Oh, I think I would rather . . .' she said, glancing around at all the other guests, so intriguingly unfamiliar.

'Yes, I know you would rather, and *that* is why you go back to Swithin,' he said blandly, and pulled her away.

CHAPTER 22

*T*here was a final flurry of leavetakings during the next few days. Swithin came to assure Kate of his eternal devotion; Rex and Foxey to remind Jane they were to be her *cicisbei* when she landed in London. Dewar, who was making the rounds of all the homes where ladies had helped him, also stopped at Stonecroft to take a formal leave. He expressed his eagerness to see the Proctors in London, which was very well received by the lady of the house.

After the party had left the neighbourhood, things settled down to some semblance of normal. There was a feeling, however, that the dull normal of old was dispersed forever. There was a group of singers now in operation, which showed no signs of disbanding. Mrs Abercrombie found a quarterly magazine that accepted her essay on Shakespearean theatre, and expressed some little interest in a similar work on Greek tragedy, so that she was deep into borrowing books from all her friends. The Hall sisters had taken the notion of organizing a spring flower show, and were busy with that. Mr Prendergast and Miss Peabody had found a cottage for rent and were making it snug for a May wedding. The Proctors had the visit to London for the Season to look forward to and to plan. Everyone, it seemed, was well occupied except Holly McCormack.

Even Mr Johnson, when he stopped at Stonecroft on his way to the orphanage, was seen to be busy and in good spirits. 'I have got the contractors coming over to see to patching up the orphan-age – the west wall that is cracked. I mean to get a good price from them, to enable us to have a closed stove as well. The house-keeper tells me we must have a closed stove. They have one at the Abbey, it seems, and Dewar put the notion into her head when he was in the kitchen one day. I wish he had left the money to buy it. You might be able to help raise funds, Miss McCormack. Our spring bazaar will be the next item on the agenda.'

What a dull item it seemed after the late proceedings – to make knitted slippers and embroidered money purses to sell at the bazaar, to speak to the Halls about potting up some cuttings from their conservatory, to make bonbons and paint cups to sell – it was so tedious she could hardly be bothered to do it. But of course it must be done. Duty did not stop because she had taken part in a play.

She was not the only one to find the winter dragging. Lady Proctor, too, discovered that, after a taste of the high life, she was bored in the country. By the end of January, she decided she would nip up to London a bit early to make the house ready for Jane's debut. Naturally, Jane must go with her to visit the modistes. Equally naturally, they could not go unattended. Sir Egbert would accompany them, sneaking home on alternate weeks to see to his swine. During his absences, Holly would be absolute mistress of Stonecroft. It was on the third day she was alone that the missive arrived from London. Its colour and odour (violet in both shade and aroma) told her the sender was her platonic lover. She was hardly more curious than vexed when she pulled it open and glanced at it. When the word 'Dewar' jumped out at her, halfway down the page, her heart did a little somer-sault, and she read quickly on to discover what Dewar was about. It settled down when she read that he was to accompany Swithin to Heron Hall with a small party, to select some *objets d'art* for inclusion in an exhibit they were planning, to raise funds for the purchase of some statue from Greece, which the government, in its sublime ignorance, considered not worth the five-thousand-

pound asking price. Swithin assured her of his continued enchant-
ment, and signed it 'your own Swithin.' There was a postscript,
cautioning her that her reply was to be directed to Heron Hall.
The note bore little resemblance to a medieval manuscript. She
had the feeling he had not put his whole heart into its production,
and was somewhat relieved.

She was uncertain in her mind whether she should reply. A
correspondence of this sort was not considered permissible except
between betrothed parties. For a single lady to write to a gentleman struck her as a daring innovation. Yet she was strongly
inclined to reply. Her interest in Grecian art was minimal, perhaps
nonexistent. Her real interest in Swithin was about as strong. As
she reread the letter, she knew that her eyes skipped over descrip-
tions of bronze fauns and such objets straight down to the words
'Dewar is with me.' This was what made her heart beat faster; this
was the only reason in the world she wished to hear more from
Heron Hall. Certainly it would be improper to answer his letter for
such an underhanded reason. Still, she found excuses to write
prowling her mind as she sat knitting a pair of ugly brown slippers
for the bazaar.

Sir Egbert had a little black vase, believed to be Grecian, on the
top shelf of his study. Her aunt would be thrilled to volunteer it to
the cause. She went to see the vase, and noticed a v-shaped nick
out of the rim facing the wall. A vase a foot high, chipped and
slightly cracked, was insufficient excuse to write.

Before she had resumed her knitting, a caller was announced.
Lady Dewar came puffing in. 'Well, Holly, as we are both
deserted, I decided to come and see you. What are you doing with
yourself, eh? Making slippers – they look very comfortable. Put an
insole in them and I'll buy them at the bazaar. A nice woolen
insole, to keep the chill from the feet. Those bootikins are the very
thing for my corns. How do you go on without your aunt and
uncle?'

'They have only been gone a few days. I have plenty to keep
me occupied.'

'Any time you're bored, come to me. Sir Laurence Digby is still at the Abbey, but he has taken to falling into a doze as soon as luncheon is over, and he don't get up till twelve, so he might as well have left with the others. I wonder what they are up to, Dewar and the rest of them. Some new rig running, I suppose.'

It was the perfect chance for Holly to discuss her letter with an older lady, and discover whether it were proper for her to reply. 'Let's have a look at it,' Lady Dewar said, holding out her hand. 'Hmph – it ain't sentimental at least. Not a *billet-doux*. Swithin is a ninnyhammer, but he is a gentleman. I see no harm in writing. In fact, as Chubbie is with him, I shall enclose a note myself. Or maybe you will be kind enough to do it for me. Tell him there is about a mountain of lumber landed in at the Abbey, and what does he want done with it. Roots mentioned a cheese barn – a temple is more like it, from the quantity of wood. Oh, and Parsons cannot make heads or tails of his scratchings for that book he is supposed to be copying out. Parsons is a fool. He spends what time Digby is awake talking to him about old dead Romans. I don't see why my son must board his pensioners at the Abbey, especially when they are such demmed crashing bores. Why don't he have any *interesting* employees?'

As soon as Lady Dewar had had her tea and taken her leave, Holly went to Sir Egbert's study to draft her reply. She could think of very few words to say to Swithin. She acknowledged receipt of his letter, mentioned the black vase, and wished him success in the exhibition, all in a paragraph. This done, she sat nibbling the end of her pen for a full quarter hour, ransacking her mind for anything else to say. The mention of the Proctors being in London and some local trivia filled a respectable half page, then she could get on with the more interesting part of the missive: Lady Dewar's visit and her messages to her son.

Another of the violet letters was delivered within the week. Swithin, his passion for monkhood beginning to switch to a passion for Grecian antiquities, wrote scarcely more than she had herself. On the bottom half of the sheet, the handwriting was different. Swithin's ornate script, enlivened in this case with birds and vines, gave way to a bolder, black slanted hand, difficult to read. Dewar was writing his own message, to be relayed to his mother.

Holly wondered that he had not written directly to the Abbey, but as she read on, with the keenest interest, she observed that the letter was as much for herself as for his mother, and wondered how on earth she was ever to show it to the countess. He wrote, 'Tell Mama (not that it is necessary, for she will never do anything anyway) to leave the lumber till my return. My plans for the temple to the Great God Cheddar are not final yet. If Parsons will begin at the beginning of my notes, he will find them legible. I wrote a very pretty hand in my youth, unlike this palsied scratch you are being subjected to. Poor Kate! How we all make use of you. And I have yet another task for you too, but it is in a good cause! I have found a fine pony for our little Bath chair Mister, and want you to be certain Dr John sees that Billie does all his exercises, so that he will be ready to ride Dobbin when I bring him home in a few weeks' time. I hope Swithin's eternity may have run out by then. *Do* let me know how Billie (and you) go on. Sincerely, Dewar.'

She read the letter six times, with a frown creasing her brow. The frown six times changed to a smile of anticipation when she came to the words 'in a few weeks' time.' He was coming back! There was no longer any pretending she was anything but delirious for his return.

Next morning, she awoke to a sky more sunny than usual, to a breeze little short of spring-like, and felt the greatest urge to be outside. The family carriage was in London, but there was a gig in the stables which she could handle. She hitched it up and drove the boys into the village for a treat. While she was in the circulating library, the countess entered.

'Now why the deuce didn't I think to stop and offer you a ride, Holly!' she exclaimed. 'Don't tell me you walked all the way from Stonecroft?'

'No, we came in the gig. Oh, and I have had a reply to your note to Dewar.'

'You might have let me know, hussy! Why didn't you come and see me, eh? You know the way well enough. I hope you don't need an engraved card. I told you to come any time, and took your absence as due to not having a drive. In fact, I meant to send the carriage for you this very day. But I'll go home with you instead, and you can come to me another time. What had Chubbie to say for himself?'

The countess returned to Stonecroft and remained for luncheon. She did not ask to see Dewar's note, but heard its contents, in a somewhat modified form. Before she left, she said, 'What time shall I send the carriage tomorrow? Afternoon would be best, as you are running the house now.'

'Yes, afternoon would be best,' Holly replied, quite overcome at the honour. This 'amount of condescension had never been bestowed, even on Lady Proctor.

The weather reverted to a gusty, cold, thoroughly miserable February day on the morrow. Holly put on her warmest gown, old and grey, and gathered up a shawl to add to her shoulders. She had tea and a long chat with the countess – just the two of them, gabbing like a pair of crones before the fire, discussing receipts and embrocations, corns and calluses, the bazaar, and all the local doings. Before she left, Sir Laurence Digby and Parsons joined them for a cup of tea.

'How does the dramatical work go on, Parsons?' Lady Dewar demanded.

'I have unlocked the secret of his handwriting,' he said, very much at home, Holly thought, from the easy way in which he took up his accustomed chair and received his tea, already sugared as he liked. 'One third of His Lordship's l's are e's, a third uncrossed t's, and the remainder are actually l's. Other than the uncertainty as to whether a 'u' is a 'w' or a 'v,' there is little else to it. It is a very interesting work. Thoroughly researched, yet not dull and dry. The best analysis of Aristophanes I have read. Of course, he wants a better translation. Dewar has got about half of *Clouds* translated. I wish he would finish the job. It is excellent. Very witty. With Aristophanes, the wording is all. He is not a terribly profound writer, but he is uniquely creative. Dewar catches the essence of it.'

'Sound a dull enough subject – clouds,' the countess said. 'One would think him an Englishman, writing a play about clouds.'

'The title is not to be taken too literally,' Parsons pointed out.

'And have you begun rounding up those Grecian things Dewar mentioned?' Lady Dewar asked.

Holly looked up, startled. This was the first indication she had that Dewar had written to the Abbey. Why did he write to her? He could have written his messages directly home. He had been at pains to demand an answer from her too. '*Do* let me know how Billie comes on.' She had spoken to Dr John and written back, again to Swithin, but assuring Dewar that Billie was doing his exercises. She had also hinted quite strongly for a reply by asking him if the matter of the pony was a secret, or if she might mention it to Billie.

When she received her answer, there was no farce of Swithin having anything to do with the letters. The missive bore Dewar's frank, and his own writing on the outside. It was a good bulky letter, full of news, with only a postscript saying that Swithin had taken the day off to dash to London to hire a hall for the exhibition, and that he would call at Belgrave Square to say how-do-you-do to the Proctors. The rest of it was purely personal, and gave a great deal of satisfaction. The few friends who had gone with them were enumerated, with not a lady in the group. He discussed the treasures being amassed for the exhibition. 'Fogle thinks we are spending more on bringing the stuff together and hiring the hall than we will make. You see, we are a vastly artistic and literary group, but need your numerate skills to bring some order to our chaos.' Toward the bottom of the page he wrote, 'I miss all my friends from Harknell. Pray send me all the news you can scrape together. Let me know how the Misses Hall and all their plants are surviving the winter, how the glee club progresses, and how develops Mrs Abercrombie's essay on Greek theatre. I have found an interesting book for her, but you had best not tell her or our clandestine correspondence will be revealed. I miss them all, not least Miss McCormack.'

She felt a very sinner to see in black and white that she was engaged in a clandestine correspondence too risqué for her friends to know about. Not with the harmless Swithin either, but with Dewar. There was no longer the excuse of relaying his messages to his mother, a very weak excuse in any case. No, she was writing to Dewar and he was writing to her, at least twice a week, with no excuse in the world but that she enjoyed it. There was nothing in the letters to be ashamed of, precisely, yet if her aunt should hear of the correspondence and demand to see the letters she knew she would blush at every sentence. Oh, but how they lightened the tedium of the long days alone at Stonecroft! February flew past, with occasional visits from Sir Egbert to oversee his estate and bring her the news.

'Missie is never at home two minutes in a row,' he boasted. 'And when she is in, the saloon is cluttered up with Sirs and lords. The Season isn't properly begun yet either. I don't see how the pace can get any hotter. They're out morning, noon, and night, but Elsa says at the height of the Season there's three and four dos a night. They are planning Missie's ball and the presentation at Court. I'll be bankrupt,' he smiled. 'At least the rest of my brood are boys – thank God for small mercies. How are Peter and Paul?' he asked, and was soon dashing up the stairs to see for himself.

Holly was in some little trepidation lest one of Dewar's letters fall into her uncle's hands, but Fate conspired to protect her. For the three days Sir Egbert was at home, no letters arrived from Dewar. This fact, while convenient, both disappointed and dismayed the would-be-recipient. Had he tired of the little game? With his love of all kinds of writing, critical works and translations and essays, had he been doing no more than passing a dullish visit at Heron Hall by writing an occasional letter to her? It was impossible for her to write again, as he had not replied to her last.

The post, waited for and watched with unabated eagerness, did bring a letter the day her uncle left, but it was from Lady Proctor, not Dewar. She tore it open, waiting with interest to read of Jane's successes. Again the name of Dewar popped out at her. He had been to call at Belgrave Square, and would return, not the next day, but the next after that. He had left Heron Hall without even telling her. For all she knew, her last letter to him sat on a salver, waiting to be seen by anyone who entered the Hall. The casual nature of his calling at Belgrave Square, to return in a few days, showed as clear as glass that he was removed to the city for the Season, again without telling her. And why should he tell her? What on earth had it to do with Miss McCormack if Lord Dewar had decided to go to the city for the Season? Nothing in the world, but still she felt betrayed, the more so as the 'few weeks' that were to see him at the Abbey had passed without bringing him.

CHAPTER 23

𝒯he day seemed interminable after reading Aunt Elsa's letter.
A visit from Mr Johnson did very little to hasten its passing. He
gave her a box of twenty-four mugs (cheap and white) to be
painted by hand with the names of local personages, in hopes that
this blatant hint for purchase would be taken, and the mugs sold
at the bazaar. She looked in vain at the list for any mention of
Dewar, knowing it would not be there. The only amusement in the
visit was that Johnson had taken the absurd notion of putting
'Lady Proctor' and 'Sir Egbert' on two of the mugs. The incon-
gruity of this elevated form on the cheap mug would not prevent
a purchase, however.

'With luck, Lord Dewar may bring a few of his friends down to
our bazaar,' Johnson droned on.

'I do not expect he will be here. My aunt said he was in London,
and planning to remain for some time, I believe.'

'He is expected home shortly,' Johnson countered, very firmly.
But, though her heart raced at the words, she could not believe his
news was more recent than her own. This was soon confirmed. 'I
had a note of him telling me he had got Billie's pony. He will be
bringing it very soon. Any day now I look for him.'

The rumour that Dewar's arrival was imminent received some
reinforcement during the afternoon. Lady Dewar again popped in,
come to the village 'to get warmed up in your arctic breezes, for

at least they ain't smoke-laden like mine. I wish you will make
Dewar get me one of those Rumford fireplaces you told him of,
Holly, for my sitting room.'

Holly had difficulty keeping her lower lip up at this unexpected
speech. When had Dewar discussed her with his mother? How
was it so calmly said, even in jest, that she could make him do
anything? 'You seem to possess a good deal more influence with
him than I do. Or maybe it is just that you take the pains to exert
your influence, for Chubbie is really obliging. Everyone tells me so.
I daresay he would have got me one before now if I had insisted.
I am not much good at insisting on things,' she admitted. 'When
you get to my age, you know, it don't seem to matter much. But
we are both glad you made him take a hand on things here in
Harknell. It is nice to have the short-cut through Evans's place –
saves a few miles.'

Her other few successful endeavours, having no direct impact
on the countess, were not quite clear in the dame's mind. 'So,
when he comes, you must hit him up for the new fireplaces.'

'Does he plan to come for the bazaar?' Holly asked, to make
her question as impersonal as possible.

'What bazaar? Lud, don't tell me it is bazaar time already?
Surely Johnson won't be fool enough to have it till the grass is
green, and a body can spend an hour outdoors without freezing to
death. No, Dewar ain't coming for the bazaar, but he is coming
soon. This week, he said. I expected him before now.'

It was Friday. His arrival 'this week' was close enough to cause
a pronounced churning inside. Lady Dewar spoke on, apparently
unaware of the blanched cheeks of her listener. 'I hope he brings
Bernier with him. My palate got quite spoiled while he was here.
The cream sauces play havoc with my digestion, but they are
worth it after all. I say, ain't you going to offer me a cup of tea,
Holly?' she asked, the matter of eating coming to mind with the
conversation.

Tea was served, then the countess bundled herself into her blankets and took her leave, with a cheery reminder that she would be

seeing Holly very soon.

She missed her son by less than fifteen minutes. While Holly was still reviewing the singular conversation, he was announced. She stood with the paintbrush in her fingers, staring in dismay at her apron, knowing she was a mess. He stood for a long minute at the door gazing at her, silent, not smiling, yet certainly not frowning either. His elegant greatcoat fell in rich folds from his shoulders. He reached up and removed it, tossing it on a chair without removing his eyes from her. 'Holly McCormack, you *wretch!*' he said in a polite, well-modulated voice. 'You knew perfectly well I was coming, and didn't even bother to brush your hair.' Then he tilted back his head and laughed. With his hands on his hips, he advanced towards her. 'Now who was the fool who said birds of a feather roost together?'

''Oh! I didn't know you were. coming,' she said.

'I told you weeks ago. I would have written telling the exact date, but I wanted to surprise you and arrive on the day you expected my letter. I was delayed by finding, when I got to London, that Sir Egbert was not there. Like a ninnyhammer, I decided to wait and see him there, but came to my wits this morning and realized that I could meet him on the road and save a day. His wife told me he always breaks for luncheon at the Green Man in Chatham. So I have seen your uncle,' he said, approaching closer.

'What did he have to say?' she asked, with a convulsive swallow. The thought was reeling in her mind that Dewar had spoken to him about an offer of marriage. It was impossible, but the light in his eyes suggested the same thing. His mother's spate of visits too. . . .

'He said yes, but hoped we could see our way clear to waiting till the Season is over. I think it a damned imposition myself, but dislike to start off on the wrong foot with the in-laws, and I know *your* sense of duty is too acute to refuse him. It seems hard to me that we have *already* had to wait till Swithin's eternity unfolded. That was a mismanaged job on your part. However, he is struck with a passion for a Miss Everley, whom he mistakes for a Grecian statue. She looks very like one, even a diffused shade of grey all over. He can convince himself of anything. He is now certain all this celibacy is no more than a selfish indulgence in the propensity to forego. Un-Greek, in short, as moderation is their guiding light. So you are freed from your vow. I have a letter telling you so that is making my jacket reek most unpleasantly of flowers.' He reached into his inner pocket and handed the violet-scented note to her.

She looked at it, using it as an excuse to keep her eyes lowered, for she hardly knew where to look. 'No need to waste time reading it now. It says – I dictated it, as his mind was not quite on the business – that he has come to realize the selfishness of his conduct, and wishes to free you from the vow. The arabesques are his own, and you have his permission, *carte blanche*, to frame or publish it, just as you wish.'

She peeped up, to see him smiling at her softly, almost shyly. All his glib chattering – it was no more than a cover-up for being a little nervous. How odd! He was actually ill at ease, rubbing his hands together in an uncharacteristic, uncertain way. She shook her head and laughed, nervous herself.

'Don't say no!' he exclaimed suddenly. 'Be impetuous for once. Let your impulses and instincts have their say. It would not be at all a bad marriage. It is not the one you envisioned, I daresay, and not the one I foresaw for myself either.'

'No, it is not at all. . . .'

'Ah, but once you are over the element of surprise, you will see all the possibilities for good. You can keep my nose to the grindstone, and I will occasionally pull yours away from it. Moderation, Kate. It is an epicurean tenet you must learn. Don't be all your life an ant. Join the grasshoppers and we'll hop. . . . This is a demmed dull analogy. And a demmed poor job of proposing too. I thought I would do better.' He stopped, sighed, then took a breath, preparatory to launching into more persuasions.

'Are you sure it's not just Lady Capulet's voice. . . .'

'Absolutely, utterly, totally, categorically convinced. I have been wrestling with it for some weeks now. If this were one of my dramatic fallings-into-love, Juliet would be the victim. It was my sort of vicarious loving of Jane *qua* Juliet that blinded me at first. I sank into the real thing without realizing it. It must be genuine, because I do not admire you for all my customary reasons. You are not – I'm sorry if I offend you, but it is an easily remedied feature – elegant. You are not very vivacious, or outrageously beautiful. You are not more than ordinarily conversable, and you are too petulant for a lady who lacks the aforementioned virtues. *Ergo*, I must love you for yourself. And to confirm all this theory, I was extremely jealous of Prendergast till I learned he was marrying someone else. Swithin I could tolerate, for I knew you would never seriously consider him.'

'As a matter of fact, I was sorely tempted to consider Heron Hall.'

'The Abbey has not its advantages to tempt you. I have not seven towers, or even one, from which to commit an heroic suicide. But if your heart is really set on leaping off something, I fancy we could get you up to the roof by means of a ladder or pulleys.'

'Oh well, I am not Sappho, after all.'

'No, you are a shrew. Kiss me, Kate!' he said, and swept her into his arms, to forget all his philosophy in an immoderate embrace that reeked more of Bacchus than Epicurus. 'Look at you,' he laughed, when he released her. 'Paint on your chin. Is that any way to start our life together?' He dabbed at the spot, unaware that he was by that time similarly adorned. 'I had better be careful, or your dowdiness will rub off on me.'

'Oh no, Chubbie. You have withstood all the onslaughts of inelegance from your mother; you can withstand mine. Should I write to Swithin?'

'Do. He will want to dance barefoot at our wedding. You will like that, but I expect *you* to wear shoes, and very likely someone else's well-used wedding gown. But I do not complain – so long as you wear my name, and a smile along with it, to prove I have tamed my shrew.'

She was already wearing the smile, and harbouring some untame ideas about their future.

Also by Joan Smith
and soon to be published:
RELUCTANT BRIDE

'I THINK IT IS A MISTAKE FOR A MAN OF UNSTABLE TEMPERAMENT TO MARRY. DON'T YOU?'

'TO MARRY A TIMID LADY, YES. YOU MUST FIND SOMEONE WHO IS NOT AFRAID OF YOUR BLUSTER-ING, ARM HER WITH A STOUT CLUB, AND MARRY HER.'

Elizabeth Braden, known as Lizzie, was settling happily into spinsterhood (she claimed she never wanted to marry anyway) when two things happened. Her carriage smashed into that of Sir Edmund Blount and someone stole her diamonds.

Between Lizzie and Sir Edmund it was hate at first sight. He was an irascible tyrant and she was a spirited nag. But for reasons not even he understood, Sir Edmund undertook to find Lizzie's stolen necklace – and found he was also looking for her heart.